FILTHY HOT PRINCE

ALLURING RULERS OF AZMIA
BOOK TWO

MAHI MISTRY

"Your eyes are like palm-groves
    refreshed by dawn's breath,
    or terraces the moon
    leaves behind."

— BADR SHAKIR AL-SAYYAB, EXCERPT OF

RAIN SONG

Dedicated to my Mom and Dad, thank you for supporting me and reminding me to have dinner.

PART I

"Can I kiss you, Khalid?"

1

KHALID

I lounged on the blue velvet armchair as if it was my obsidian throne. Lifting the fragile China cup to my mouth, I took a sip, relishing the burn of whiskey from the half empty bottle before the interview started. I already had the half bottle before the art show started and needless to say, I was tipsy as fuck.

"What's the inspiration behind your paintings?" She asked, the cameras zooming in on my face.

I answered with a straight face. "Suffering and fucking."

The female interviewer turned into a flustered mess, people whispering to each other as my agent glared at me, imitating as if he was slicing his throat. He either meant he wanted to die or wanted me to cut it out.

I gulped down the whiskey from the cup. I couldn't care less what the art critics had to say about me or the interview when it airs. I was Khalid Al Latif. A Prince and an artist. If they didn't want my honest answers, they could go fuck themselves while I watch.

Talking about fucking.

I eyed the people walking slowly among the crowd, hoping

for a certain someone to arrive and to take her to the suite. It had been some time since I got laid. About a few months. I had been busy with my brother's marriage, Sultan of Azmia, and making sure our palace was well protected before I could travel to London for my art show.

The interviewer cleared her throat and gestured the camera crew to roll as she crossed her legs, her skirt inching up her thigh. I wished she would hurry up with the questions instead of fluttering her lashes at me.

"Your painting, *Limerence*," she started. *Finally.* Her tone remained professional despite the way her eyes raked over my dark suit, the top of my shirt where I had unbuttoned top two buttons. She licked her lips before continuing, "It has been auctioned for two-hundred million dollars. More than Pablo Picasso's *Women of Algiers Version O.* That is certainly an enormous deal in the art industry and for your country as well. Do you think the fame of the painting has any relation with you being the Prince and the brother of Sultan of Azmia?"

I had sketched and painted *Limerence*, my most famous painting yet, when I was nineteen. I had painted it after the night I killed my father with his sword, a family heirloom that my brother, Zain, the Sultan of Azmia, possessed. All I could see was the flashes of crimson blood coating my shirt and his tunic, the nightgown of my little sister, and the beige wall splattered with his blood.

Flashes of red blood, and bright golden red hair with a toothy grin had conjured in my head. The image of the young girl I had met at fifteen and the living nightmare of murdering my father had made me want to pour it all out on a canvas.

Clenching my jaw, I answered in deep voice, "I didn't want *Limerence* to be released to the public, but my family, my brother and sister, urged me to. My royalty certainly gave advantage for it to be recognised and I am proud that it offers more appreciation to my culture and Azmia."

After the art show, I knew my agent would be thrilled for the smooth reply without cursing again on the live telecast.

"That is lovely. Are you seeing anyone at the moment, Your Highness? Our fans, especially the youngsters, are quite curious if there's someone in your mind who could be a future Princess of Azmia."

I resisted the urge to roll my eyes.

I glanced at the abstract painting I had finished before landing in London. I wasn't going to display that painting in the gallery, but my agent had insisted. I was surprised by the attention it had garnered in a few moments. It was nothing but slashes of paints and a unique form of a figure in blue. I had to paint it after waking up from a nightmare.

The interviewer waited for my answer patiently.

I replied without hesitation. "No, I am not dating anyone, nor do I plan to. Will that be all?"

I was only capable of loving my family and my country.

Besides, who in the world would want to love a monster who had killed his own father?

👑

SOPHIA GORA HUMMED IN HER SULTRY VOICE, EXAMINING THE framed painting before us. Her manicured black painted nails hovered over the canvas as she traced an invisible line of the shades of paint.

"It looks brilliant, Khalid. You have outdone yourself this time."

The corner of my lips curled, receiving the flat praise from our sponsor's daughter, also a famous lingerie model.

I bowed my head a little. "Thank you, Ms Gora."

She scrunched her nose, her dark red painted lips pouting at me. "You can call me by my first name, you know? You don't always have to be so posh and royal."

We walked side by side to see the next painting. The marble chrome tiles matched with the deep navy velvet folds of the wall where all my paintings were displayed with a dim lighting. Tucking my hands in the pockets of the suit pants, I mindlessly examined the people who were invited for the event. Celebrities, models, art patrons, musicians, art critics, and a few art hungry students scribbling notes as they gaped at the paintings.

My cheeks slashed with color. My paintings weren't *that* good that people took notes of them.

Amongst all, I missed my sister and family who couldn't visit the art show. Zain was the Sultan of Azmia and he couldn't leave when Nasrin, his wife and the Sultana, was pregnant. Zara, my sister, was hopefully safe, travelling Sri Lanka and volunteering in an elephant farm, having the best time of her life playing with baby elephants, her favourite animal.

The heavy, fruity perfume made me pull out of my thoughts as Sophia leaned closer. It would have looked normal if her round breasts weren't pressing against my arm, but it seemed awkward because of my six feet five tall frame. I loomed over her lean frame as she pretended she wasn't doing that on purpose while examining the painting.

"What inspired you to paint this?" Her voice floated in my ears.

I smirked, glancing at the painting filled with warm blue tones.

"*Lust.*"

Her dark eyes widened and color bloomed in her cheeks. "Oh, really?"

I leaned down, shamelessly roving my eyes over the ample cleavage of her dress, and whispered in her ear. "*Yes,* indeed."

Her pupils dilated. Before I could plan getting us into a suite in the hotel, the trace of *that* scent wafted past me.

I straightened up, ignoring the small frown on Sophia as I

looked around, wanting to know who wore *that* scent. My eyes zeroed in on the woman in red.

Thoughts disappeared from my head as I raked my eyes over her dress. Just a few shades darker than her ginger hair. Beautiful, glorious hair that flowed down her back. My heart-beat pounded in my ears as I marched towards her, wanting to know her. My hands ached with the need to touch her, command her to tell me why *that* particular scent.

The scent that reminded me of my mother and the day spent in the backyard of the foster house, talking to the little girl. The girl who had become my muse for *Limerence*.

"Excuse me?" I said, my hand halting to hover over her arm when I saw the cane in her hand.

My eyes went to hers, and I noticed the dark glasses. *She can't see.* Swallowing the gulp in my throat, I pulled back my hand, my body flooding with warmth when she faced my direction. The scent of roses and ocean was overpowering. The same delicate fragrance of sunshine and freshly cut grass.

It was nostalgic.

"Yes?" she said. Her voice was soft, heavy with English accent but gentle. Delicate. Just like she looked.

Despite the stunning red dress hugging her curves, her face was crafted with softness. I could notice her long lashes blinking in my direction, her green eyes cloudy. Freckles dusted over her small pert nose and the high of her cheek-bones. Her soft chin and pillowy lips tilting up to me, as she asked, "Who are you?"

Fuck. I wanted to touch her, close the distance between us and take her to my apartment and spend a week with her. *Naked.*

"I am Khalid Al Latif," I said, not knowing why my voice had turned husky. I was definitely attracted to her.

She blinked at me, a small smile curling at her lips as red color spread over her cheeks. Shock and surprise rippled through me the longer I stared at her. Her freckled face. Her smile. Her hair. I remembered it somehow. They seemed familiar. Even her sweet presence felt like a blanket of warmth placed over me.

"It's an honor to meet you, Prince Khalid," she said. Hearing her say my name made me stir in my pants. "I have heard remarkable things about your paintings. I am Valeria."

I eyed her dainty hands, her nimble fingers as I wrapped my hand around her. Shock trembled through my skin, the hair on my arms and nape of the neck rising as my large hand fitted around her much smaller one. By the small shudder in her breath, I knew it affected her too.

"I wanted to ask you about the perfume that you are wearing. It reminded me of someone." I leaned forward, the scent of her making me insane.

My eyes darted to the pink tongue as it seeped out to wet her lips. I resisted the urge to kiss her. "I've always loved the scent of roses, it's one of my favorite—"

"*Valeria!*" A loud noise interrupted us. A man in suit walked towards us, eyeing our adjoined hands and frowning. Valeria let go of my hand, taking a step back. Towards him.

"I was looking for you. Here, I got you champagne," he said, glancing between the two of us. "I am Brandon, her date."

I nodded at him, hiding my fist in my pocket.

She has a date with this guy? She can do better. Me.

Valeria declined the champagne flute, and I took it from him when he insisted her to drink it. I swallowed the bubbly alcohol, offering him an awfully sweet smile.

If Zayed, my close friend, was here, he would mock me for being jealous and even childish.

Before I could ask her to show her around the art gallery and maybe my bedroom as well, he beat me to it. "It's nice to meet you, Mr Khalid, but we have to leave or we will be late for our dinner reservation."

Valeria gave him a look when he held her hand in front of me. I reminded myself to be civil.

You are not a caveman, Khalid. You can't take her over your shoulder and call her yours.

"I hope we will meet again soon, Valeria," I said, giving her a small smile, winking at Brandon, who glared at me. Date or not, he was jealous of the little exchange Valeria and I had.

"You should try more woody notes instead of oriental," Valeria said, bowing her head and leaving in the arms of another man. "Just a suggestion, Prince Khalid."

Woody notes? Huh.

I made my way to the agent, asking him to bring me the guest list of the art show, my eyes scanning for a particular name.

"Where is Valeria? What's her last name?" I demanded as he ended a call with *BBC News*, apologising for my cursing during the live interview.

Sophia leaned closer to me, her fingers creeping up my arm.

I pulled away, "I am busy tonight, Sophia."

"Busy?" she huffed, pulling away. "With what?"

"Work," I replied, and repeated my question to the agent. "What is Valeria's last name?"

"You mean the red hair you met earlier?" Sophia asked, her eyes darting from my face to the guest list.

"Yes, *her*. Do you know her?"

"Of course, I know her. She is the first blind entrepreneur to be on the *Forbes 30 under 30*," she said with a grin. "I love the perfumes made by her company."

"Perfume?" I prodded, wanting to know more about Valeria. She seemed intriguing the more I knew about her.

"*Delicate Dew*, Khalid. It's like you are living under a rock." She shook her head, naming the famous brand I have heard before. As Azmia was famous for its own exotic fragrance oils, lotions and perfumes, we had to know about the competition.

"Her last name is Dunne. She's Valeria Dunne. I wished she had stayed longer. I wanted to talk—"

I droned out of her talk, repeating her name. Valeria Dunne. That's her name. The woman in red was a CEO of a perfume company.

"Cancel my flight for Azmia, I have serious business to do," I said to my agent, who let out a long sigh. "Thank you, Sophia, remind me to treat you with dinner when we meet again." I kissed her cheek, smiling at her.

I left the art show early. I had to call her and set up an arrangement to meet her.

I wanted to be with Valeria.

2

VALERIA

I couldn't stop thinking about a certain Prince who smelled of whiskey and rich pine while I had dinner with my date. Brandon was the CFO of my company, and he had asked me on a date to the art show two weeks ago. I had agreed because it had been a long time since I felt intimacy of any kind. I wanted to try something, anything at all instead of moping around my house even on weekends.

"Are you sure you don't want anything to drink?" Brandon asked as I sat on his couch, making sure I didn't bump with anything as I laid my cane beside me.

"Yes, I am sure," I replied.

I didn't drink. The last time I drank beer I was sixteen. Almost a decade. Ever since that incident, I hated alcohol. It made me nauseous.

I could hear Brandon shuffling around his kitchen. My thoughts drifting to Khalid Al Latif. There was something familiar about him, especially how deep his voice was. Husky and masculine, it had made me very aware of how fast my heart beat pulsed when he had leaned closer. I could taste the musk in the air, his scent surrounding me.

He smelt of whiskey and trouble. I couldn't help steering my attraction towards him.

All evening I had been hearing his praise of paintings, how handsome and talented he was, some even comparing him to a God, putting him on a pedestal. I had giggled hearing his answer during his interview while others gossiped of him being with multiple people. Sometimes at *once*.

I had flushed and walked away with Brandon as he talked about the brand initiatives I could do. I didn't want to talk about my company when I was on a date. I wanted to talk about the paintings, ask him to explain them to me but I didn't want to be pitied if I brought it up.

"Here, it's a glass of cold water, I am having a can of beer."

I felt the dip on the couch as he sat beside me, my fingers wrapping around the cold glass. I heard the hiss of a beer can opening as he gulped from it while I took a sip.

What happens now? Do I have to do something?

What would I do if Khalid were here? Maybe I would hold his large hand, caress the callouses I had felt, and laugh at the size difference between his hand and mine. I would kiss his smile. Yes, I would. He smelt so good and masculine. I wanted to kiss him. Feel his hands on my skin and his scent wrapping around me while he whispered dirty words in his velvety smooth voice.

I snapped out of my thoughts and swallowed the cold water. *Jesus, what's wrong with me?* I am on a date with Brandon, yet I can't stop thinking about a certain Prince for a few minutes.

I focused on my date and asked him about his childhood. He talked to me about his parents, his normal life and his love for numbers. When the same question was directed at me, I hesitated.

"I was orphaned. Born and raised in a foster house," I

replied, thinking about the sad and happy memories. The adoption, the accident, losing parents and my sight. "You know Mr Benjamin and Mabel?"

"Yes, I know. I thought they were your parents," Brandon questioned.

"They were my foster parents. After a bad incident with my adoption, they adopted me," I said, fumbling with my fingers.

He hummed, and I felt him lean closer. I held my breath. His clammy hand touched mine. He was nervous. "You know, Valeria, I have been attracted to you since I joined the company," he whispered, my lips pressing into a thin line when he moved my hair over my shoulder, his lips landing on my skin. I squeezed his hand, not knowing what to do and how to react. "You don't know how incredibly hot you are. So fucking sexy."

I wanted to say something. *Yes? No? Maybe? Move away?* I quelled down the terror that was surfacing, my body screaming at me to move away, run, scream for help. But it was okay. I wasn't in danger. I was safe. *I am safe.* Brandon wouldn't do that. I had my cane and pepper spray with me.

But I didn't want him to touch me.

I pulled back, bringing some distance between us, but still held his hand. "Can we take this slow? I don't... I don't want to—"

"It's our third date, Valeria," he said, closing in on me once again, but didn't touch me, his fingers rubbing over my arm. "We don't need to have sex but I want to—"

I shook my head. "Stop Brandon. I don't feel comfortable to... to do all this stuff yet."

Would he understand? If I tried to tell him, would he? No. He might mock me that I was drunk or—

"Okay," he said, moving back, his hand leaving mine. "*Okay,*" he repeated to himself, his voice low as he sighed.

I heard him stand up and walk around his apartment as I

relaxed on the couch. I should have asked him to put on a movie on Netflix so we could enjoy spending time together. I could at least distract myself with audio descriptions of the movie and forget about the world for an hour or two.

I heard the light click of a lighter, the scent of smoke wafting in my nose.

My entire body tensed.

"I am smoking. Hope you don't mind," he murmured carelessly.

Yes, I did mind. I couldn't handle the smoke. The scent of cheap beer, the stench of smoke hovering in the room, the mocking laughter of his friends when they puffed it at me as if it was all fun and games.

I suppressed the urge to tell him to stop smoking and decided to leave. I didn't want to bother him with tiny things that he wanted to do just because I hated it. He wouldn't understand. He was already sulking around and smoking when I denied him little intimacy.

"I can drive you home after I finish," he answered, already picking up his car keys.

I shuddered to think about being in the same car and the stench of smoke around me. "It's okay, I will call my driver."

"Oh… *okay.*" I could hear the disappointment and sadness in his voice. "Should I walk you down? Stay with you until—"

"It's okay, Brandon. Thank you for taking me to the art show and the delicious meal. I will see you on Monday." I rushed out of the door.

I sighed in the elevator, pressing the button of ground floor.

When will these fears go away?

Khalid

"Hello?" the soft voice asked curiously.

"I am sorry for calling you at this hour, Valeria. But I

needed to talk to you," I said, my knuckles turning white from where I was clutching the cold marble of the balcony, waiting for her response.

Why were my hands so clammy? Was I nervous? No, I couldn't be. I could count the number of times I had ever been nervous in thirty-two years of my life in one hand.

Four times, if I remembered precisely.

First, when I held baby Zara for the first time, afraid I would drop her. Second, when I met and talked with the adorable little girl in the backyard of an orphanage and helped her draw. I was a teenager back then and utterly infatuated with her because she had amused me and that had made me nervous. Third, when I had sex at seventeen, afraid that I would hurt the woman. And the fourth time, when I murdered my father in front of my family, afraid they would see me as the monster I was.

But it would seem that I had to add number five to it. Calling Valeria Dunne late at night to hear her sweet voice.

I was aware of how close I was holding the phone to my ear, smiling, when I heard her take a slow, steady breath. *Good.* I wasn't the only one who was nervous.

"I certainly wasn't expecting a call from a handsome Prince such as you." I could hear her smiling.

I grinned at the night sky. "How do you know I am handsome?"

"I have heard about you from other people."

"They could all be lying and I could be ugly with rotted teeth for all you know."

She giggled, the sound adorable. I rubbed my chest, confused to why I was feeling so warm in my chest.

This never happens.

"I don't believe you are ugly," she whispered. "I liked how you smell."

"You liked how I smell?"

"*Mhmm,*" I heard the small shuffle, and I imagined her on her bed, laying down on the pillow as she talked with me. *Hopefully naked.* "And your voice."

On instinct, my voice lowered to an octave. "You like my voice, dear Valeria?"

I heard her take a sharp intake of breath, and I knew I had her. So sweet and innocent.

"Why did you call me at this hour, Khalid?" Her voice was breathy.

I licked my lips, imaging her doing filthy things I tell her to do through the phone, her face flushed of embarrassment and lust.

"I want to meet you."

"Right now?"

The excitement and shock in her voice made me chuckle. "Not now, you greedy girl," I purred. "Tomorrow at seven in the evening."

"Why?"

"I want to have dinner with you."

And have you as my dessert if the dinner goes well.

Valeria didn't reply for a few moments. "If I said no?"

I chuckled, wishing she would deny me so I would know what lengths I would go to have dinner with her. Because I was afraid I would do *anything* just to spend a few hours alone with her.

"I dare you to, sweet one," I crooned.

I heard her swallow. "Fine. Meet me at *Ambrosial.* Second floor. Tomorrow at seven in the evening."

I grinned widely, resisting the urge to jump. "Yes, ma'am."

"If you are a second later, I will leave."

"I won't be late, Valeria. Wear your hair down. I will see you tomorrow. Sweet dreams."

Before she could reply, I ended the call. No one had ever

demanded a place to meet me, but a young woman named Valeria dared and even told me to be on time.

I couldn't wait to dine with her and fuck her.

3

VALERIA

My body quivered with an adrenaline rush when he ended the call. A giddy grin tugged on my lips as I let out fits of giggle, covering my mouth.

"I can't believe you just did that!"

I remember how I had called him by his first name. A Prince!

Ahhhhh

I fell on the sheets of the bed that felt like how I imagined clouds would feel like. Extremely soft and warm. My red hair splayed across the huge pillows where I planted my face and let out excited squeals. I was acting like a teenage girl who got asked out by her crush for the prom night. Not a twenty-six-year-old tycoon and founder of *Delicate Dew*, a perfume brand, I had started after graduating with a bachelor's degree in business and no job offerings because I was visually impaired.

"Valeria!"

Startled by Benjamin, my loyal guardian, seeing me acting out like that made me roll over. Unfortunately, it caused me to tangle my legs in the blanket and fall over on the other side of the bed, causing a very loud *thump* as my head hit something hard.

Benjamin winced. "Are you okay, Valeria? I didn't mean to startle you."

I sat up, patting my unruly red hair and ignored the small itch of pain on my forehead. I had momentarily forgotten that there was a nightstand placed on the left side of the bed.

"It's okay, Mr Benjamin. I was just… *um*, I talked to Prince Khalid, and he wants to dine with me tomorrow at *Ambrosial*," I said, my cheeks scorching with blood. I must resemble a tomato with my cheeks the same color as my hair.

"That Prince Khalid you talked about?"

I nodded in his direction. I had told him and Mabel, his wife, also my guardian, that I met the Prince of Azmia. "He asked you out for a dinner? That's nice, I suppose."

I turned towards the deep, raspy voice and smiled. Patting the edge of the bed, I stood up and fixed the blanket. "It is more than nice. I will have dinner with a Prince tomorrow!"

Valeria.

My body still hummed with little goosebumps when he had said my name in his deep voice. It was rich with a little English accent. His voice made me feel warm. Like I was wearing a thick cashmere sweater on Friday night and drinking hot cocoa while it snowed outside. I wanted to hear his smooth voice again, especially hear him call me by my name.

"Tomorrow? But you have the meeting with the factory manufacturer to talk about the new launch—"

"I know it's important, Mr Benjamin, but can you please move it on Tuesday? Or else I won't be able to meet him."

I could sense the hint of a smile in his voice when he replied, "Of course, my dear. I will prepare for your dinner with the Prince and postpone the meeting."

I gave him my best toothy grin.

"It's so good to see you smile like that, love," he said, joy lacing his voice. "Goodnight."

I waved toward my bedroom door, trying to remember how his face looked when he smiled at me. After more than a decade of not having my sight, it was hard to remember the faces of the people who took care of me. Especially Mr Benjamin. *Did his hair color change? Were there wrinkles on his face? How did his eyes react when he heard his wife laughing? Did they gleam with happiness?*

"Goodnight, Mr Benjamin."

I shook out the sadness that weighed heavy on my shoulders and mentally counted the steps towards the balcony. Holding the cold latch, I shut the doors closed and huffed out a sigh when London's wind stopped weaving inside my bedroom. After settling under the warm blanket, I wondered if Khalid Al Latif was as excited as I was.

In only a matter of few hours, I would be sitting across him.

Khalid

I tightened the golden cuff links of my shirt before donning a suit of the similar color as my obsidian eyes. I was wearing the latest watch from *Patek Philippe*. I had taken time to trim my stubble neatly. Heeding Valeria's advice, I sprayed a mild musky, woodsy scented cologne from Azmia, a custom-made scent just for me. The top two buttons of the white shirt were unbuttoned, giving a glimpse of my tanned skin. Donning the shiny black shoes, I was ready.

I had put an effort to look good in front of Miss Valeria Dunne. *For the dinner and one-night-stand,* I reminded myself, checking my watch for the umpteenth time.

As the driver drove the sleek back car towards the venue of the restaurant, I impatiently checked the internet again, searching her name like a teenager. I couldn't help myself. I was curious. Being a royal for over thirty-two years, there were only a few things that made me curious and not bored. And Valeria made me extremely curious.

I was impressed reading about her upbringing as a foster child, losing her sight in a car accident, dealing with unemployment even though she had a Business Degree from a reputable University just because she was blind. The reason behind having her own perfume brand, sharing her story through her social media and various interviews.

By the time we reached the restaurant, my respect for her had increased tenfold. She was rich yet humble, delicate yet daring enough to demand me to meet her even though I had asked her out.

The staff of the luxurious restaurant led me to the upper level which overlooked the city of London. It had a stunning view of street and building lights with clear night sky. Despite the opulent setting of the floor, it was odd that it was empty of staff and people.

"Where is everyone?"

"Miss Valeria reserved the second floor for the evening. She doesn't like crowds, and this is much better for her," the server answered with a small smile as if he was remembering the past encounters with the woman I was curious about.

I settled down at the table placed in the center of the floor, underneath a dimly lit chandelier. The warm and rich environment reminded me of the dining hall back in the Palace of Azmia where I had countless dinners and lunches with my family. Valeria had a great taste, but not when it came to dating.

I sipped on red wine, lazily waiting for her to arrive.

Finally, the clock struck seven.

Valeria

My loud sniffle echoed in the room as I turned to the other side, holding in my wince and making sure the bandage wasn't misplaced.

"Please don't cry dear, I am sure he will understand." Mabel, Mr Benjamin's wife, said in a soothing voice. It made me feel more guilty. They both were doing so much for me.

I tugged the blankets over my head. I didn't want them to see me like that, even though they both had been with me since the beginning. They always took care of me when something like that happened.

An hour ago, I was wearing a slim white dress, small diamond studs in my ears with my waist length red hair curled in silky waves. Mabel had told me I looked like a beautiful angel after I had applied minimal makeup. I had learned to do it on my own since high school. I had thanked her for the compliment, knowing she had called me angel when I was at my worst, after the accident that robbed me of my sight.

But as soon as I had stood up from the stool, my head had throbbed painfully with my eyes. I had almost fainted.

The doctor told us that my headaches were getting worse because of the corneal blindness and the only cure was to implant new corneas in my eyes. But I wouldn't agree with it. I didn't deserve it.

The headache was my fault, anyway.

It was half past seven with me crying on the bed because I hit my head after getting too excited over a call with the Prince of Azmia, Khalid Al Latif.

I groaned, wishing I was sitting across from him and hearing him talk.

"Are you okay? Do your eyes still hurt?" Mr Benjamin asked.

"No. I wish I could apologize, but I am too ashamed to even call him." I pouted, the spot between my ribs aching. "He must be cussing me."

I was ashamed. *Deeply* ashamed. I had told him not to be late and yet I was the one who couldn't meet him. I had never once been late in my life to any meeting. I was always on time. I hated tardiness. But curse my throbbing head and eyes. I had begged both of them to let me go and meet Khalid, but the doctor insisted me to get some rest.

"Why don't you call him over?" Mabel asked. "I will cook something delicious and have dinner here. He's a Prince, Valeria, you should have dinner with him."

I groaned, "Exactly, Mabel. I don't want him to see me like this."

I didn't want his pity. Not from him.

Mabel petted my hair. "At some point, you have to accept it and let others accept it too, Valeria."

Frowning at her words, I buried my face in the pillows.

I heard Mr Benjamin moving around the room and closing the windows to stop the cold air from entering. "Get some rest, I will talk to him and reschedule the dinner."

Peeking from the blankets, I looked toward his raspy voice, trying to remember the lines on his face from childhood when I had my sight. Even though the image of his face was blurry in my mind, I remembered his kind blue eyes and the small wrinkles around them.

"Thank you, Mr Benjamin. I don't know what I would do without you." My eyes burned with tears, throat clogging up as I tried my hardest not to cry. My tears would upset him.

"Valeria, don't cry, my dear. You are like my daughter and as your guardian, it is my duty to care for my child."

I sniffled, thanking him once more as he patted my head.

I hope Prince Khalid gives me another chance to meet him.

Khalid

I was trying not to show my impatience, anger, irritation

and concern, taking a sip of wine. I did not enjoy the bitter, stingy taste it left in my throat. *Did she dare stood me up? Me? Prince of Azmia?* How dare someone waste my time like that? But I stayed seated on the chair, glaring at the empty seat across from me.

I wanted to see if she would arrive hastily, apologizing for her delay or if she wouldn't arrive at all.

Most of all, I was concerned that something might have happened to her. I didn't know why, but I knew the Valeria Dunne I talked to last night was an intelligent, sweet woman who wouldn't be late if something hadn't happened to her. She had insisted that I shouldn't be late.

Is she okay? Should I call her? Ask her to reschedule or check up on her in person?

I was about to reach for my phone when it started ringing. Relief passed through me when I saw it was the same number. Without hesitation, I picked it and asked,

"Where are you?"

"I am at home, your grace, if you must know. Thank you for asking."

Gritting my teeth in annoyance, I said, "Where is Valeria? She told me to meet her at seven. She's late."

Benjamin had called me that morning to ask me about my intentions with his daughter. I had been honest that I wanted to have dinner with her. I didn't tell him what I had planned to do with Valeria afterwards.

He cleared his throat. "About that, Mr Khalid. Valeria is extremely apologetic for not being able to meet you this evening. She was disappointed because of the circumstances—"

"What circumstances? If she was busy, she could've called me earlier." Letting out a frustrated sigh, I looked over at the enormous view of London. "Did something happen? Is she okay?"

Why was I so concerned? She is a stranger.

"I am not sure how she will behave if I let you know about this, but if you insist, I will tell you. Valeria was ready to meet you when she had to postpone this meeting because of a sudden medical emergency regarding her health."

My heart started pounding in my ears. I urged, "Will she be okay?"

"Yes, the doctor told her to rest, which made her throw a fit. I believe she will be well by tomorrow."

"Good. Tell her to meet me at *Laziz* restaurant. Tomorrow. At seven."

Before I could hear Benjamin's reply, I ended the call, hoping she would be able to make it.

I had to see her before I left for Azmia.

4

VALERIA

Drink this.

I'll take care of you.

Sh, it's okay, Valeria. Fuck, you're so hot.

It's okay, a few more—

I woke up with a gasp. Memories of that night playing in my head. The scent of cheap beers, the stench of smoke, the thick air. Sweat sheeted my body as I sighed, running my hands through my pajamas, feeling the satin bedsheets underneath me. I clutched the pillow and bit my lip when I made sure I had my underwear on.

Thank God.

"You are safe, Valeria," I muttered to myself. "It has been a decade. You are safe. I am safe. I am okay."

I laid back on the bed, asking *Siri* for the time. It was half past midnight. That meant I would meet Khalid in a few hours. Cuddling my pillow, I played his latest interview, falling asleep to his deep voice whispering in my ear, soothing me.

I WAS A LITTLE NERVOUS AFTER SENDING THE TEXT TO BRANDON. Rejecting his idea to meet up for another date.

I reminded myself that I had to do it. I wasn't attracted to him and after the time at his apartment and his smoking, I couldn't date him.

The smell of roses wafted in my room, making me smile and relaxing my nerves. Khalid had sent a bouquet of roses that morning, with a letter in Braille for me. I was extremely touched by the gesture, the pads of my fingers moving over the little bumps on the card.

To My Sweet Rose, Valeria,

I hope you are ready to meet me today. If not, don't worry, I have it all planned. Until then, take care of yourself.

Your Handsome Date,

Khalid

Grinning, I clutched the little card to my chest. I couldn't wait to meet him.

Mabel helped me pick out a dress as I changed and took my time applying the makeup. When I turned fifteen, every girl in my school was obsessed with makeup, and I had asked Mabel to help me with it. Since then, I had taught myself to use and apply it. I had marked every product with Braille to know what I was using.

Fetching the circular tube with a textured droplet on the packaging, I swirled it open and gently applied the mascara. For the final touch, I took a *Dyson* air wrap to curl my ginger hair in waves.

"How do I look?" I asked Mabel when she entered my room.

Her lips pressed on my forehead. "Like an angel. Khalid is going to forget he is a Prince after seeing you."

I chuckled at her and applied light red lipstick at her suggestion. My finger traced the slight bruise on the upper right of my head. Hopefully, it won't be noticeable.

Pinning the two locks of strands on the crown, I donned a

comfortable, elegant dress. It hugged my lithe, tall frame, ending just above my knees. Mabel had commented that the navy dress suited me well and Prince Khalid would propose marriage to me just by the looks.

I sprayed my signature perfume and layered it with other subtle one so it would last longer, the scent of roses and freshly cut grass with a hint of spice.

Now I feel ready.

I felt nerves racking up my body as my driver drove me and Mr Benjamin to *Laziz* restaurant. It was well known for its luxurious interior and lavish cuisine. The cost of one course dish was more expensive than the heels I wore.

I fidgeted in the car seat, feeling the wooden box. A heavy and very expensive painter set to gift him and apologize for not arriving the day before.

"Will you be okay? Your cane is with you, right?"

I nodded at Mr Benjamin when the car stopped to a halt. "Would you please help me find the table?"

"Of course, my dear."

Khalid

I glanced around the crowd of the restaurant. Even on a Tuesday evening, it was filled with rich celebrities, employees and couples. I had postponed my visit to Azmia till next week, and although Zain was not happy hearing about the news, he was being extremely nosy. I knew he wanted me to be present and look over the country while he took care of Nasrin, who was five months pregnant. He wanted to spend some time alone with her before the baby shower. Zain and Nasrin deserved it.

I wished to find the deeper love like them, but I knew that no man like me would ever find peace with his demons.

I thought back to the letter I had written for Valeria and internally cringed at my sweet rose.

Who the fuck calls their date a sweet rose?

I was definitely *way* behind in the dating scene.

Zara had called me the night before. I was more than delighted to see my little sister having the time of her life in Australia. She had been travelling the world, so it wasn't a surprise that she flew from Sri Lanka to Australia. Her hair was still a shortish pixie, making her cheekbones and pert nose stand out. She was on a beach, her pale skin sun bathing as she asked me if I was having fun.

I had shrugged.

"You need to loosen up, Khalid," she had said, scrunching her nose at me as if she was disappointed with my answer. "You need to live, brother. You are thirty-two so have fun before your hair turns grey. Ask Zayed to help you."

Zara had said with a mocking grin, the beauty spot on the corner of her lip, looking adorable, with her hazel eyes gleaming in the sun. I missed her. I told her to keep me and Zain updated on her whereabouts and give us an emergency call if anything else happened.

No one knew where she was except our family. As a royal princess, it was her wish to stay anonymous, travel the world and learn photography. I just hoped she would take care of herself.

I didn't have the courage to tell her I couldn't ask Zayed to have fun. *How could I have fun when I had taken someone's life?*

I snapped back to reality when the server asked me if I would like to order a bottle of wine. I dismissed him, still drowning in my thoughts about the past when my eyes pinned on the stunning redhead who entered the restaurant with an air of elegance. Hot blood thrummed in my veins as I shame-lessly raked my eyes over her body, covered in navy blue.

Lust.

Images of the blue painting flashed in my head the longer I gazed at her. Her long legs were bare beneath the knees, delicate sandal heels donning her ankles. Her glowing skin was as pale as alabaster, her bright copper hair falling in waves around her shoulders, a small smile curving on her pillowy red lips.

My body reacted in a primal way when I noticed someone old, possibly her father, holding her arm. I had never felt that way before.

"Hello, Prince Khalid."

I stood up, counting the adorable freckles on her nose and cheeks. Cute. I couldn't wait to kiss them.

"Hello, Valeria."

Angel. Her face was of an angel.

Even though stunning sunglasses covered her eyes, I could notice her long lashes blinking in my direction. Color red dusting her cheeks as she smiled at me.

Fuck me.

"This is Mr Benjamin," she introduced the old man by her side.

"Of course," I replied.

I couldn't stop staring at her.

"Should I stay, Valeria?"

With a great amount of effort, I managed to look away from her and to the man standing beside her. Benjamin. The man who called himself her father, who had asked me for my intentions. *Why was he here with her?*

Valeria gave Benjamin a smile. I narrowed my eyes. I wanted to be on the receiving end of that smile. I quickly shook off the ridiculous idea.

I must be going insane.

"I will be okay, thank you, Mr Benjamin."

I had the urge to step closer to her and shield her from others' view, protect her. "I will take care of her and drive her back... if Valeria is okay with it. Or my driver can drive her home."

She turned towards me, her cheeks pink. I took a deep breath to control myself and glared at my shoes. She was too precious to look at.

Fuck. Why am I acting like a teenager with a crush?

"You don't have to trouble yourself—"

"It's no trouble at all." I gave her a brief smile, even though I knew she couldn't see it. "It would be my honor."

Benjamin cleared his throat. I glared at him for interrupting us. "I'll be leaving then. Have a good night, Valeria. Mr Khalid."

With a nod, he left us alone, standing closer to each other in a crowded restaurant.

Valeria

I forced myself not to lean up and take a long whiff of Khalid's smoky, woodsy cologne. He smelt nice. *Really* nice. Something musky and exotic and very male. The kind of nice that would make you nostalgic after a few years and fill you with warmth. It made my stomach churn with an odd feeling. Perhaps it was giddiness.

"I want to apologize for asking you to meet here," Khalid said, standing beside me.

I turned in the direction of his deep voice tinged with a little English accent.

Hearing an apology from him made me feel weird because his tone told me he wasn't used to saying sorry to anyone.

Every inch of my body was aware of the closeness between us, the air charged with static electricity, making my nerves hum with anticipation. I could feel him looming over me. Towering me even though I was fairly tall, even in heels.

Before I could open my mouth, he asked me if he could touch me.

Blood rushed to my face, my legs tensing at his smooth

question. *Did he want to touch me in front of so many people? He was truly a player like those articles I had heard—*

"What?" I managed to utter, mentally shaking off the dirty visuals repeating in my head with my naked body sprawled across a table for his full course meal.

I was sure I was red from head to toe.

Khalid cleared his throat. "My guards have cleared the second floor for us if that's okay with you?"

His guards? Of course, he would have guards. He *is* a Prince. But he did what? *Did he do that for me?* Maybe he wanted privacy during our dinner.

Not touch me privately, of course.

I lifted my palm. "Here."

If it was someone else guiding me, I would ask for their elbow, but not with Khalid. I *wanted* to hold his hand.

Warm, powerful hand engulfed my hand. I could feel the small tingles when his long fingers held my smaller palm in his larger one. I traced the pads of his fingers absentmindedly, noticing the small callouses from where he might grip his paint brushes for long hours. His hands were not soft as I had imagined a painter's hand would be. They were calloused, roughened.

I adored it.

He slowly led me to the stairs, aware of my cane in my right hand. He made sure to tell me about the railing, clutching my hand with each stair I climbed. As if he was afraid to make me fall and staying close to make sure I didn't. I tried hiding my burning face behind the curtain of my hair, but the strands pinned on my scalp didn't help.

After climbing the stairs, I thanked him.

"No need to thank me. I hope I didn't trouble you."

I could sense the hesitation in his rich voice.

"It's alright, Khalid. It was just a minor headache but my doctor urged me to take a day off."

Why am I smiling so much? My cheeks hurt, and I wanted to press my cold hands on my face to calm them down.

Khalid

I pulled a chair for her, her subtle feminine perfume wafting in my nose as she sat down, gripping the edge of the table. I tried not to take a whiff of her silky copper hair, which smelt like roses. I had to control myself and not creep her out.

"Can you please bring water for me? Thank you," Valeria said to the waiter with a warm smile that had his ears turn pink. He poured me a glass of the expensive white wine that I had ordered and excused himself to bring her water.

"You don't drink wine?"

Her eyes flickered in my direction as she removed the glasses. "No, I don't like alcohol."

I swallowed a big gulp. She was my complete opposite.

I could barely take my eyes off of her. They had given her the menu in Braille, the soft pads of her fingers running across it.

My right hand still felt tingles from before. Her hand was smaller than mine and I had to force my eyes on the stairs when she had traced my fingers. I knew she did it mindlessly, but it felt intimate to me. Almost erotic for her to caress my fingers like that.

I wondered how it would feel if she caressed a different, *harder* part of my anatomy. For the umpteenth time, I had to shuffle in the confines of my pants, remembering her soft touch.

This was a new low for me. Getting turned on by holding hands.

After giving our orders, Valeria looked at me, her voice shy. "I have something for you."

I watched as she leaned down to open her handbag and pull out a big wooden box with a small red bow.

"This is for not being able to meet you yesterday. I hope these are the ones you like. I didn't know which one to choose from. I can barely draw a straight stick figure so I apologize beforehand if you don't like them. So, *um*, let me know which one to get—"

I took the box from her before she could lose her breath. "Thank you very much, Valeria. But you don't need to do this for having a medical emergency. I should be the one to get you something."

She gave me a slow nod, her lips pursed together as she waited expectantly for my reaction. I didn't want to make her wait and opened the box. My eyes widened when I saw the expensive oil paints in a wooden carved box from a very luxurious brand. It must have cost a pretty penny to gift me this.

"Thank you, Valeria," I said, my voice a husky whisper as I awed at the colors. I couldn't wait to try them and feel the texture smoothen underneath the pressure of the paintbrush. "The colors look so vibrant and rich, I can't wait to paint using them. It's very thoughtful of you."

If it was even possible, her cheeks reddened further, a gorgeous smile curving her lips. "You're welcome, I am glad you like them."

We were interrupted when the server brought our food. I didn't tell her that everything cooked was tested healthy and without any poison by my royal taster. My family and I decided that it was a risk to ignore the event of last year when Nasrin, my brother's wife, was almost poisoned by the food cooked for her.

I watched in awe how easily she maneuvered the different types of spoons and forks as if she remembered how and where everything is placed. I was very impressed.

"You seem close to Benjamin," I said, wanting to know more about the man who was so protective of her.

Valeria nodded. "He and Mabel are my guardians. My parents, you could say, as they took me in growing up. I was dropped on their foster home when I was a baby."

I took a sharp breath. I could never understand why someone would ever do that.

"If it's not too much, can I ask what happened to your sight?" I wanted to know if she could see through a fog or darkness.

Zara's mother, Isabella, was born blind, and she had a foggy vision. I wanted to know if Valeria did, too.

She took a shaky breath, and I knew it was a hard question. "I lost my sight in a car accident when I was eleven. A truck driver ran past the traffic lights, lost his control and it slammed with our car. The couple who had adopted me a year before that didn't survive. I hit my head and my world went black. I woke up with corneal blindness."

I clenched the spoon in my hand, cursing at the circumstances, but I knew better than to blame it all on the circumstances.

"Shouldn't you get new corneas to treat it?" I knew about it because I often visited charities involved with treating disabled children. After death, eye donors donate their eyes and the donated corneas helps the children with corneal blindness get their sight back.

"Of course. But I would rather have children get their sight back than me. I... I wouldn't know what I would do when and if I get my sight back."

The server came back with the main course. The air around us tense and heavy. It was a serious subject, but I couldn't imagine living without sight for a day. I had tried painting covering my eyes, but it was a terrible process. Not knowing which colors I am using, which colors I am mixing, which lines I am stroking on the canvas.

Valeria broke the silence first. "About the paintings. Does the inspiration really come from suffering and..." She waved her hand, her face turning scarlet.

I smirked, leaning on the table. "Suffering and?"

"You know... the answer that you gave to the interviewer."

"I don't remember, Valeria. Suffering *and*?" I asked again, innocence lacing my voice while my eyes dared her to say the word she was embarrassed to.

Fucking.

"I know you are teasing me," she grumbled and whispered quickly, "*Fucking*. Suffering and fucking."

I grinned, very pleased with her reply. "Not really. I like to make my agent angry and I was bored at the art show, especially with the interview. I said it to piss them off."

Valeria tilted her head, her red hair sliding over her shoulder and revealing her slender, pale neck. I could see the pulse beating in her neck. Before my filthy thoughts could fill my mind, I looked away.

"I thought every art came from a little of suffering... and intimacy." She chose her words carefully.

I hummed, taking a sip of wine. "It could, but it also means having fun. It is a lengthy process and despite the efforts, whatever that may be in other's case, most of the artists are happy when they are creating what they want to make."

I didn't tell her that I was an exception. I hadn't made anything while I was having 'fun', I only painted after having sex, heady with alcohol or waking up from nightmares, suffering with the demons of my past.

She bit her lip, my hazel eyes watching the fullness of her bottom lip before she replied. "I understand, Khalid. Like the process of turning a scent into a bottle of glass."

I took a sharp breath when Valeria gave me a bright smile. If she kept smiling at me like that, I was sure I would fall for her. I placed my hand over my chest, rubbing the material of the shirt to calm my pounding heart underneath.

Wait, fall for her? Where did that come from?

I couldn't fall for her, I won't.

But I knew, at that moment, I was lying to myself.

Valeria

I clutched his hand when he helped me down the stairs after we had our dessert. I had asked him which painting was the hardest to paint. Walking out of the restaurant together, I breathed in the fresh air of night.

"Every painting was hardest to do," he hummed, thinking about his answer. His deep voice making me shiver. "It would be my next painting."

Why did I sense a hint of smugness in his voice?

"Will you tell me what it's about?" I asked sweetly, my mind full of curiosity. I couldn't wait for him to finish the painting and hear Benjamin explain it. Or better yet, hear Khalid explain it to me.

Khalid crooned, his warm breath brushing the shell of my ear. "You would have to try harder than that, Valeria."

I let out a small laugh and squeezed his hand when he announced his driver was waiting for us. I settled in the warm leather seat of the car and felt Khalid's presence beside me, closing the door after laying my cane on the side. I told my address to the driver, the car turning on with a smooth purr, and started moving.

"What about *Limerence*? Was it hard to paint?" It was among his best paintings, after all.

There was a moment of silence before Khalid answered. "No. I finished sketching it in a day and painted it within next two days."

I could sense the hint of hardness in his voice, which was absent when he talked to me before. My question must have evoked some kind of bad memory to him while he painted *Limerence.*

Without hesitation, I placed my palm on his hand. Or rather, I wanted to place my palm on his hand to console him but landed on his muscular thigh. Without embarrassing myself further, I said, "I apologize if my question was rude. I was getting too curious."

Oh, I am curious, alright.

I scolded myself for being so rude while feeling the hot, strong skin underneath the touch of my hand clad in silk pants. I froze when his thigh muscle tensed, and before I could take my hand away, he covered my palm with his.

"You weren't rude." He asked, "How do you feel—"

"We have arrived at Miss Valeria's home, your grace," the driver interrupted us.

Khalid squeezed my hand. "Come on, I will walk you to your door."

I led the way, having the path to my house mapped out in my mind. He had asked me about my work, and he seemed impressed when I talked about *Delicate Dew*. It had a profitable launch two years ago, with doubling profits each month ever since it was launched.

I had a terrible date night because the fragrance I was wearing made me feel uncomfortable. It was supposed to be the best perfume of that year, with a reputable brand, but it didn't suit my skin. With my business degree, I decided that I would make my brand of perfume for every gender with simple notes to wear every day. Half of the royalties went to fund the fundraiser and charities for disabled people.

"The rosy, delicate perfume that you are wearing right now, is it from your brand?" He asked, the scent of his cologne in the night air making me want to press my face against his chest.

Why does he have to smell so good?

"It is. It lasts for hours."

"My mom used to wear it that's why I wanted to talk to you about it at the art show," he said and I could feel the sadness in his voice. Everyone knew about the death of his mothers, the two Sultanas dying in a plane crash. "The notes have changed, but it made me nostalgic."

I rubbed my thumb on his pulse. "I layer it with other perfume to match with my body. I found the name of the brand when I was a kid and asked a lady and she was kind enough to give me her own travel size bottle."

"You are wearing the woodsy notes," I said. "It suits you."

"I had to take the suggestion of a beautiful lady," he said, the vibrations of his voice sending chills over my body. "I would like to invest in your company. Try out some of the perfumes myself."

I faced him. "You would? But… we just met and you want to offer a partnership to my company?"

When he didn't reply, I giggled. "You nodded, didn't you?"

"I… I am so sorry. Yes, I nodded." Khalid let out a small chuckle, his warm breath caressing the bare skin of my neck.

He continued, "Knowing most of the profit goes to the charities, I know my investments will be in excellent hands. Even the beautiful CEO of the company seems very charming and caring."

I didn't reply, our feet coming to a halt in front of the main door of my house. I knew he was looking over the gardens that were mainly handled by Mabel and Mr Benjamin.

"Were you going to ask me about something? Before we arrived?"

"Yes, but it can wait. Goodnight, Valeria. I will see you soon."

I was not expecting his hot body pressing against me, a pair of warm lips kissing my cheek. I gaped and pressed my fingers to where Khalid had kissed me. My entire body felt like it was about to melt when I heard him walk away.

Not fair. I wanted to kiss him goodnight, too.

Kiss *his cheek*. Not anything else.

Nothing else.

5
KHALID

I let out a sharp exhale, my body clenching with need and pleasure. I watched with half-lidded eyes as my hand stroked the velvety skin of my cock, moving it back and forth with firm pressure. Warm palettes of water pattered across my broad shoulders, the muscles on my body tensing with pure lust.

The deltoids of my muscular back moved when I leaned on the tile across me, squeezing my eyes shut. Instantly, my mind flashed with images of the stunning red-haired woman who had captured my mind, body and soul within one meeting.

Valeria Dunne.

"*Valeria,*" I groaned out, my husky voice echoing in the empty bathroom.

In my mind, I hadn't been a gentleman and walked her home. *No,* I had captured her soft palm on my thigh and trailed it upwards. To make her feel how fucking *hard* her one touch had made me. She would gasp as I would use her hand to stroke myself over my pants, the friction causing me to groan her name and embrace her lips in a heated kiss.

There would be no one but us in the backseat of my car, kissing and touching each other's bodies and fucking.

Lots of fucking.

I imagined how beautiful she would look spread out beneath me. All bare and flushed for me. Whimpering and moaning and clutching my shoulders when I thrust inside her tight pussy again and again. Oh, how wonderful her moans would sound against my ears. How her warm walls would clench me.

I came with a long moan, hissing her name as I released thick spurts of seed in the shower. With a sharp exhale, I leaned back on the cold tiles, swallowing the lump in my throat.

I was truly going mad. Over a woman, nonetheless. Zayed would definitely make fun of me if I ever told him.

My muscles relaxed, my mind still floating with the filthy fantasies I had for Valeria. Guilt washed over me and I cleaned myself quickly, getting out of the shower and angrily wearing some clothes to hide my nudity.

I felt sick. Ashamed. Guilty. I shouldn't have, but I did. Valeria was six years younger than me and even though our age didn't matter, she seemed innocent. Far too innocent. She didn't know that I killed my own father without any remorse. And I would do it again if I had to.

She was better off without me.

Then why did I feel the need to be with her? Why did the ache of her absence cause a hollowness in my heart? Most of all, *why did she seem so familiar?*

⚜

MY CAR SMELT LIKE ROSES, MY DRIVER DRIVING THE CAR WHILE I checked the map to the address Benjamin had given me after much reluctance. After the morning shower, I had gone to see

Valeria, but she wasn't at her home when I had knocked at eleven in the morning with a bouquet of roses in my hands. Benjamin had opened the door with a smile and asked if the flowers were for him.

He wishes.

Benjamin told me that Valeria was volunteering for the day at the foster care he and his wife, Mabel—who was a sweet, plum lady and not at all like Benjamin—had started. After asking him for the address, I had left Valeria's beautiful house in search of her.

So she was a self-made millionaire, beautiful like an angel, supported charities and volunteered in a foster house.

Each day, I discovered something new about Valeria, who was slowly turning into my muse.

After reaching the foster house, I took the bouquet of roses with me and looked over a whitewashed building. Few of the people stared at me when I entered through the gate. I was used to the looks because of my tall height, my skin tone and my face.

I had an aquiline pointed nose, stern face with a chiseled jaw and sharp cheekbones. My dark brows and hooded onyx eyes made me look intimidating. Even Zain had commented that I looked more like a Sultan of Azmia than he ever did.

But I always denied it. Looks didn't matter. Looks *never* matter. It was the inside that mattered, and mine was rotted with dark memories and past sins.

I stopped in the hallway, looking around for the cozy feeling the house gave of. The smiling photographs of children and babies made me smile. It made me remember how I used to visit foster homes with my mother as a child. How happy it made me to spend that time with her, watching her treat others with kindness. The scent of roses and freshly cut grass.

Why was I here? What was I doing here? What was my purpose in knowing more about Valeria Dunne when I had to be in my country?

I let out a sigh, raking my hand through my hair. I shouldn't have come chasing her at the foster care. I knew it from the first moment I saw her. Valeria was nothing like me. She reminded me of all the good things in my life.

And why I didn't deserve any of it.

I was about to drop the roses in a nearby empty vase and leave when I heard the commotion from the backyard. The loud, cheerful laughter of the familiar soft lilting voice.

I couldn't help myself but follow the sound, and I was glad that I did.

There you are.

Her long red hair burnt like a shinning copper in the sunlight as kids surrounded her, running and playing with her while still being careful. She laughed again when the little Asian boy whispered something in her ear. Her face was bare of any makeup, making her look younger. Far younger than her real age. My eyes traced the edges of her lips, her pert nose red with laughter, with her cheeks dusted pink.

It was decided. Valeria was my muse, and I would do anything to paint her.

Or *on* her.

Valeria

I huffed out a breath when the children continued to giggle and run around me. I should be helping the others in the kitchen or in the laundry and volunteer but instead, I was with the kids who had dragged me in the backyard to play as soon as I had arrived with home-baked cookies.

I had a prickle of sensation that someone might be watching me, but I ignored it. It could be one of the kid—

"Who's that tall man, Valy?" Keon, a four-year-old boy, asked, tugging on my white tee shirt.

I had my wardrobe set up according to the colors from light to pastels to dark so on most occasions, I knew which colored clothes I was wearing.

"Which tall man?" I asked, turning around, "Is someone there? Keon wants to meet you—"

"Hello Valeria."

I was not expecting to hear someone reply. I was especially not expecting Khalid's velvety smooth voice to reply.

"Khalid? You are here. I... *hello*." I tugged on my loose white tee shirt nervously. I was wearing a tee, jeans and sneakers in front of the Prince of Azmia.

Last night, I had a boost of confidence because I knew I looked good in a dress with my hair styled and face donned in minimal makeup. But at that moment, I had no makeup on and my hair was all over the place. Only if I had known that he might see me so soon then I would have—

What the hell was I thinking? So what if he saw me in a tee shirt and jeans? I was still wearing my signature scent. I knew I still looked good without makeup or my hair styled. I didn't need to make myself presentable. Especially while volunteering.

I looked decent, and the kids adored me, and that was enough.

"Yes, I am here. I came to visit you this morning, but Benjamin told me that you would be here. So I came."

Khalid's voice became clear and loud as he got closer, standing directly across from me. He smelt of his musky male cologne and... roses. It was distinctive, but I had noticed.

The night before, I was wearing heels. But standing across Khalid Al Latif in sneakers, I realized how tall he must be to make me feel tiny just by standing close. I remembered searching his name on the web page and hearing *Siri* describe his attribute, especially that he was six feet five.

My brain took some time processing what he meant. I sputtered, "You came to my house? You talked with Benjamin and he said… you came here to *meet me?*"

I felt him smiling as he answered, "Yes, sweet one. I had to see you this morning, so here I am." The scent of roses wafted through my nose as Khalid gently placed my palm around something. "This is a bouquet of roses."

"Oh." I smiled and took a long sniff from the smooth petals. "They smell lovely!"

"They are for you, Valeria."

My face must be the same color as the roses. "Why?"

My belly churned with an unknown warm emotion when I heard Khalid laugh for the first time. It was low, soft and everything more than I could handle. It made me happy hearing his laugh. I wanted to record it and hear it over and over again. His laugh was adorably precious.

"Of course, it's for you," he managed to say through his laugh.

I was still spell bound from hearing his laughter. "I like your laugh," I whispered. "You should do it more often, Khalid."

I heard him take a sharp breath, and I didn't know what his expression said at that moment. I wished, just for a moment, to have my sight back so I could decipher what he was thinking, what he looked like, or if his cheeks get warm like mine when he gets flustered.

To end the weird silence between them, I introduced Khalid to the kids and handed each one of them a rose to take care of. They took it happily and thanked Khalid for them.

"It's lunchtime!" one of the volunteers yelled and like a hoard of sheep, all the children ran towards the dining with hoots and cheers.

I glanced in his direction. "Would you like to join us, Khalid?"

Khalid

"Come back soon, Valeria. The kids miss you," one of the older women with white streaks in her hair said to the smiling woman standing beside me, patting her red hair with her palm.

"I will. Soon!"

I watched as she embraced the older woman in a hug and bid her goodbye. I bowed my head and walked alongside Valeria, staying close. But she knew how many steps the gate was from the main door. I had told her that I would drop her home. I opened the door for her and kept a palm under the edge of the roof of the car when Valeria bent to sit down. I didn't want to get her hurt by hitting her head.

When the driver started the car, I noticed that she was struggling with the belt.

"May I?" I asked, her striking green eyes peering at me. *She was not wearing sunglasses today.* Beautiful eyes. I swallowed the lump in my throat the longer her eyes gazed across my face. Her lower lashes looked so soft and pretty.

What the absolute fuck, Khalid? Lower lashes? You are whipped by lower lashes? Un-fucking-believable.

"Sure."

I leaned close, wrapping my hand around the belt and dragging it towards the buckle and latching onto it. But curse my eyes for staying on the slender curve of her pale neck, the way her tee shirt tightened over her chest as her breathing got heavier. She smelt like flowers and something feminine. I wanted to untangle her copper tendrils from the low bun on her neck and let my hand run through the length of them.

I quickly latched the buckle and cleared my throat when she mumbled a small 'thank you.'

"Would you like to visit the art gallery with me?"

Why were my hands getting sweaty? Why was I nervous?

"With you? Of course, Khalid. It would be my honor, but you know I don't have sight."

I clenched my hand. "I will try my best to explain the paintings to you. If that's okay with you?"

Valeria's smile reached her eyes. My heart stumbling yet again at the sight. "Sure."

⚜

"AND THIS IS *NOX*. I DIDN'T NAME IT. IT IS PAINTED IN NEUTRALS with a landscape of night from my house back in Azmia." Valeria nodded, intently hearing every word I spoke, wanting to know more about my paintings.

It was evening when we had arrived at the empty art gallery. I had told the driver to take his leave, I would drop her home and then take a cab.

I was showing her around, our silent feet padding side by side. My low baritone voice speaking just over her ear, making her shiver. It felt intimate and extremely touching that she trusted me to show her around an empty art gallery.

My warm fingers cradled her dainty wrist. "Here, point out your index finger."

She did what I asked, gasping when my tall body pressed against her side, careful not to touch her anywhere inappropriately, even though my body begged to fuck her between my paintings against an empty wall.

I stretched her arm towards the canvas. Her finger touched the texture of fabric, her face glowing as if she had solved a hard puzzle.

Adorable.

"Is that your—"

My warm breath caressed her cheek. "Yes. It's the painting.

This is a shaded grey color." I traced her finger lower. Letting her feel the stroke of the brush, "meeting a darker color of land at night. And when you go up," our clasped hands trailed up, "it's the color white of the clear sky. Of purity and clarity."

I opened her palm and lightly trailed all her fingers over the middle part of the painting. Letting her touch all the small little dots, dents and grainy texture.

"These are sand dunes mixed with grey, white, black and darker colors, creating a contrasting yet simple painting. This was the easiest among all the others presented here."

"Wow," Valeria breathed out, her fingers squeezing mine. "It sounds beautiful."

We moved to other paintings. Each time, I held her hand and let her explore the painting on her own. Sometimes stepping back and enjoying watching her. Her eyebrows scrunched with concentration when she gently touched my paintings. She was so careful and gentle, as if she was caressing expensive China.

It arose a new feeling in my body. A new sensation. It was erotic in nature. I loved watching her explore my paintings. As if she was exploring me, my body, with her gentle fingers.

Fuck, what I wouldn't do to feel that.

When she asked me for the colors, I tried to explain to her as much as I could, giving an example of nature and fruits and feelings. I wished to spend the night in the gallery explaining the paintings to her all night, but it was getting late and when we stepped out of the gallery, the sky had turned grey with rain pattering hard on the ground.

"I love the smell of wet sand!" Valeria giggled as cold water started pattering over us.

I held her close, not wanting her to fall. But it seemed like she wanted to enjoy the rain a bit more, and I was too whipped to ever deny anything to her.

I peered at Valeria when she shook out her hair and let it

get wet. She looked at the sky with a big grin and closed her eyes, her lashes getting wet.

"Khalid, come on, join me!"

As I couldn't deny her anything, I decided to step out of the nearby shade and join her even though I hated rain.

Valeria surprised me when she held my hand and told me to mirror her and face the sky with a big smile.

"Are you doing it?"

I lied to her for the first time. "Yes."

I was busy watching *her*.

"How does it feel?"

"I feel… alive."

For the first time in years, I truly felt *alive*.

6

KHALID

I noticed the bus stop close to the gallery and held her close as I led her towards it. I felt a little guilty for stopping her from enjoying in the rain, but the carefree look on her face still remained.

My eyes averted to the couple of drunk men leering at women as they passed by. My hold tightened on Valeria's hand, the sound of rain falling on the ground and her cane tapping surrounding us.

"Look at that wet little thing," one of the men whistled, walking towards us. They blocked our path. Two of his friends surrounding us, reeking of cheap beer.

Valeria pressed closer to me, my hand tightening as I felt how tense her body had become. She was afraid. Her icy fingers squeezed mine as she whispered, "Let's go, Khalid."

"You heard the lady." I eyed the three men. "Let us pass."

But they were too drunk to process what I said as one of them lifted his hand towards Valeria. I grabbed his wrist and glared down at him.

Drawing a slow, steady breath, I said in a controlled tone, "I said, let us pass. I won't repeat it again."

"She's so fucking wet for us!" the other guy cackled.

My jaw clenched and before I could call the police to let it end smoothly, I heard the small *thump* behind me. Valeria gasped as they pushed away her cane and grabbed her arm.

My pulse sped up, muscles and veins straining against my skin as I violently pushed the man I was holding towards his friend.

Adrenaline rushed through my head as I prowled towards the man who was holding her arm. I grabbed it and pried away his hand from her. My nose flared at the red markings on her pale arm.

"K-Khalid, let's go, please," she stuttered, her voice small as she fetched her phone, trying to call for help even though her body was shaking.

My head threw back as pain coursed through my cheek. I shook my head and spit out blood, glancing at the man who had punched me. I held him by the collar of his shirt, rewarding him with a punch, relishing in the crunch of his nose breaking. My knuckles zinged with pain, but I ignored it and kicked his stomach.

"*Khalid,*" Valeria called for me to stop, but I couldn't.

I wanted to hurt him.

He coughed, blood spluttering out of his mouth as I took the cane he had taken away from my Valeria. I hit him with the cane, sighing when it broke after hitting his back, a scream tearing out of his mouth.

"Stop it, man! We will leave you alone." His two friends held my arms, but I wasn't done yet. I thrashed against them, kicking and punching the sensitive points of their body, their ribs, the back of their knees, their faces.

Huffing a breath, I leaned down on the previous man, who had grabbed Valeria. I punched him, holding him up by his collar.

I snarled, "How *dare* you touch her."

Rage simmered through me, flashes of my father grabbing Zara's dainty wrist erupting in my head.

I hit him again, his eyes swelling shut, blood pouring out of his nose and lips.

"How dare you touch what's *mine*," I said, my voice cold and guttural. I held his head, ready to smash it against the pavement.

"*Khalid!*" Valeria cried out, grabbing my arm. "Please. Stop. *Please.*"

I took a deep breath, the man whimpering as I let him go. "If I see you out here leering at anyone again… I *will* kill you," I threatened, standing up and wiping my face on the sleeve of my shirt as police glanced at the three beaten men and at me.

A sense of release washed over me when I glared at their cowering faces and the shocked glances of people surrounding us. Some of them had their phones on, taking videos and pictures. Somehow, I didn't give a shit about the consequences of being a Prince of Azmia and getting into a fight.

They had touched Valeria. Even when I warned them to let us pass. They deserved it.

My eyes zeroed on her, her wide eyes, her shaking hands and her wet clothes. Removing my shirt, I draped it over her, my blood smeared over the sleeve as she tugged it closer to her.

"Come with me," I said to her, holding her hand.

I would deal with the fight, the police. My guards had been notified about it as my *Rolls-Royce* stopped to a halt. I asked her to sit inside, telling her I would be back in a minute and demanding one of my guards to bring her some water.

Talking to the police, I confessed that they had started the fight. The witnesses took my side.

"We need to talk to the lady to confirm—"

I looked down at him. "No, you don't *need* to. I confirmed it. If you still want to talk to her, give me a call tomorrow morning and we will sort this out, officer."

I gave him a charming smile because he knew who I was and walked away, asking the guard to clear up anything else the cops wanted to ask me.

Being a prince certainly came in handy during some times.

♔

"I AM SORRY FOR WHAT HAPPENED," I SAID TO VALERIA IN THE car, her gaze distant as she looked out of the car window. I wished I had hailed a cab as soon as we walked out of the art gallery. But I wanted to spend some more time with her, wait at the bus stop and talk to her.

"What are you sorry for?" She asked, still not looking at me.

My left cheek hurt as I said, "For letting you hear all that. I should have hailed a cab."

Valeria didn't reply as she pulled my shirt around herself and pushed her hand through the armholes, wearing it. My cheekbones slashed with color as I noticed the dark-colored bra visible through her wet tee.

I should have noticed that before those idiots did. But it was not her fault, it was their fault.

When I glanced at her after a few moments, her fingers were fumbling with the buttons of the shirt, which was unfamiliar to her.

I broke the silence. "May I?"

She nodded, biting her bottom lip when my hands placed over hers, my breath lightly fanning over her arms when I carefully buttoned the shirt. My face was so close to hers. I could count the freckles on her face. Her cheeks dusted pink. I watched in amusement when her ears turned fiery red.

What are you thinking about, sweet one?

I tried my best not to let my eyes wander on her wet skin and focused on buttoning the shirt. Her slow warm breath brushed on my cheek and I forced my mind to stop my body from reacting. I had to remind myself how sweet and innocent she was.

When I pulled back, she gave me a small nod in return. She managed to look gorgeous even wearing my shirt that looked enormous on her little body. But I knew she would look gorgeous with or without the clothes.

My cock ached to be released from the confines of the jeans as I shuffled in my seat when the images of her bare body on my bed flashed in my mind.

To avert my attention, I forced myself to look out of the window, watching the building lights flickering against the soft patter of the shower.

I couldn't help but notice *her*. Her delicate scent, her wet hair, as if she was wrapped all around me. I wanted her to wrap around me when I plunge my c—

"Where are we going?"

I didn't want that day to end. I wanted to be with her for a few more moments. At least for a night.

I glanced over at her and knew what I wanted. "Do you want to come over to my apartment?"

Valeria flushed visibly, her fingers twirling with the hem of my shirt on her lap. Her brows furrowed, thinking over my suggestion.

I had to take it slow with her, I couldn't allow myself to know her body and get it over with in a night. I wanted to take my time with her. A night wasn't enough for that.

She finally replied. "Yes, we need to talk, Khalid."

Valeria

"You can change in here, here's the lock. I am in the kitchen. Let me know if you need anything, okay?" Khalid's deep voice resonated through me, feeling more intimate than usual while I explored the bathroom, familiarizing myself with the surrounding and mapping it out in my brain.

My cane was useless because *someone* had bad temper and broke it in a fight. But I didn't plan to visit Khalid's apartment in the evening. I had to use my hands to touch and make sure I didn't trip.

We had arrived at his apartment few moments ago and he had been extremely calm, explaining the layout of his house as if the fight had never happened. The space around me was spacious and opulent. Simple yet filled with the unique taste of antiques, paintings and little sculptures. The kitchen had a big island and all the usual necessities. There were two rooms, and he had been kind enough to explain the master suite and let me use the enormous bathroom in it. It had its own jacuzzi, shower and steam cubicle.

I clutched the cotton fabric of his clothes. A fresh tee shirt and sweatpants, which he had given me to change into so I wouldn't get cold.

"Thank you, Khalid." I hoped he couldn't decipher how small my voice had become. I was in a new space with him. Alone. With my clothes drenched. His own bloody shirt covering me.

Oh God.

I heard him close the door and let out an enormous sigh of relief. I could use some time alone before joining him in the kitchen. I needed to talk to him about what had happened. The way he had reacted towards someone catcalling me as if I hadn't gone through it before. The sound of bone crunching and hard muscle hitting the skin rang through my ears as I stood under the shower.

He hadn't thought twice before punching them and starting a fight instead of calling for help or police. As if he didn't care he got hurt or what people and media will talk about him, the Prince of Azmia, getting into a street fight. All because of *me*.

I wished I hadn't panicked when the stranger had grabbed my hand, I wished I had kicked him or screamed for help or called the police sooner. I wished I hadn't frozen the second the reek of cheap beer surrounded me. I wished I had done something instead of just standing by and hearing Khalid being hit and fighting.

All because of me.

I wiped away the stupid, useless tears and angrily washed my body, hating how I could still feel the strange touch on my arm as I scrubbed it until I felt clean. My skin burning and sensitive.

It all happened because of me.

Khalid

"Sit down," Valeria ordered me, her cheeks puffing with anger.

I bit back my grin and sat down on my couch. She didn't look angry, she looked adorable. So small and tiny in my large clothes. She even had to roll up the sweatpants. I could kiss her and tuck her in my pocket.

"Give me your hand," she demanded, placing a medical kit on the coffee table.

I raised my eyebrow, but followed her command. Despite the cuteness that seeped out of every pore of her body, I wanted to follow her commands. All her commands.

Her gentle fingers touched my red knuckles as if she knew I had hurt them during the fight. The thought made me bite the inside of my cheek.

"Why are you doing this, Valeria?" I tried to pull my hand back, but her hold was firm. "It's okay, they are small cuts—"

She glared in my direction, her finger rubbing over the pulse of my wrist as she looked down at my hand as if she couldn't believe she was holding it.

"Pain needs care, Khalid," she whispered softly as she continued to clean my cuts and bandage them.

Her words resonated through my body, and I let her clean them up. I didn't know what to say to her. If pain needed care, then why did I still feel hurt and guilt after what I had done? If pain truly needed care, then why didn't I feel comfortable in my own skin until… *her*.

I stared at her red hair, her long lashes, and her nimble fingers. *Why now do I feel cared for? Why her? Why with Valeria?*

Her hand raised to my face, her fingers hovering in front of my eyes. I forced myself to say, "It's okay, I am fine, Valeria."

She pulled back, keeping everything as it was placed in the medical kit.

"Where did you learn to bandage like this?" I asked, rubbing my hands where she had held me with her soft fingers.

"I used to fall a lot when I lost my sight at the beginning. I didn't want to bother Mabel or Benjamin every time I got a wound so I learnt it on my own."

I wanted to say something, offer her some type of comfort, but the only way I knew was physical and I knew after what had happened, she wouldn't want that.

"You shouldn't have fought with them," she muttered after a few moments of silence, her eyes burning towards me.

I clenched my jaw. "It was my choice to fight them. They tried to touch you without—"

"I could have handled it without violence, Khalid," she said, her voice full of emotions. I looked away from her. "Don't… don't fight for me."

"Why not?"

"Because I am telling you not to."

"That's bullshit," I said, and glared at her. Taking a deep breath, I softened my voice and took her hands in mine. I stroked her soft skin, lightly tracing the red marks of that man's hold on her arm. "I am sorry if you don't like violence. If it scares you, my sweet. But I won't apologize for my choice to protect you… or anyone I care about, in my own way."

"But now people will shame you because you are a Prince and you fought them because of me."

I smiled at her frowning face. "You forgot an important detail, Valeria. I am a Prince of Azmia, I would like to see them try to shame me."

She sighed, mumbling, "So arrogant."

I eyed the dark red streaks of her hair. "You would catch cold with your hair damp. Here, let me pat them dry for you."

Before Valeria could protest, I stood up to bring another clean towel. I didn't want her to get sick.

"Is this okay?" My deep voice whispered softly from her side as I gently patted strands of her hair with a towel.

She hummed, arching her head back at me. I licked my lips at the sight of her slender neck, her beating pulse throbbing fast. *Did the closeness between us affect her, too? Was her heart beating as loudly as mine was whenever we were together?*

"I smell cheese," she sniffed out, her pert nose scrunching adorably, making me smile. "Did you make something?"

"Yes, there's a grilled cheese sandwich on the coffee table. I hope you are not lactose intolerant."

"Not at all. It smells delicious." Valeria hungrily took the bite from the sandwich, making me look away when she let out a soft hum.

Stay in control, Khalid. You are thirty-two, for fuck's sake.

I had made both of us sandwiches while she was taking a shower and brought the plates to the living room. The dim lamps gave the spacious room a soft glow as rain kept pattering against the large windows of my apartment. The view of London city lights at night, especially during rain, was marvelous.

We both ate the sandwich in comfortable silence, listening to the rain showering outside. It was weird how I had never sat in silence with anyone other than my family and my friend Zayed.

I needed to tell her. Ask her. I couldn't wait anymore.

"I have a favor to ask."

"I want to ask something from you, Khalid."

We both said at the same time, breaking the silence.

I asked, "What is it, Valeria?"

I would give anything she asked me.

Valeria tucked her hair behind her flushed ears and asked, "I wanted to, um, touch your face, if it's not too much to ask?"

I raised my eyebrows, my dark eyes roving over her face, asking me something so little with so much innocence. I raised my hand and traced the soft curve of her cheek, eyeing and remembering the freckles splattered on her nose and cheeks. Valeria shivered underneath my touch, her warm breath caressing my hand as I traced it lower, before twirling it around a stand of her copper hair.

"Only on one condition," I whispered back, allured with the sweet, innocent beauty in front of me.

Was she a virgin?

Get those thoughts out of your filthy mind, Khalid.

Blood ran to her cheeks, making them hot. She stuttered, "Wh-what condition?"

"It's simple. Describe my features when you touch me." There was a pause which made me think of my *other* features, effectively making me fluster. I continued after clearing my throat, "I mean, my face. I will sketch it. I want to know how I look in your mind."

She nodded, almost too nervously, "Sure! I am okay with that."

So there we were, sitting close to each other on the couch, our limbs brushing each other. I was clutching my sketchbook and pencil tightly when Valeria leaned up on her knees, her chest so close to my face. I cursed in my head for noticing that she wasn't even wearing a bra.

It might have drenched too, so she must have worn just my tee shirt. Which didn't help because her perky breasts with hardened nipples were poking through the fabric, enticing and torturing me in every delicious way.

But the look on Valeria's face was of pure innocence and curiosity. Guilt coursed through me, and I hated myself for being such a man and thinking like that when all she wanted to know was how I looked.

Valeria giggled nervously, "Just close your eyes so that I don't poke them."

I followed her command and clenched my jaw when her fingers touched my hair.

So soft, Valeria thought. She wanted to run her fingers through it as she described his hair to him.

"It smells amazing! Is it dark brown like chocolate?" She asked.

I smiled. No one had commented on my hair before. "It is black. Obsidian. Just like my eyes."

"I wonder what they look like." Valeria said in the moment, not realizing that no one had ever paid attention to me like that before.

Valeria wanted to see my eyes. It made me giddy in a way I shouldn't feel. They were just eyes, after all.

Her fingers traced my smooth forehead, the slashing brows and my hooded closed eyes. She lowered her fingers to my nose. Her soft voice describing the feel of my lashes, smoothness of my skin and my aquiline nose. She was smiling when her fingers grazed over the sides of my face, a tremble of shiver spiraling across her body. She explained my high cheekbones, my jaw covered in stubble, a five o'clock shadow, scratching teasingly across her palm.

I clenched the pencil so tightly that I was scared I might break it. I was looking at her, her eyes closed when she touched me so intimately, caressing me with such gentleness that I never wanted her to stop. Her hands cupped my face, her shaky voice whispering at the sharpness of my face.

I watched in horror when she was about to pull away and acted on pure instinct, holding her wrist.

"You missed something, Valeria." My voice was heavy with arousal.

"I did?" Her voice was breathy.

I pulled her closer. "I can't finish my sketch without one thing."

We both knew what I was referring to.

Valeria swallowed the lump in her throat. "Are you okay with it?"

My response was to place her fingers on my lips. I watched her face with half-lidded eyes, her teeth sinking into the pink flesh of her bottom lip, wishing I was the one doing that. Thank God I was covering myself with the sketchbook, or she might have known that I was going hard with just a small touch of hers on my lips. That I might just combust if she kissed me.

The heavy air around us sizzled with sparks. It felt raw. Intimate. Vulnerable.

Valeria shyly trailed her hands from my lips to cup my jaw. My heart rate doubled over as I heard her say,

"Can I... Can I kiss you, Khalid?"

PART II

"I want to paint you, Valeria."

7

VALERIA

Everything became muffled in his living room when I whispered those sweet words. It felt as if a membrane had dropped around us, caging us in a heady sensation.

'*Can I... Can I kiss you, Khalid?*'

I let out a small gasp when I felt his hand wrap around my waist and pull me closer to him, settling me on his lap. My first impression of Khalid was how hard he was—*no, not there*, but how strongly built he must be. Like a concrete wall. And how broad his shoulders were when my hands fisted the material of his shirt. He was large, larger than anyone I had ever known, caging me on his lap, his muscular arms with corded veins wrapped around my waist.

But his touch was gentle, like a wind brushing petals of rose. He was gentle. It made my heart ache.

Then I *felt* him. The hard bulge underneath my thigh. *Did I cause that?* A pulse throbbed violently between my legs. White hot lust turned into a melting sensation in my lower belly. I was aching painfully, wanting and waiting.

With my hands on his jaw, I could make out the sensual line

of his mouth. I had the sudden urge to lick those lines and please him. My skin prickled with anticipation, trying to be patient with his answer. His heart was racing when I smelt his scent. Exotic and musky and pure male.

It was purely vulgar and filthy, in the sense I had never known.

I felt his head move slowly in a nod. My breathing grew erratic, as if I might hyperventilate. My skin burnt with fire when his large palm cupped the side of my face, his thumb rubbing my cheek. I was hot. Fiery. It felt overwhelming, and I didn't know what to do.

Khalid said in a low voice, "Yes, my sweet one."

Before I could react, his arm pushed me towards him, our bodies pressing into each other. Melting into one. He anchored my head towards him and pressed his mouth against mine, stealing my breath.

My eyes squeezed shut when I felt the gentle press of his lips, his hand deep in my hair, holding me close. I kissed him back, my own fingers trailing up to feel his hot skin and the wild pulse in his neck and settling on to his hair. I wanted more. *Needed* more when he pulsed beneath me.

I moaned into the kiss.

With a small groan, Khalid plunged his tongue into my mouth. As if my moan had driven him to the edge. My legs clenched around him when he took the kiss from zero to one hundred. It was no more a gentle, exploratory kiss.

It was explicit. Raw. Wicked.

I didn't know what I was feeling anymore. Adrenaline and delicious pleasure coursed through my blood. It made my body aware of how hot and hard he was. How soft and willing I was. It made my skin tingle with awareness. My heating core tightened with extreme need.

I registered after a while that his hand was under my tee shirt, caressing my back softly, my spine sending shivers down my body making my toes curl at his touch. I felt something in me when his mouth left mine, allowing me to gulp down a deep breath when his lips trailed down over my jaw, kissing my neck.

My head tipped back, eyes closed. I was smiling. My entire body was reduced to a frantic, urgent need that I felt crawling beneath me. And Khalid stroked that exact need to make me feel alive.

I was alive.

I felt drugged and dizzy with that feeling. It was consuming me.

"Khalid…"

Khalid

I heard her sultry whisper and looked up at her through my diamond like black eyes. Her face was flushed and her lips were swollen red with the kiss we had shared. She looked dizzy with a small smile on her lips.

I had to hold on to her so that I wouldn't combust. She was my anchor.

I took a deep breath, urging myself down, not wanting to taint her innocence with my raging need. It felt wrong to me even though what we had just shared… I had never felt like that before.

I removed my hand from the tee shirt, not knowing when I had done that, and rubbed her back, patting down her mussed hair.

"Are you okay, Valeria?"

My voice wrapped around her name in a rich timber. I felt the small clench of her legs, and I knew she was as much aroused as I was. If not more, judging by her dizzy expression.

She hummed, her fingers playing with hair on the back of my neck. It made me heady. If she kept doing that…

"I want to do it again."

"What?"

Valeria looked away, clearing her throat. "The kiss, I mean. I… I want to feel like that again, Khalid."

I understood her. Fuck, how much I understood what she meant.

But I asked anyway, "Feel like what?"

"*Alive.*"

I wanted to make her feel alive again. Make us both feel alive and more. But I was afraid that if I kissed her once more, I wouldn't be able to stop.

"We can't right now, my sweet one," I said in a low voice that she could have barely heard it. My lips pressed over her cheek as I settled her on the couch.

Valeria visibly sulked, a small pout forming on her lips. *Fucking adorable.* "Can I ask why not?"

I wanted to kiss away her small pout. I tapped her nose and picked up the sketchbook to finish where I left off. "I said we can't right now. It's just not the right moment… the right place. Setting."

I didn't know how to explain it to her. In those few days, Valeria had become too precious to me. I didn't want to lay her down and pleasure her in one of my apartments in London. It was not what she deserved. And I always wanted to strive to offer her the best.

Valeria

"Then where is the right place? The right moment?" My voice was laced with frustration that we both felt. I didn't understand him. He was hard. I was wet. *We were aroused, then why didn't he… not like I would know how this works.*

"Somewhere that is not here." Khalid let out a sigh and

paused for a moment. I felt his eyes on me as he continued, "Are you a virgin, Valeria?"

I blinked in his direction and looked away, my hands clenching tightly in my palm. I didn't think he would ask that. I said truthfully, "No, I am not a virgin if that is what you are worried about."

I felt his hand lay on top of mine. I faced him. "Okay, I just wanted to know. I didn't want to cause you pain if you were."

I swallowed the lump in my throat and nodded back. I felt safe and comfortable around him. I knew Khalid would never cause me pain. Not willingly anyway, like making me feel... empty without his touch and embrace.

It was driving me crazy.

"This is not the right time because I want to paint you, Valeria," He whispered in his deep velvety voice.

"P-paint me?"

I could smell his musky scent when he crooned in my ear. "Yes. *Naked.*"

I trembled, my body reacting acutely to his teasing words.

He continued in his low voice, his finger trailing over my neck, "I want to paint your pale skin. Your neck. Your sensual body. Your stunning eyes. Your lush lips. Your red copper hair."

Khalid flicked my ear with his tongue, making me gasp when he whispered dirtily, "Your *tits.*"

"I can paint on you too, my sweet one." He planted a soft kiss below my ear. My breathing grew erratic. My breasts—*tits*, as he called them, aching to be touched by him. "Lay your naked body on my bed and paint on your bare skin with my hands. Would you like that, Valeria?"

I was clenching my legs tightly, melting passionate desire gushing my underwear. I licked my lips, my heart beating loudly. "I... I would love that, Khalid."

When I didn't heart him reply, I sought him out and

touched his face, feeling the warm skin beneath my palm. "Please tell me what are you thinking?"

He covered my hand with his, kissing my palm and squeezing it lightly. "I want you to come with me to my country. To Azmia. Tomorrow."

I never even dreamt that he would ever ask me to come with him. Invite me with him to go to his country. It felt surreal.

I let out a nervous laugh. "Are you sure? Why? Why Azmia?"

Khalid confessed, "Because it's the only place where I am truly free to paint. I have my studio, a place where I go to paint and nowhere else. It's a force of habit. And I want to take you there with me."

I processed his words and considered them for a moment. I had never taken a day off from working and visiting factories to make sure every perfume bottle of my brand was made perfect, from the scent to its packaging. I had been thinking about a mini-vacation, even Mabel and Mr Benjamin wanted me to take some time off.

I could do that. Go to Azmia. Be with Khalid. Let him paint me. Let him paint *on* me.

The opportunities were endless.

I leaned up, wanting to kiss him on his cheek, but my calculations were misjudged and the kiss landed on his lips. Too flustered, I pulled back and blurted, "Yes. I would like to come with you, Khalid. To Azmia. But I would need to make some calls and talk to Brandon before we leave."

"Good." He kissed my forehead. "I will let Benjamin know. You don't need to pack any clothes."

I turned red hearing his words and felt him smirking when he dialed the number.

8

KHALID

"Meet your new mother," my father's gruff voice rumbled through the room, a pale woman standing beside him, holding a cane in her hand. "Her name is Isabella."

I glared at her, scoffing and crossing my arms in my hand. *So this is why he was absent from the Palace for three months.* He went and married someone else even though mother was his wife.

Zain squeezed my shoulder, giving me a look to *behave* and stepped ahead to introduce himself. Father smiled proudly at him, even ruffling his hair.

He never did that to me.

"Pst, pst, Khal!"

I glanced over my shoulder at the curls of Zayed's hair. He was hiding behind a pillar and calling me over to play with horses. I smiled at his dimple and was about to sneak over to him when my father's voice stopped me.

"Khalid Al Latif," I mentally winced at his harsh tone saying my full name. "Have I not taught you any manners?"

I clenched my jaw and glared at his dark eyes. Isabella was

smiling in my direction but she wasn't looking at me. I had heard my mother's maid gossip how Isabella couldn't see. That she was born blind.

So I poked my tongue at her and ignoring father's shout, I ran away with Zayed to play with the horses.

The dark room shifted and I was in the bed, frowning at the throbbing pain in my right foot.

"Your father told me you fell from the horse," Isabella said, walking towards my bed, her cane tapping against the floor.

"Why did you marry my father?"

She laughed. I hadn't heard someone laugh like that before. Softly and gently. Nowadays my mothers' laugh seemed forced even though Zain and I tried our best to make her happy.

"I like his voice," she stated, sitting on the edge of the bed, looking in my direction with that annoying little smile. She looked at me as if she could see through me. I hated that.

"That's it? He sounds grumpy to me."

"I like his charm, leadership and honesty." Isabella placed her palm on the cast of my foot. "You are a lot like him."

"No, I am not!"

She lifted her hand as if shocked by my outburst and placed her hand on her lap. "I didn't mean to anger you, Prince Khalid."

I glared at her but decided it was of no use if she couldn't see I was glaring at her. I glanced at her cane. "You know... he is not even handsome. He is getting old."

"You really dislike your father, don't you?" Isabella chuckled, her voice lilting. "I didn't marry him for his looks, Prince. He offered me love and safety."

I didn't reply to her, watching her leave my room as I wondered how he took everything he had promised to offer her.

How he ignored that Isabella was unfit to be a mother yet forced her to carry a child for nine months. How my father hated her and refused to hold my little sister, letting my mother comfort Isabella. How he moved Isabella to a closeted chambers with Zara, stealing what little freedom she had. How he beat my mother, Zain and me for his own hatred, greed and delusion of having another male heir.

It drove him insane. It pushed our mother to depression and Isabella to isolation.

My world fogged and I whirled until I saw him hold my sister's dainty wrist, tears streaming down her pale face as she cried, calling her brother's name. All I could see was flashes of my father hurting my mother and Isabella. Beating Zain, scolding him to be a better man, a better leader, a better Sultan until he refused to feel anything.

I couldn't let that monster hurt my sister. Not my Zara. I had promised Isabella that I would take care of her when she had left with my mother to London and died in a plane crash. It was a death promise.

But it was Zain who moved first, who yelled at father, stood his grounds. I pulled Zara's small body towards me, tears threatening my eyes when I saw the red marks of his finger-prints on her skin.

"I won't let him hurt you," I promised to her, wiping tears from her cheeks and pulling her behind me as she clutched my legs.

My father, Salman Al Latif, had hit his Zain on the head with his cane. I clenched my fists, my hands shaking as I met my own father's eyes. Dark and angry and mad. He was not my father anymore. Just a shell of a person driven by greed, jealousy, anger and hatred toward his own six years old daughter.

He wanted to hurt my mother. Isabella. Zain and me. He wanted to hurt my sister. A kid.

I had tried to come up with excuses for his actions but I couldn't anymore.

I have had enough.

My father was a terrible person and he didn't deserve to live.

I held the hilt of his sword from the wall where it was hung for display, the family heirloom that was passed on from generation to generation. I squared my shoulder, begging him to stop when he called Zara a witch, a monster. But he didn't hear me.

I could only stop him by driving the sword through his chest, tears running down my face as I looked at the man who had caused so much pain and misery to my loved ones.

For a moment, all I felt was relief.

Good. He won't be able to hurt us anymore. He won't ever hurt Zara. She will be able to roam freely around the palace. She will be able to step out and go see the desert on a horse. She won't be restricted to her room anymore.

Then I felt the trickle of warm blood on my hands, the gasp of my sister as my father's blood sprayed on both of us, the wall painting red. So much red.

Red. I had seen that red before. When I was fifteen, on that backyard with her. Carrot pin on her hair. Sketching with her.

"I want to go back to that orphanage," I remembered telling my mother in the car wishing I had asked that girl her name.

My mother smiled at me and ruffled my hair. "Give her roses when we visit again, Khalid."

I promised I would. That's what gentlemen do when they want to impress a woman.

Red.

That night the memories of red blended in my head and I cried for the first time in ages and painted *Limerence* in my room. I had killed my father. I had taken someone's life.

I woke up next morning with my bedsheet drenched in my sweat. Sighing, I held my head in my palms. Over a decade had passed and yet those nightmares troubled me.

I took a few deep breaths and checked the time. Right. I had to wake up Valeria from the guest room and drive to the airport. I shook off the flashes of nightmare and took a cold shower.

Valeria. I will focus on her. Not my past. At least for a month.

♔

I LOOKED AT THE CLOUDY VIEW FROM THE WINDOW OF THE private plane, my skin prickling with nervousness to get back to my country. With a woman I adored.

A secret smile curled my lips when I looked across the seat and found her dozing off against the neck pillow I had gently laid to support her head. Her pink lips, the ones which I had devoured the night before, were a little parted. Her breathing was even with her lashes, making shadows on her soft cheeks.

I had woken her up from the guest bedroom early morning after spending the night shuffling on my bed. I wasn't able to sleep when Valeria was sleeping in the next room. I wanted to cuddle her, hug her to my chest and smell the roses from her hair the first thing in the morning. But I had controlled all my urges.

I had thanked Benjamin and Mabel for packing her a suitcase and handing me a box of chocolate chip cookies with a secret recipe of Mabel's which Valeria loved to devour. I had politely asked for the recipe and Mabel had given it to me with a big smile.

Zain knew that I wouldn't arrive at the palace straight away. I had a business to do.

By business, I meant Valeria.

Valeria

I covered my mouth, stifling a yawn when the plane trembled with turbulence. The air hostess had offered sweet dates, and I had passed out after eating a few of them. I tried to pat down my hair as much as I could, feeling Khalid's eyes on me. It was a warm sensation that made my body respond differently. I had never felt it before.

After my business took off, I had given dating a try, but I could never feel comfortable with my date, and if I did, he would try to get in my pants at the end of the second date.

With Khalid, I wanted to have sex with him the night we met. It's crazy how sexually attracted I was towards him.

Khalid took my palm as we descended from the plane, his hold tight. I was clutching the cane he had gifted me in my other hand even though I didn't need it when he was with me.

Heat washed over me like a caress. It felt heavy and freeing at the same time. It was afternoon, and I could feel the sweltering sun looming above us, perspiration forming on my brow.

"We usually cover our head and face with a *keffiyeh* during the noon, but there's no need of it because we will drive to the oasis by a car," Khalid explained when I heard a car door open. I knew what *keffiyeh* was, a cotton scarf that wrapped around the head to help keep you cool during the scorching heat.

I sat down on the soft leather of the car seat and sighed in relief when I felt the other door close, and Khalid sat beside me. I knew it was him by his exotic musky scent, which was more potent than before, and the way his large body settled beside me. He was always gentle and slow, never surprising me with suddenness which might shock me otherwise. Especially because of how tall and large he was compared to me.

When the car started moving, I looked in his direction and asked, "We are going to an oasis?"

Khalid

I should have told her beforehand. "Yes, we are going to a private oasis. We will stay there for a while to get started with the painting," I said, omitting how I planned to woo and seduce her at the oasis. "If that is okay with you. We can go to the palace if that's what you want."

Her fingers fumbled in her lap. She did that a lot when she was thinking. A nervous tick, probably. Valeria offered me a small smile. "Sure, I want to know how you are going to start the painting. I am excited about it."

I could hear in her honeyed voice how excited she was.

Leaning closer to her, I breathed in her sweet feminine perfume and whispered, "*Naked*, my sweet one. I don't want any clothes on you while I paint you." I watched her slender, pale throat bob when she gulped, the tips of her ear turning pink. I smirked and pulled away. "But don't worry, we can have a demo today before we start. *With* the clothes on."

I watched Valeria with a dark gleam in my eyes when red flush creeped over the neck of her tee shirt, to her cheeks. I wanted to remove that fabric and see where else she was flushed and lick every inch of her soft skin.

Forcing my mind to something else, I looked away from her clenched legs and controlled my urges. We weren't even alone yet and my body was reacting wildly to her being there. Beside me. In my country. I felt more primal and intimate, as if I couldn't help being a civil man for once and stake claim on her like a wild beast.

I clenched my fists, focusing on my breath, and calmed myself down. *What was happening to me?* I had never lost control before. Well, I had once. But never like *this*. Never due to lust and physical attraction.

I peered at the woman who leaned her head outside the window, feeling the wind run through her red hair, which gleamed golden red in the sunlight, a soft smile donning her face. She looked carefree and innocent. *Pure.* Everything opposite of what I was and more. But I knew it was not just physical attraction with her. If it was, I would have taken her on the couch last night.

It was more. Something special.

I, Khalid Al Latif, was afraid to know what made Valeria Dunne so special and precious to me.

"WELCOME TO THE OASIS, VALERIA," I SAID, HOLDING HER HAND while my people in white long tunics bowed at us, helping with our luggage and taking it in the manor. It was more of a smaller palace than a manor, with large open spaces, only to be closed during a sandstorm. I had checked the weather and one would arrive later that week.

The air felt cool on the oasis. It felt wild and free. The smell of fresh water and something musty like wet sand surrounded us as I took her to explore the oasis while the staff set up her room.

There, in my country, surrounded by my people, I felt something like a warm blanket settle over me. Valeria looked womanly, tall, even in the casual clothes. Her red hair glowed like a carnelian crystal does under the sunlight, red and orange and auburn. Her alabaster skin was pale and flawless, the dotted freckles on her cheeks making her look younger.

Every minute with her was a sweet, delicious torture that I was glad to have, even though it made other parts of my body ache with need.

"I hear water. Is there a pond nearby?" Valeria asked with a grin on her face.

"Yes, there's a swimming pool and a spa on the lower floor but I also have a private pool on the balcony of the master suite. Come on, I will take you there."

Valeria

My body was on override from hearing Khalid's deep, soothing voice when he explained the interior of the small palace. I had managed to swallow my shock when he casually mentioned it had a home theatre and a tennis court. Who needed tennis court in the middle of the desert? Apparently, royals of Azmia were competitive when it came to sports and needed one at the oasis.

It was built over a hundred years ago to keep an eye on their neighboring area, but The Golden Sand War was long over and they had rebuilt it with some modern taste to spend some time away from the capital. I could feel the lush opulence as soon as I had entered through the humongous gates Khalid had explained to me with security stations.

I could hear lots of people walking, the staff who took care of the oasis. I knew they were his people, but didn't know how to greet them. Khalid told me that they were busy setting up our things so I wouldn't be able to greet them at that moment. We walked past the hallway to the kitchen, from where I could smell the exotic spices and something delicious cooking. My mouth watered. I couldn't wait to taste the spicy cuisine.

I could feel that we were in a deep end in the dark cold hallway. I stepped closer to him, wanting to make sure I wasn't lost without him, even though I had my cane with me. His body heat warmed me. He squeezed my hand in reassurance, leading the way.

"This is my art studio. I am sorry it's a bit cold as it's open to all the elements." Khalid's voice was deeper and louder in the studio.

So this is where the magic happens.

9

KHALID

I watched Valeria turn around, her hands brushing the empty oak wood table. I told her where all the paint tubes and brushes were kept with large bottles of paint placed in the shelf at the corner of the room. I had decorated the walls with some of my smaller paintings, stacks of panels and canvases stored at the back of the studio. Faint scent of the paint thinner and oil lingered in the air.

Her hand touched the large pillars on our left with heavy doors open. The view was nothing but endless sand dunes. I remembered sitting there at night and staring at the sky.

"It feels different in this room," Valeria muttered.

I walked beside her, warning her about the chaise lounge before she could stumble into it. The end of her cane gently tapping against it.

It was navy blue in color, looking black in certain lighting. The arms of chaise were intricate in gold, making it look elegant. It was the only piece of furniture which stood out the most in my art studio.

I never painted figures, especially nude models, since my art school. But I wanted to try it with Valeria. I could just imagine how gorgeous she would look, draped over the lounger. Without any clothes.

I swallowed the lump in my throat and made her touch my wooden easel. She giggled, feeling the rough strokes of pain that were splashed across it. I wondered how big the painting would be. I would need an enormous canvas for what I had in mind.

I walked her upstairs, showing her the master suite. It was my room. I opened the French doors with intricate designs and told her about the color scheme. Black and golden. All the material was velvet or satin with golden lace, which matched with the subtle decor. Abstract artwork and antiques were decorated throughout the ancient building, with soft Egyptian rugs adorning the floors.

The bed was the center of attraction of the large space. It was set up higher than the floor, with black satin draping down from the center to its drapes tied on the long legs of the bed with golden lace strings. It was rich and opulent.

The balcony could be compared to a terrace as it had its own lower sitting dining area with lanterns and a pool.

"Be careful," I warned when Valeria excitedly walked towards the sound of the water.

I bent down beside her when she dipped her hand on the gleaming surface of clean water. I wanted to make sure she wouldn't trip down and make her clothes wet…

Her face was so serene. The freckles dotting her face seemed to sparkle when she closed her eyes. She must love water a lot. I wanted to paint her portrait, capture the moment on a canvas and keep it with me to look back in time and remember Valeria and torture myself by missing her because she wouldn't be a part of my life at that time.

I had to remind myself about the differences of her pure world and the demons of my past that I still bore. No one needed to know about them. Not even my family, and especially not Valeria. I would finish the painting, get her out of my system, and eventually move on with the chemistry we have after sending her back to London.

"You can come bathe in here anytime you want," I said in a teasing tone.

She splashed cold water across my face. I shook my hair at her face that was dripping with water.

Valeria laughed, pushing me away. "You are filthy, Prince Khalid."

I grinned at her, wiping the water droplets. "Sh, you love it, my sweet one."

Valeria

My sweet one.

I tried not to melt every time he called me that in his velvety voice. I wondered why he called me that. Or if he had endearments for everyone he met.

Khalid led me to my room, staying with me while I mapped it out in my mind. He mentioned that it was like his but with ruby and golden color scheme. The balcony had the dining area and my bathroom felt like another room with a sink and bath carved out from a dark, cold rock.

I felt like a Princess in a castle, getting spoilt by the lovely Prince. The fact that Khalid, Prince of Azmia, might be spoiling me made me feel giddy. I wanted to laugh and hide my face in the pillow.

He left, assuring me that I could send my maid to him anytime I wanted.

My own personal maid? Oh Christ.

Wanting to relax and take a bath, I went to the bathroom and stripped out of my clothes. I had found a few small bottles of oils in the cabinet and used the one which smelt like roses in the bath. I let out a long sigh when my body dipped in the warm water, my muscles relaxing.

My mind raced back to the night before. The passionate kiss that burned my core as soon as I thought about it. My lips tingled at the memory. I wanted to kiss Khalid again. The thought of kissing him without clothes made me shiver with pleasure. I wanted to feel his strong arms around me when we embraced each other. How safe and protected I would feel in his arms.

Would he be gentle?

My heated sex clenched with need.

I shook my head, wanting to stop all the hot images going through my head. Being there with Khalid was making me feel wild and carefree. As if the inhibitions of the real world fell apart in the old palace of the oasis. The feeling was raw and pure need.

I got out of the bath, my body smelling like musky, sweet roses as I dried myself and covered my body with a robe that was hanging in the bathroom. I was surprised that the maid had taken time to arrange the closet in the color scheme I had always preferred. Each piece of clothing was placed in the same way as it had been placed in my closet back at my house. Yet another thing Khalid was thoughtful of.

I tried not to mull too much over it as I got dressed in a sundress that was cool against my skin. I combed through my wet hair and had let it down over my shoulders when someone knocked on the door.

Someone with light feet entered when I opened the door. I knew it was not Khalid. The scent was different, too. It was the maid, asking me if I needed anything.

"Where is Khalid?"

The maid, whose name was Tamara, replied, "Prince Khalid is in his studio. He wanted to meet you before the dinner is served."

Khalid

I looked up from the sketchbook, halting the movements of the pencil, when Valeria came into my view. She looked stunning wearing the white dress, her damp red hair piled up in a bun with few tendrils brushing her bare shoulder.

"Khalid?" her voice called out, small yet confused.

I stood up from the stool. "I am here. I wanted to try a demo sketch with you if it's not too much to ask?"

"I wouldn't mind having my painting made by world famous painter." Valeria instinctively touched my arm, smiling up at me. "Are we… are we starting today?"

I didn't miss the small whisper of her question. I had told her that I wanted to paint her naked after all. I trailed my finger on her cheek, wanting to press my lips against hers, feel them give in and taste them.

"Don't worry, this is just a trial so you get used to it."

Entwining my fingers with her small ones, I took her to the dark chaise lounge. Her white dress and her alabaster skin glowed against the obsidian chaise.

She looked like an angel.

"What do I have to do?"

"Look wherever you want to and be still if you can." I kissed her cheek, walking back to the stool, and watched the angle and posture of her body. Seeing her in my studio, sitting across me, made me feel something warm in my chest.

It was clear that Valeria was tense and nervous. Her lashes kept fluttering everywhere.

"Valeria," her eyes jumped in my direction and I tried to keep my voice even and soft. "Are you okay, sweet? We don't have to do this now."

I wished I could help her stay still and ease whatever was worrying her to be so tense.

A small frown etched between her brows, "I want to, but I

don't know where to look. Whether I should keep my eyes closed or open."

It was rather a difficult thing. I had always practiced to start a figure painting or sketch from the eyes. Even the nude one when I was in university. Because if the eyes were perfect, catching the emotion in them, then the whole painting would be perfect too. But Valeria would get nervous with her eyes open and I couldn't sketch them first.

I had always liked challenges. I would love to try and see how I would sketch her body before her eyes.

Keeping the sketchbook away, I walked back to her, her eyes following the direction of my footsteps. I cupped her face, her eyes fluttering closed when my thumb brushed over her cheekbone.

"You don't have to worry about anything. You had a long day. Come on, let's have dinner."

We walked to the dining area the staff had arranged hand in hand. Valeria was quiet and I was worried that she was getting anxious regarding the painting.

"Khalid," she whispered, looking down. "I... I am sorry to disappoint you."

I froze. Wrapping my hand around her wrist, I pulled her small body closer and cupped her cheek. I glared down at her dainty, bare face. "You can never ever disappoint me, Valeria. Leave everything about the painting to me, and all you have to do is enjoy your time here. I don't want you to worry, is that understood?"

Valeria

I nodded, the sound of his commanding voice making my heartbeat increase. My skin scorched with prickling heat when his thumb rubbed along the seam of my bottom lip.

He asked in his deep, low voice, "Say you understand me,

my sweet one. Or I have other methods to make you understand."

I wanted to take his thumb in my mouth and suckle on it. I wanted to know what another methods Khalid was talking about.

We both stepped back when we heard someone walking down the hallway and heard Tamara say, "Oh, Prince Khalid, Miss Valeria! I was just about to walk down to the studio to let you both know that the dinner is served."

We thanked her and walked together, the surrounding air charged with our attraction. I leaned up to him and whispered, "I don't understand, Khalid. Please make me understand tomorrow."

10

KHALID

I watched in surprised awe when my muse grinned, turning away and walking to the dining area with a bounce in her step. Valeria Dunne was something else. She made me feel everything that had been dead and buried under my rotten body for so long.

I had to remind myself that we were there for the painting. And nothing else.

I shouldn't—I *couldn't* have feelings for her.

I followed Valeria, entering the lantern lit area. The table was low and, on either side, deep red satin coverings were placed. Valeria was moving her head in a different direction when plates of steaming exotic food with delicious scent were placed on the carved table, teasing both of us to devour everything.

Instead of sitting across her, I sat beside her, crossing my legs which brushed with her bare knees. The lantern lights cast a soft glow, making the area look more intimate. The staff left as soon as the platter of food was placed, giving us privacy and to have their own food in the castle dining area. I had asked them before to place their dining in the sitting area outside the master suite.

The water rustled in the tiled pool with wind whistling around us. The sun had already set and the moon looked brighter with stars twinkling around it.

I served the different curries and bread on her plate, letting her touch the bread with her fingers and explaining to her to eat it with her hands. She tucked the stray piece of her hair behind her ear. My fingers itched to undo the knot of her vibrant hair and let it fall around her shoulders and down her back.

I held back the urge and diverted my attention to her confused face.

"How do I eat it with my hands?" Her voice was small, shy and curious.

I tore a piece of bread and smeared it with the delicious red curry full of spices. I held it across her and said with a husky voice, "I'll feed it to you."

Valeria's breathing grew erratic when her nostril wafted with the scent of curry. She parted her lips as I fed the bite to her. My eyes lowered when she leaned forward, her full breasts swaying with the movement, making my body sizzle. I couldn't tear my gaze from the unrestricted view of her barely covered breasts. So full and round.

My attention went to her mouth when she let out a small moan of pleasure. It did a terrible thing to my body. I wanted to push away the food and haul her on the table, claiming her then and there.

Fuck, I was aching badly for her.

"This food is delicious!" Valeria announced, "Here, you should taste it."

I blinked at her, watching her with amusement when she tore a piece of bread and tried to dip it in the curry. I held her hand and slowly folded her fingers to make a small shovel out of the bread and then dip it in the curry. She thanked me and lifted the morsel towards me.

I stared at it with an open mouth.

"What are you waiting for, Khalid?" She grinned. She looked stunning. It made my heart ache too. "Eat it before it gets cold."

No one had ever fed me since my mother passed away. Only she had ever fed me. Ignoring the sad memories, I leaned down and ate the bite from her fingers.

Before I could take the bite, she was pulling her hand back. A small frown on her face. I closed my palm around her wrist, stopping her. Her lips parted when my mouth wrapped around her fingers. My hot, wet tongue licking away the curry, smearing the pads of her fingers. I smirked, watching her cheeks burn red, definitely aroused. I wanted to tell her that she wasn't alone. I had been teased to my edge just by having her beside me.

I pulled away, letting her hand go. I whispered in a low voice, "It is delicious, my sweet one."

Her cheeks were flaming when I poured a glass of champagne. As she didn't like alcohol, I poured her a glass of cold water. She took a sip as soon as I handed it to her. I watched the long, graceful column of her throat work, my eyes taking in the erratic, beating pulse. She didn't look a day over eighteen without any makeup or jewelry donning her.

We talked about her work, how she managed to turn the small fragrance brand to a worldwide profitable business. She had been in many magazine articles, fashion blogs, and galas since then.

Valeria

Since the dinner, I had learned two things. One, Khalid Al Latif, was a beautiful, teasing man. Two, I loved his little teases, especially how my body reacted to it. My sex was throbbing and burning, since he had erotically licked my fingers when I fed him.

When my cheeks burned, I stubbornly thought that it must be the spices from the curry I had. But I knew better. It was the mutual burning chemistry between us that made me fluster and become hot and wet with need.

I was silent when Khalid walked me back to my room even though I had mapped out the distance between our room was six paces. I wanted to know if I was only imagining the connection between us during the dinner or if he had felt it too.

"Sleep well, my sweet one." His warm lips pressed against my forehead and before I could recover from the warm feeling of them, I heard his footsteps descend to his room, the doors shutting close.

So he didn't want to sleep with me. Not that I was hoping he would, of course. Khalid was the Prince of Azmia and he had many other women… or men willing to warm his bed at night. Or whenever he wanted.

Taking a deep breath, I lifted my chin and walked into my room, closing the doors behind me. I sent a quick voicemail to Mr Benjamin to let them know I was doing well and removed the pin holding my red hair in a bun. Running my hand through the soft strands, I leaned on the railing in the balcony before the atmosphere got too cold.

I kept the windows open and sat down on the bed, the sheets soft and cool. It made my skin tingle. I lazily stretched out on the bed, which was large enough for a soccer team.

More than enough for two people.

Shaking my head at the dirty thoughts, I slid the blankets over my body, wondering what was Khalid doing at that hour. *Maybe taking a relaxing shower before sleeping?*

"You are being rude, Valeria!" I scolded myself, hiding my

flaming face in a pillow when thoughts of Khalid wet with water filled my head.

I hoped that I could survive another day with him. Alone and naked in his art studio.

♛

I COULD HEAR *HIS* SOFT VOICE IN MY ROOM, HIS NEW SHOES shuffling as he looked around my closet while I frowned on the bed. "Come to the party with me."

Even though I had already denied, he was always insistent. The familiar scent of citrus overwhelmed me. I could feel him looming over my bed. "Come on, Val. you know it's going to be fun. Everyone from our high school is going."

He knelt down, my cheeks warming at his attention. The golden boy of the school, my close friend, my crush, gazing at me.

"I will be with you," he whispered. "I promise."

I fumbled in the darkness, grabbing his hand, my cane in my other hand as I tried to pull the sleeve of an oversized shirt I had worn over the dress he had chosen for me. The stench of cheap beer was strong. The bustling of people, the taste of acid and smoke in the air.

He laughed with his friends when I coughed, taking a small drag, but brought me a cup of something bitter and strong.

"Here, drink this. It's beer and sprite."

I felt dizzy.

My head rolling as I moved between the bodies, trying to make sense of the world. Of the universe. *Is this what being drunk feels like?* It's fun. I felt loose. Almost unhinged.

I giggled, my arms and body swaying with others to the loud music. He told me colorful neon lights were all around us. That my red hair looked purple and my skin looked green. I had almost forgotten how colors looked. I burst into laughter when he said, 'Like an alien.'

So alive.

I felt lightheaded and free. As if my soul was out of me, floating in the ceiling until I fell.

But *he* held me. He never let me fall down. He always protected me.

"Come with me, you can rest here."

The stench of sweat and alcohol surrounded us. I was floating even though my feet felt heavy. I told him I didn't feel so good, I wanted to go home and sleep for a week straight.

Of course I didn't feel so good. I never had alcohol before. I tried to call Mr Benjamin, but I was slurring my words, and I didn't want him to worry. He told me to keep my phone down and rest on the bed. That he would look after me. Make sure no one entered the room.

I followed his advice like a lost puppy. Massaging my head, I flopped down on the bed. The sheets smelled of orange detergent. I told him that, laughing and clutching my stomach.

Floating and bobbing in the endless darkness, I thought, *so naïve, so stupid.*

The reek of beer brushed over my face, the warm fingers inching my dress up.

What are you doing? I mumbled sleepily, and it felt like I was speaking another language.

Everything felt foggy and suffocating and constricting. I couldn't speak because my tongue was heavy, my mouth too dry. My limbs were tired with exhaustion, or maybe the alcohol.

Sh, it's okay, Valeria. Fuck, you're so hot. He whispered back, holding down my wrists when I tried to bat his hands away.

It was of no use.

It was really happening. He was—

No, I had said.

Yes, he had groaned.

Stop, I moaned in pain.

It's okay, a few more—See? You love it, he whispered.

Please don't, it hurts. No, I cried out.

I blacked out again.

The dryness in my throat woke me up, my mind a jumbled mess of throbbing headache and—something sticky between my thighs. I wanted to puke. My thighs coated with it as I panicked, wincing when the soreness between my legs felt prominent.

My memories were jumbled. Maybe it was a stupid nightmare. Yes, that must be it.

"Let me clean you up, Val. You have beer all over your thighs," *he* lied to me, leading me to the bathroom and gently holding my arms and patting my hair when he cleaned me up.

No beer could be that thick.

It must be a bad dream. He wouldn't… *no*. He wouldn't. I was drunk, and it was a bad dream.

But my dress was torn from the side, my bra unclasped. The shirt I had worn before was missing and so was *my underwear*.

"Did something happen?" I asked him in a low voice, scared.

Scared of what? There was nothing to be scared of. He was my best-friend. The Golden Boy in the school was my best-friend.

His citrus scent overpowered me as he stood up, washed my hands, and fixed my dress with soft fingers. His voice was gentle but firm. "Nothing happened, Valeria."

Right. Of course. I was overthinking. He could *never* do that. He would always protect me—

But why were his friends faking concern about me? Why did *they* have my shirt? Why were they asking me to smoke with them? Why were they laughing?

"Where are we going?" I asked, trying to turn on my phone, but the broken glass of the mobile was visible. It was brand new and Mr Benjamin and Mabel had bought it for me last month on my sixteenth birthday.

He drove the car, offering me his phone to call. "I am taking you home, Val. Where else would I take you? Your parents trusted me to take care of you. I will *always* take care of you."

I nodded, thankful for his sweet words.

His song played in the car, the radio station host complimenting him. His band was doing well.

He would never do that.

But my underwear was still missing.

And it was blood that had coated my thighs, not beer.

"Valeria. Wake up!"

"*Stop!*" I pushed hard at the broad shoulders, didn't want *him* to touch me again.

Not again. No, never again. *Oh God.*

"It's me, Khalid. It's okay, Valeria. It's just a dream."

I woke up with a start, my heart beating too loudly under my palm as I touched my chest. I sighed in relief. I was wearing clothes, especially my underwear.

It was okay. I am okay.

"Valeria? Are you okay?"

No, I am not okay.

It was Khalid. Not *him*. Khalid was there with me. I was in Azmia. I was with him at the oasis. Relief washed over my body when I wrapped my arms around his neck, hiding my face in the crook. All I cared about at that moment was that I was safe with him.

Khalid Al Latif would never harm me.

He pulled me closer, stroking my hair and back gently, kissing the top of my hair and muttering sweet words in his hoarse, rich voice. He must have heard my pleads and my crying.

I didn't want to let go of him, of his warmth, so I pulled

away only a little to look in the direction of his face. "I... I am sorry for waking you up like this. I—"

Khalid

I cupped her face, tucking back the hair which was framing her face because of perspiration. "Don't apologize for it. I got worried something happened to you and I walked in to see you having a nightmare."

I had thought it was Zara. My little sister's voice crying for help at night. The door to Valeria's room was unlocked, and I had found her thrashing on the bed, whimpering and yelling at someone in her nightmares. I wanted to hurt the person who dared to even think about causing pain to Valeria. To trouble her with nightmares.

Her body was still shivering. I pulled her closer, making sure her hands didn't wander down my back. That would create too many questions. I had forgotten to wear my shirt when I rushed in to check up on her. It didn't seem like Valeria cared as she laid her face on my chest. She had never looked so fragile and vulnerable and small.

I swore to God that I would enjoy hurting the piece of shit who caused it. I had nightmares about my past, and I knew how terrible and torturous they all were. To be stuck in your own head, helplessly calling out for help, to stop the pain. It never faded away, welcoming itself at night to trouble the soul.

"You're okay, you're with me, sweet one," I whispered once more, both to her and me.

I poured her a glass of water from the tumbler and unclenched my jaw when she gulped down the water.

"Thank you," she whispered, her voice back to normal. It was shaky and stuttering before. "For being here. With me. Thank you, Khalid."

She closed her small palms around my hand. I looked at our

hands and at the dainty face with the red nose. "You don't have to thank me for this, Valeria. You would have done the same."

"Do you want to talk about it?" I asked in a low voice.

She quickly shook her head, her red hair fanning out. "No."

I nodded. "Okay. Will you be okay? Should I—"

Valeria clutched my hand harder. "Please stay. I don't want to be alone tonight." She let go of my hand, "Um, only if you don't mind."

"Of course, my sweet one. Anything you want."

The small smile curling her lips was to die for.

I was afraid that if she had asked me to carve out my heart to make her smile, I would have.

Fool. I was turning into a complete, utter fool.

But what worried me more was that it didn't affect me at all.

After turning off the lantern lamps on either side of the bed, I closed the door and slid inside the blankets. She had kept the windows open, so the room was getting cold. I was thankful for her choice because it made us sleep closer to each other to stay warm.

Her fingers had entwined with mine, the feeling far more intimate than it should have been. I couldn't remember the last time I shared a bed with a woman and just held hands. I don't think it ever happened.

But holding Valeria's hand, I was happy and content. Knowing that I would be there to fight off her demons and keep her safe. She would never have to worry about getting hurt when she was here. In Azmia. But especially with me. No one would dare touch her and I would like to see someone try just to give off an example of what would happen if they did.

I knew that even though Valeria was not mine to protect, I would, because she was precious to me.

11

VALERIA

I hummed sleepily, snuggling closer to the warm heat that surrounded me. Strong hands traced the skin of my arms, going up and down to the crooks of my elbows. I shivered, tingles of heat following the path of his touch.

I could feel his burning gaze on me as he traced my cheekbones. My lashes fluttered when his hand descended down to my slender neck. *Lower.* To the soft peak of my breasts.

"Khalid…" I sighed, my voice sultry because of the sleep. I felt his breath fanning on my neck, our bodies touching each other, when his hand trailed across the neckline of my dress.

"*Mhmm,*" he hummed, his voice hoarse and masculine. My toes curled hearing his rich voice. "Good morning, Valeria."

My name had never sounded so beautiful. So soft yet hot. His tongue wrapped around my name, striking a chord deep in my belly.

Khalid's hand traced the curve of my body in the soft fabric of the dress. I took a deep breath when his hand found the hem of my dress, trailing it up to reveal the soft pale thighs.

He paused, "Valeria?"

I breathed out. "Please don't stop now."

My body arched up to him, wanting to be touched and kissed. His hands scrunched the fabric of dress and took it off of me, my arms lifting to help him remove it.

Heat creeped up my neck to my face. My hands flew instinctively to shield myself from the burning gaze of Khalid. I felt the hot, warm sensation in my underwear and lazily rubbed my legs together, wanting to stop the increasingly growing heat.

Khalid
(Khalid first person, Valeria third person)

My mouth watered at the sight of her bare skin against the dark ruby sheets. I watched her angelic face through my half-lidded eyes, gleaming with arousal and lust. I wanted to touch myself at the sight of wetness polling in the white lace underwear.

I held her wrists and gently pulled them away from her body, revealing her perfectly round breasts. The pink tips of her nipples arching towards me, her breath getting caught in her throat.

"Let me see you, my sweet one." My rich, velvety voice brushed through her ears, allowing her to relax under my gaze.

My fingers raked through her silky russet waves, tucking them softly behind her ear and pressing a soft kiss on the corner of her lips. Valeria's body pressed against me, her soft breasts squishing against my muscular, hard chest. The tent in my trousers brushed her thigh, making me clench the sheet.

My lips descended on her neck, kissing and tasting the pale skin, licking her pulse and enjoying the way her body responded so quickly to me. My hands trailed down the valley between her breasts, circling each bud. Valeria gasped when my hot mouth wrapped around her nipple, lazily sucking it and biting the nub with my teeth.

I wanted to get drunk on the sweet moans coming out of her lips when I suckled on her breasts. My hand pinched the nipple and squeezed the soft flesh while the other hand trailed over the curve of her waist, soothing her. Valeria whimpered underneath my large body. My hot mouth repeated the actions on other breast until they were flushed.

I pulled back, proud at the sight of her sensitized breasts, and pressed a sweet kiss to the tips before moving my mouth towards where I wanted the most. Goosebumps raised on her body when I watched her through my lashes. Clenching my jaw, I parted her legs and pressed my middle finger against her heating sex.

Valeria took a sharp breath at the new sensation of being touched and caressed so intimately. Her teeth sunk into the seam of her bottom lip when my finger moved lazily through the lace.

My eyes didn't leave her face when I fisted the hem of little lace covering her and tore it apart.

She gasped.

My eyes zeroed on the bare sight of her sex, the wetness oozing out of her, her musky scent surrounding us. I flung away the shredded lace somewhere in the bedroom and held her thighs to really look at her.

My voice was deep and husky when I groaned out, "So wet and pink. I want to taste you, Valeria."

Valeria squirmed under my heavy gaze on her bare sex. Her breath quickened and the sensation coursing through her tightened into a coil, the pressure growing and growing until I relieved it for her.

By touching her where she wanted the most.

"Khalid," she moaned quietly, turning her face.

I trailed my fingers over her slicked lips, finding the little nub of pleasure and rolling it around experimentally. I wished she could see herself at that moment. Sunlight was peeking through the curtains, making her body glow when my finger pushed inside her warm heat.

She is so fucking tight.

I let out a groan and found her hand to entwine my fingers with hers. I slowly thrust my finger in and out of her velvety walls, adding another finger. Valeria's body arched up to me, her hips moving towards me and clenching my hand.

Valeria was feeling the coil inside her unwind and flutter when my fingers moved inside her. She wanted more. *So much more.*

I could sense her impatience, feel the pressure increasing in her body, but I was selfish. I wanted to drag out her climax before watching her come apart. My aching cock was pressing against the confines of my trousers, wanting to feel her warm heat clench around me the way it did around my fingers.

I leaned down, her musky feminine scent wafting in my nose as I pressed a small kiss on her sensitive sex. She squeezed my hand, a gasp tearing out of her throat before turning into a loud moan when my hot lips found her pleasure bud, sucking it in my mouth and licking it at the same time, my fingers thrusting inside her.

Her moans, the rocking of her hips, and her scent were making me heady with lust. My body was burning and aching for a release. I pulled away, leaving her feeling empty when I removed my fingers. I pressed them carefully against her slightly parted lips, and her sex clenched at the scent of herself.

She wanted to hide her flushed face, but she stopped herself when I spoke in a guttural tone.

"*Suck*," I ordered. The primal part of me enjoyed the way her naked body squirmed underneath me. So sweet and erotic. "Taste yourself, Valeria."

Like a good girl, she parted her lips. I watched in awe, twitching in my pants. With my eyes on her face and her hollowed cheeks as she tasted herself, I leaned down and licked the sweet nectar from her bare sex.

I groaned and closed my eyes at the heady, musky taste of her, and repeated my actions with more pressure on my tongue. Valeria responded quickly, her muffled moans causing me to remove my fingers and push her hips down so I could lick her properly.

She tasted just as sweet as she looked, if not more.

"You taste like fucking heaven, my sweet," I whispered in deep voice, my warm breath sensitizing her more. "I can get drunk off of you."

Valeria's reply was a plea which I gladly obeyed, licking her and eating her out gently. My fingers pushed inside her, my tongue flicking the clitoris, making her reach out and hold on to my soft, thick hair.

I increased my pace and fucked her relentlessly with my digits, her arousal coating them while my tongue took solace in making gentle, soft circles around her swollen pink nub.

The maddening pace of both gentle and rough was making Valeria tether to edge.

I squeezed her hand. "Let go, sweetheart."

She mumbled something incoherent and came apart on my mouth and fingers when they curled inside her. The pressure growing inside her exploded and made her skin burn hot. Melting arousal pooled out of her and she couldn't stop when her eyes watered with pleasure, tiny explosions of heat spiraling through her body.

It was maddening.

She loved it.

I watched in absolute awe, watching her fall apart. Her wild red hair spread out on the pillows, her lips parted when she breathed out my name, and her eyes watering. I kissed away her tears, the saltiness coating my lips as I soothed her down. I trailed my hand through her trembling legs and kissed her when she lifted her head to touch me. Her fingers ran through my hair and pulled me closer, deeper, her sensitized breasts pressing against my hot body.

Valeria

I had never felt something like this.

I had never felt more alive.

I wanted to—

I pulled away when his large hands cupped my face with a gentleness I had never felt before.

"Is that you?"

Khalid's cheeks warmed when she felt his bulge brushing over her thigh. His pupils dilated when she spread her legs, pulling him closer. He let out a soft grunt when his hardened length pressed over her melting heat.

He rasped out, "Valeria."

The hoarse sound of his voice and the fiery feeling on my core sent a jolt through my body, my back arching off the bed.

"Please," I begged, not knowing what I was begging him for. My head was fussy, and I wanted him all over me, to make me combust with that feeling again.

I wanted Khalid. In all the ways possible.

Khalid

I couldn't think straight at the pleading, sultry tone of Valeria. She was alluring. Writhing beneath me, her nails digging into my shoulders, her thighs spread wide. I leaned down, about to capture her lower lip, but jolted back when I heard the shrill sound of my cell phone ringing.

I let out a defeated sigh and kissed her sweet neck before pulling back. "I am sorry, sweet, I have to take that. It must be my brother or sister."

Only my family knew where I was at the moment and they knew better not to disturb me while I was here, so it must be something urgent.

But the naked sight of Valeria spread out on dark ruby sheets made me want to ignore the call and warm my body with hers.

"O-of course, I was… I was about to go take a shower, anyway."

I raised my eyebrow at the small stutter when she covered herself with the thin sheets, her copper hair tousled and falling in waves over her shoulders.

I couldn't believe that she was the same woman who was pleading me to pleasure her seconds ago. Now she was being shy and sweet as if I didn't know what she tastes like. Her musky scent was still overpowering my senses.

I leaned closer to her, her eyes looking in my direction and twirled my finger around a red strand, lightly tugging on it and pressing my lips over hers.

"I wish I could join you, wash you with my hands…" I said in a low voice and promised. "We will continue this later, my sweet one."

Giving her one last glance, I pulled back and straightened myself in the trousers. I walked out of her room mustering all the self-control I had. No one tested my control like she did without even doing anything.

Valeria was overpowering all my senses, and I didn't know if I liked that or not.

12

KHALID

I answered the phone and closed the doors of my room behind me.

"How is my dear brother doing?" Zain, my elder brother and the Sultan of Azmia drawled in his deep voice.

I rolled my eyes. Zain cockblocked me with Valeria just to ask me how I am doing?

"What do you want, Zain? I was… I was doing something important." *Or I was about to, anyway.*

"Something important or someone?"

I could hear the smirk in his voice.

"Some*one* important," I corrected him. "Now, tell me, why are you calling me? You know I am at the oasis."

"You have never brought anyone at the oasis before. Not even your own brother. Not even Zara." He couldn't hide the disbelief in his tone.

I scratched the back of my neck. "I am painting."

"Are you painting that someone important? Or are you painting *on her?*"

I planned to do that soon.

"Zain, I do not want to talk about this with you right now. Why did you call? Is Nasrin okay? *Jadati (grandmother)?*"

I heard him sigh through the phone. "Yes, everyone is alright, including me, thanks for asking. I called to ask you about Zara. She is not responding to any of my calls, and I don't know which country she is travelling right now, let alone where she is and if she is safe or not."

I could feel his worry. Zara was our little sister and also the only Princess of Azmia. She had been travelling the world as soon as she turned nineteen. She knew how to take care of herself, but it didn't make us less worried about her. Zara never stayed in the same country, let alone a place for more than a couple of months, so it was hard to track her down and make sure she was doing fine.

"I will try calling her and talk to her. Last I heard, she was in Australia." I remembered her video call while she was on a beach, her cheerful face relieving me of the brotherly stress.

"Call her as soon as you can and let her know that if she misses the baby shower, I will never forgive her. Nasrin wants Zara to be here. Even grandma is worried."

I let out a soft chuckle. "She is more worried about the man who would dare to marry our sister."

We both knew that as long as I was alive, Zara wasn't going to get married. Even if she liked someone, I would make sure that her partner was capable before allowing him or her to see my sister.

I won't ever let someone hurt her again. Like how our father did.

"I pray for the man who falls for our little Zara." Zain said in a mocking tone.

"When do I have to arrive at the palace?" I asked, wondering if I could finish the painting before that and if I could bring Valeria with me.

I heard the shuffles of paper as Rahim, our advisor, talked with him. I sighed. Zain was working overtime once again.

"In a week, if you can. I want to spend some time alone with my lovely wife, but handling the country with her due date coming soon and the celebration of the baby shower is taking a toll on me. I would appreciate your help, Khalid. Especially with the security and protection."

He seemed tired. Zain had been handling the country since the age of twenty, after the death of our father because of me. We had all watched him die. But Zain never gave me too much responsibility, even though I was only a year younger than him.

Ignoring the bitter memories, I replied, "Of course, brother. You don't have to ask. I will be there in a week. I will try to finish the painting before that if I can."

"Thank you, Khalid. Bring your muse along if you want to," he teased.

"Her name is Valeria. I will ask her although I am sure she would love to visit the palace."

He added, "And warm your bed."

"*Zain*," I warned him. "She is… she is not like that."

Zain didn't say anything for a while, which made me frown at the phone.

"Do you like her? Valeria?"

I looked at the pool on the balcony, remembering the big grin on her face when she splashed water on me. *Did I like her? Yes, I want to have sex with her, but… did I like her more than that?*

"That is none of your busine—"

"Admit it, little brother. You like Valeria," he chuckled. "I cannot wait to meet her and see why does my brother seem so whipped."

I hung up on the Sultan of Azmia, cursing him at the teasing laugh. I wasn't sure if I could name the feelings I had for Valeria. I adored her. I was impressed by her. I respected her. I wanted to fuck her too, but she was special to me. *Precious.*

Whatever the feeling was, I was sure it wasn't just about me liking her. I couldn't put it into words, so I would pour it out in the canvas with paint.

Valeria

I patted my wet body with the lush towel. The sweet scent of roses and the exotic oil which I had added in the bath wafted from my soft skin. My cheeks would start aching if I kept smiling and grinning like a silly person. When I walked out of the bathroom, I bit my lip at the tingling sensation throbbing between my legs.

I loved how wild and untethered I had felt when Khalid had touched my innermost sensitive parts and ravished them. My arms brushed my breasts and blood creeped along my neck when the nipples turned hard, remembering the lick of his tongue and bite of his teeth. I shook my head, attempting to clear the thought and dressed myself in a long-sleeved tee shirt with trousers.

Tamara, the maid, had brought eggs, bread, sliced fruits with a big glass of juice for the breakfast, informing me to meet Khalid in the studio once I was done. I had never finished my breakfast so quickly before that day. I told myself that I didn't want to make him wait, but deep down, I knew that I couldn't wait to be around him again. Hear his rich deep voice and… and maybe kiss him too.

There was a subtle bounce in my step as I guided myself to the studio with the cane. The morning fresh air lifted my mood as a wide smile curled my lips. I was simply too excited to be with Khalid. I could only hope that he would be excited to see me as well.

"Good morning, Khalid," I said as soon as I walked inside the cool studio. As it was open to all the elements, the room was much cooler than other rooms I had been.

Warmth spread over my body when I felt him lean closer, twirling his finger around the tendril of my loose hair. "Good morning, Valeria," he purred in his smooth voice, his breath caressing my face when he kissed my cheek before stepping back. "Are you ready to start the painting?"

Too nervous and excited to utter anything, I nodded.

"I am hoping to finish the rough sketch before lunch." He guided me towards the chaise. "All you have to do is sit in a certain position and let me know if you are uncomfortable, okay?"

I squeezed his hand, the pads of my fingers making small patterns on his knuckles. "I understand."

"You can remove your clothes and keep them on this table."

I didn't know if I imagined his voice turn deeper, lowering an octave or not.

"All of my clothes?"

"I want to paint you naked, Valeria," he said in a low voice. "Unless you don't want to—"

"No, I... I trust you. I am okay with it."

I forced myself to move. Khalid had already seen me naked. He wouldn't care, he is a professional artist. I took a few deep breaths and tried to calm down my body.

It's okay, no one's going to hurt me. I am safe with Khalid.

Khalid

I tried to control myself as I closed the doors of the studio, mentally counting till ten when I heard the soft rustles of clothes. I had sketched with nude models before, but it had been during practice and they were models. I didn't see them as anything else but shades of different colors, light hitting the different curves and how to perceive them differently and turn it into a painting.

I didn't have feelings for the models.

But it was Valeria who was willing to be my muse, be nude in front of me for hours even though she was extremely shy. She had agreed to this because she completely trusted me.

I hope I can maintain myself around her and get this painting done quickly.

"I am ready."

Her shy, soft voice called out to me.

I turned around and clenched my hands in fists, my piercing obsidian eyes darkening as they raked over her elegant figure sitting on the onyx chaise. Her striking green eyes were blinking in my direction, her hands on her thighs—her creamy naked thighs which I had held that morning, eating her out. I prowled towards her, my skin prickling with the heat that was growing inside me to claim the woman in front of me.

Her red hair glowed in the sunlight, falling in tumbles of waves around her and brushing over the peak of her round breasts. Her flat stomach was taut with nerves and her hands were placed modestly in front of her, her legs together, to cover herself.

As if I hadn't seen every inch of her that she was hiding.

"I am going to touch you to have you sit in a pose, okay?" I managed to voice out with a cold tone, mentally wincing at how harsh I sounded. I didn't want to, but I had to because my attraction towards Valeria might cause trouble during the painting sessions.

"O… Okay."

Great, you already scared the poor girl!

I gently touched her shoulder and told her to lean back on the lounger, her elbow resting on the intricate arm. Her legs were positioned on the chaise, with her arm draped over the curve of her waist. I would paint something later to hide her sex, but at the moment, I told her to relax as much as she could in that position. I draped a white lace fabric on the furniture. For the last touch, I tucked her hair over her shoulder with a few tendrils framing her face and brushing her decolletage.

I saw her bite her bottom lip at the proximity. I cupped her face, rubbing the pad of my thumb over the seam of her lip to make her release it, and asked, "Are you comfortable with this?"

She swallowed and nodded. "I am. I will try to stay as still as I can."

"Thank you," I whispered, meaning more than just regarding the painting.

Valeria surprised both of us by leaning up and pressing her lips against mine. I ignored the tension in my stomach and kissed her, my hot tongue licking her lips, giving them a soft bite. Her thighs clenched and before we could take it further, I pulled away.

"You are a tease, my sweet." My voice was heavy with arousal. I stood up, my dark gaze lingering at the pebbled pink tips of her breasts. "Now, stay still."

13

VALERIA

I tried not to tremble when I felt his tall, large body looming over me. I knew Khalid could see how aroused I was, naked in front of him, while he was fully clothed in a room filled with paints and brushes. I clenched and unclenched my fingers in a fist when a cool breeze whispered through the room, roving over my bare body, making my skin prickle.

How will I be able to sit still for hours?

I could feel the tension increasing in my body. My arms and shoulders feeling heavy, as if someone was physically pushing me down. I felt small. Almost afraid. Like the night—

No. Khalid is with me. He is a good person. I am okay. I am safe. I am fine.

The sound of charcoal moving across the canvas made me well aware of his burning gaze. He had already started sketching me. Khalid Al Latif was taking a nude sketch of me.

Should I look at him?

But I could only hear whispers of the charcoal, and it made my body tense with nervousness. I didn't know what to do, where to look, my eyes had been blanketed with darkness since the accident. That night. Cold and dizzy. Crying. Arms holding me down. Missing underwear. Sticky thighs—

"*Valeria.*"

I gasped, pulling back when I felt another presence, my eyes blinking. Musky cologne. The woodsy scent of pine. Deep voice.

Khalid.

"Oh, I am not staying still, right? I am sorry, I am just worried about where to look and I don't—"

"Shh," he hushed me. I bit my lip from apologizing again. "I can see you panicking, my sweet. Are you sure you are okay? Comfortable? Is something bothering you?"

I shook my head, rubbing my arms and looking away from his direction. I didn't like the warm feeling glowing in my chest. "I am not panicking. I don't know where to look."

Khalid didn't reply for a few seconds, as if he was assessing me. I wanted to tell him to stop.

"Does being naked with me bother you?" He questioned, as if he was asking if I liked apples or not. "Should I bring in Tamara?"

"No. I am okay, Khalid. I am… I don't mind being naked and alone with you." I flushed, saying the words, my head dipping as I twirled my fingers.

I heard him shift and say, "If you ever feel uncomfortable, today or tomorrow or whenever we are together, let me know, okay?"

I nodded, licking my lips.

Was it weird that the concern he had for me turned me on?

I was sure that at the rate we were going, I would orgasm if Khalid breathed over me.

Forcing dirty images out of my head, I focused on his presence as he moved around the studio as if he was looking for something.

"Now I remember telling you about not to worry, or I

would make you understand it with other methods. Remember Valeria?" His voice seemed closer, softer, but full with the promise of teasing.

The hair on the back of my neck rose as I dipped my head.

"This is one of my methods," he whispered, kneeling down across me. I shivered, his warm breath caressing my bare breast. My mouth turned dry. My hands ached to touch him. "Let me know if this feels comfortable."

I felt the soft satin material being pressed over my eyelids, temple, my hair. His warm skin inches away from me as he tied a knot behind my head, asking me if it was too tight.

Khalid blindfolded me. I could understand his reason. My eyes would stop blinking and flickering around, and I would feel calmer with the blindfold on. Stay still and not panic.

Despite that, it felt extremely erotic and sensual. Lounging naked and blindfolded in Khalid's art studio.

His fingers were gentle as he fixed my hair, one strand brushing over the pebbled nipple of my breast making me take a shuddering breath. His finger lowered towards it, brushing his knuckles on my breast. I didn't pull away, leaning closer to his touch.

I gasped when he palmed the flesh, pinching the nipple. He stopped rolling the hard tip with his thumb and forefinger when I held onto his wrist, urging him closer. I would go insane if he stopped touching me.

"Would you enjoy getting your hands tied up?" Khalid said, his voice serious yet full of mischief.

I pulled away my hand from his wrist. "I didn't know that the Prince of Azmia was into that stuff."

Khalid let out a soft chuckle that did terrible things to my body. "Oh, sweet one, I am into all types of stuff."

He gently tugged a piece of my hair, kissing my cheek as he stood up. "Don't worry, we have a lot of time to explore and play with all kinds of stuff."

Khalid

I sat down on the stool once again. The canvas had rough lines and strokes of the chaise and her body. My eyes fleeted from her still body to the canvas. I would have to finish sketching and painting the eyes once everything else was painted. I had never done it before.

I usually finished sketching the eyes at first so that all the other features of face and body could be sketched and painted proportionally and not seem cartoonish. But Valeria was panicking for some reason, and I didn't want to make her anxious. Telling her to close her eyes would make her feel bad, and I didn't want her to feel discouraged because of her lack of sight. She was more than enough for the painting and I could adjust anything for her.

Seeing her relaxed body lounging on the chaise with her eyes blindfolded in a black satin, different thoughts took over my mind. Dirty, filthy thoughts. So much so that I had to force myself down and focus on the sketching.

I picked up the charcoal stick for sketching and worked on the sketch. Black lines in curves and waves traced on the canvas as the Sun rose higher.

Valeria's alabaster skin began to glow when the sun rays fell over her, her body shifting ever so lightly, a small sigh leaving her lips. I tried not to stare at those lips for too long and sketched her dainty face, skipping her eyes until I finished drawing everything. Her hair fell in waves and traced the soft tendril down to her round breast.

I felt tortured and relieved at the same time while drawing her. Her delicious lithe body was inviting me to do whatever I wished. Claim her on the chaise like a wild man.

Ignoring those thoughts and feelings, I felt proud of how much she trusted me. I felt honored to earn her trust to be naked and blindfolded and alone in a different country when she didn't have her sight.

I finished the rough sketch before lunch and kept the charcoal back in its place, cleaning the black ash of charcoal coating my fingers with a cloth.

"You can relax, my sweet," I said to her. "I will be right back. I need to wash my hands."

I ignored the long sigh of hers when I walked to the attached bathroom and rinsed my hands. I stared at my reflection. My hair had been tousled because I had run my hand over it during the sketching. The pupils of my eyes were dilated, and they were shining like dark orbs. I shook my head and splashed cold water on my face.

Who was I kidding? I was definitely aroused.

"Khalid," her sweet voice called out to me.

I cursed at myself for getting lost in my head and quickly made my way towards her.

Valeria was still sitting on the chaise, a soft glow on her face and over her body. She was still naked. With her eyes blindfolded.

"Should I remove this?" She asked, her fingers brushing the dark cloth over her eyes.

I bent down in front of her, careful not to touch her anywhere else. "I'll do it for you." My voice was low when I leaned closer to untie the blindfold.

Seductive, musky scent of roses and something feminine wafted in my nose when I removed the satin. I pulled back and covered her body with a blanket I had placed earlier on the table.

"Did you finish the sketch?" She asked, thankful for the warm blanket surrounding her.

"I did, but I am not letting you touch it until I finish the painting," I said with a teasing but firm voice. I eyed the small flush on her cheeks and told her to get dressed for lunch.

"I love this so much," Valeria giggled, letting her hand run through the soft mane of the horse.

"Hold on to the reins, Valeria," I scolded her, concern lacing my voice. "I don't want you to fall."

She turned around, our faces inches apart as she smiled up at me. "I trust you. You would never let me fall, Khalid."

I tightened my hold on her waist.

I had entered her room early evening, asking her if she wanted to visit a nearby lake with me. She had agreed instantly. When I had announced that we were going to ride on a horse, she was more than excited. She had never ridden on a horse before and she wanted to know how it felt. I had explained the breed of the horse, Kamil, and his beautiful dark coat as we rode.

Valeria's back rested against me, our bodies touching each other as I held the reins and commanded the horse. She could feel the hard muscles through her back and tried not to let it affect her. As if she hadn't known what it felt like when our bodies had embraced each other that morning. Valeria tried not to squirm when she felt my strong thighs tense and relax. My other arm was wrapped tightly around her waist when I guided the horse, the soft breeze kissing our bare skin.

The air was cool and fresh, but I told her to cover her nose with *keffiyeh* because of the sand. She complied, so I wouldn't worry. Although she wished she could feel the air on her face and breathe it in.

"When did you ride a horse for the first time?" She asked, leaning back on me, my masculine, musky cologne with the cool air making her feel heady.

I smiled down at Valeria, pulling her closer when she leaned back on me, her *keffiyeh* covering her mouth and glorious red hair. I knew she was smiling up at me like she always did.

"I was seven. Our father wanted me and my brother, Zain, to train from the early age. We learnt how to ride horses and sword fighting even though we didn't have any need of it."

"Did you enjoy it?" Valeria could sense that I hated learning all of it at such a young age. She wished she knew how to fight to protect herself.

I looked at the bleeding setting sun. "No. Neither of us enjoyed learning any of that. Our father... he was strict."

Valeria tensed. She knew what that meant. She covered my palm on her waist with hers and asked in a low voice, "Did he... did he hurt you?"

Yes. Yes, he did. He hurt all of us.

I glared at the sand beneath us, hearing her question. I didn't want to taint Valeria by letting her know about my past, but her question was sincere as if she knew what it was like. I prayed that no one had ever and would ever do that to her.

"Yes," I gritted through my teeth. "But he hurt our mothers the most. And my sister. He could never appreciate the love they had for him."

"They?"

I entwined our hands together. "He had two wives. Zain and I were conceived before his second marriage to Isabella. She was a daughter of a wealthy surgeon in London. Isabella was my sister, Zara's, mother. She was born blind, and we adored her because we would lead her all around the palace with Zara and describe everything to her. Both of our mothers loved us in a way our father never did."

Her voice was barely audible when she said, "I wish I could meet them."

"They would have adored you," I said truthfully. Especially my mother. She would pinch my ear if I ever even dared to think about breaking her heart and ask me to marry her.

But my mother wasn't with me anymore and times had changed.

"Really?" Valeria's cheeks warmed with blood.

I squeezed her hand. "Yes. They would make various sweets too and delicious *roz bel laban*, rice pudding, for you."

"That sounds really sweet." She kissed my knuckles. "I want to learn to make it."

I raised my eyebrows at her. "Why?"

She shrugged, looking away. "So that I can have it whenever I want." I was secretly amused. Valeria didn't have the courage to tell me that she wanted to learn to cook *roz bel laban* to please me.

"Is the sun setting?" Valeria asked.

I hummed looking at the sunset. "It is setting down, disappearing down the sand dunes."

"Explain it to me." She demanded.

I smiled down at her, wanting to smother her face with kisses. Shaking the thought, I fulfilled her wish. "It's orange. The whole sky is a canvas of orange and blue. Even little bit of red. It is refreshing, tropical, but it feels comforting."

She hummed, "Orange gives me warmth and security."

I was surprised by her reply. "What about blue?"

"Blue is like the sound of water. It is cold like ice," she giggled. "I love ice-cream but it's sweet. Blue is not… sweet. It seems clear. Calm. Relaxing. I would swim in blue if I could."

"You are always welcome to swim in the pool, Valeria," I said.

She shook her head at me and asked, "And you? What do you think of red?"

I gazed at her hair, the silky strands and the rich color. "Lust. It reminds me of passion. It is purely sexual for me."

Her breathing increased as she shuffled on the saddle. I bit back my groan when I felt her pressing against me.

"How so?" She asked innocently.

I leaned down closer to her ear, lightly caressing her arms. "It makes my body warm, as if a fire is burning inside me. Right now, all I can think about is the rich color of your hair. How your cheeks look when you blush with embarrassment—" Valeria's cheeks flushed, a smirk formed on my lips. "—just like that, or with sexual excitement."

She squirmed again.

I exhaled sharply, my fingers threatening to slide inside her pants as I caressed her stomach under her top. "Are you excited, Valeria?" I whispered in her ear. "If I slide my fingers inside your underwear, would your pussy be wet and pink for me just like this morning, *hm?*"

She gasped, her hips bucking, wanting more. "*Khalid,*" Valeria pleaded, her voice sultry.

"Tell me what you want, my sweet," I said, my voice husky as I breathed in her rosy delicate scent. "Say it."

"Please touch me."

"Touch you where?"

I wanted to hear her say it. See her cheeks turn red.

But Valeria had another thing in mind. She held my hand that was on her stomach and lowered it down her hips, over her lace covered mound.

"*Here,*" she whispered, her voice full of arousal.

Cupping her, I squeezed her pussy, groaning at the feel of wetness. "Already wet for me, sweet girl."

Valeria whimpered, leaning back when I slid her underwear to the side and rubbed her slicked slit. She felt my hardness poking her lower back and gasped when I palmed her breast with my other hand. The muscles of her thighs relaxed and tensed when I played with her clit, my lips descending on her neck, licking her beating pulse.

She moaned in my arms as I lowered her *keffiyeh* and watched her heady expression through my half-lidded eyes. She looked so fucking hot, begging and squirming in my arms.

Her breathy voice and her needy body arched in my arms as if she couldn't wait for more. As if she needed me. *Wanted* me.

I inserted a finger inside her wet folds, sinking my teeth into the soft skin of her neck when she clenched me. "I can't wait to ravish you, Valeria," I grunted, her soft gasps getting louder and louder when I slid another finger into her heat.

"*Please*," she begged again, her eyes squeezing shut.

I tweaked her nipple through her thin shirt. "Ride my fingers, sweet one."

Her freckles became prominent when light pink dusted over her cheeks. "I have—"

I could sense the hesitation in her voice. Softly fondling her breast, I whispered, "Go on, you can ride my fingers and fuck yourself or you can wait till you get to ride my cock."

Surprise, shock and arousal were clear on her face, her pussy clenching my fingers. "I get to ride your…?"

I chuckled softly, licking her ear. "You have to earn it, Valeria."

"Earn it?" Her cheeks turned a darker shade of red as she looked away, squirming in my hand. "You are so arrogant—*ah!*"

I pressed my thumb on her clitoris, slowly rolling it around with little pressure. Her fingers dug into my forearms when I repeated my actions. "It's your choice, my sweet one. You can ride my fingers here *or wait*. Which one will it be?"

Valeria didn't answer me. She closed her eyes and slowly bucked her hips against my fingers, holding my arms as leverage to ride herself to orgasm. I smirked, proud of her, and continued playing with her breasts, watching her chest flush and heave as her breathing increased.

"That's my good girl," I purred, kissing her jaw. She was clamping my fingers as if her life depended on it. "You're going to cum riding my fingers, aren't you, *hm?*"

"*Yes.*"

"Yes, *what?*"

Valeria looked at my face, pulling out her bottom lip from between her teeth. "Yes, my filthy Prince," she crooned.

I crushed my lips against hers, swallowing her groans when I thrust my fingers inside her cunt. I threaded my fingers through her hair and held her as I claimed her mouth, exploring it with my tongue while my fingers curled, rubbing over her sensitive spot.

She whimpered, pressing down on my hand as her wetness coated it, her body shuddering. I kissed her through her orgasm, her lips going pliant, her hands caressing my arms, the finger marks she had given me.

I pulled away, both of us gasping for air. Her lips were swollen with our kisses and her expression seemed dizzy with her orgasm. I caressed her body, soothing her down as she came down to earth, going lax in my arms, her breathing slowing down.

Licking away her juices, I tried not to make my hard on prominent even though I wished to do something about it.

"What are you thinking?" She asked after a few moments.

"I am thinking of stripping you naked and ravishing you in the desert."

14

VALERIA

"I am thinking of stripping you naked and ravishing you in the desert."

I swallowed the lump in my throat after hearing Khalid's words. He certainly had a way with them. Even though I had reached my peak a few moments ago, my body wanted him again.

It was crazy how much he affected me.

It was even crazier that I was about to ask him to strip me naked and ravish me in the desert.

But my words died in my throat when I heard the rustling of water. We were close to the lake he wanted to take me to.

Khalid helped me down the horse, and I felt embarrassed to look in his direction, remembering how he had told me to ride his hand or wait for his... *argh*, so so arrogant. Even though a small part of me enjoyed when he demanded me to do it.

"Is it safe to swim here?" I asked, the scent of fresh water and cool air kissing my bare skin.

Khalid pressed his hand on my lower back as he led me to the lake. "Very safe. Even the local kids come here to swim now and then. Why?" His hot lips pressed against my ear, making me shiver when he purred, "Are you thinking of skinny dipping in the lake, Valeria?"

My body zinged with excitement at the thought of swimming naked in a lake, alone with Khalid. *Maybe I can repay him with some teasing, or try to tease him for before.*

I walked out of his reach and grinned at him. "Yes, Prince Khalid, I am going to skinny dip."

Feeling brave, I crossed my arms, and holding the hem of my top, I removed it. Cool air brushed across my bare breasts, making my nipples hard. I shivered and removed my pants along with the underwear. I took a deep breath and straightened up, standing naked in front of Khalid.

I heard him taking slow steps towards me and held my breath. My body scorched under his heated gaze as I tried not to take a step back. I was very aware of how alone I felt with his looming presence in the desert. There was on one around. Just both of us.

But I didn't feel scared, I felt excited. Turned on. I wanted to know what he would do.

"You are a terrible tease, Valeria," he said, his voice heavy as his fingers ran through my hair. I licked my lips, waiting and wanting. His warm lips pressed against my forehead. "Go on then, take a swim. I will wait here."

Huh?

I tried not to frown as I asked, "You won't join me?"

"Sadly, no, love." Khalid took a step back. "I will watch over you. Just don't swim too far."

I understood his decision not to swim with me, but I still felt disappointed that he didn't want to join me.

"Okay," I muttered and walked towards the lake, my bare feet sinking in the wet mud. I let out the breath I was holding and relaxed as the cold water surrounded my body.

If Khalid wanted to be a party-pooper, I didn't care. I would still have fun in the lake. It had been a long time since I swam.

Khalid

I sighed sadly as I watched Valeria's pale body swim in the lake. I wanted to join her... but my back. I knew if I went to skinny dip with her, which I really wanted to, we would end up making out and touching each other. That meant her hands touching all over my body. Especially my back.

I didn't want to make her freak out if she touched me. There was a reason I never removed my shirt in front of anyone. Even in private. I didn't want anyone, including my family and especially Valeria, to see my back.

None of them needed to know about that.

So I watched her, kept an eye on her as she teased me while she backstroked. Her nipples flushed and pointed as she swam lazily, her wet hair clung to her body. Such a fucking tease.

I closed my eyes and forced myself to stay calm. Taking a deep breath, I opened my eyes and—

"Valeria?" I said, quickly standing up from the sand. "Valeria," I called out to her once more when I couldn't see her swimming in the lake.

Where the fuck did she go?

My heartbeat pounded in my ears as I quickly removed my shoes and walked inside the lake. Clothes be damned.

"Valeria!" I shouted, water reaching to my shirt, its material clinging to my chest. I looked all around but couldn't find her. Taking a deep breath, I dove into the lake.

I panted, swimming all around the lake. "Valeria, where did you go?" I kept calling her name, but she didn't reply.

Fuck. Look what you have done, Khalid. Couldn't even take care of one person.

"Valeria!"

Such a fucking coward and calling yourself a Prince. You should be ashamed of yourself. Someone might die because of your carelessness.

"Valeria, where are you?!"

You already killed your father. Now you have killed Val—

"Valeria!"

Please be safe. Please be safe. Please be safe. Please don't die. I can't lose you too.

She is blind and you let her drown. You let her down. You promised to take care of her. So fucking shameful. Why don't you kill yoursel—

"Surprise!"

Cold water splashed across my face, my body freezing as I heard the familiar soft laughter. I opened my eyes, droplets of water falling down my lashes as I stared at her grinning face. The ringing in my ear slowed down.

Valeria is okay.

My heartbeat slowly dropped to normal. My breathing became easier, the fog clearing from my head.

She is safe, and she is grinning at me.

I glared at her, my emotions all over the place. Her smile dropped when I didn't react. I didn't know how to react. I was relieved that she was safe and well, but I was furious at her for pranking me like that.

"Khalid?" she asked, swimming closer and lightly touching my stiff arm. "Are you ok—"

Wrapping my hand around her wrist, I dragged her closer. "What the *fuck* were you thinking?" I seethed, my nose flaring with anger.

Her eyes widened at my tone, but I didn't care. I was angry at her for scaring me like that. I was angry at myself for being so fucking careless.

"Why the fuck would you do that? You know I am responsible for you while you are here. I thought you fucking drowned when I closed my eyes just for a second. Fucking hell, Valeria."

I let go of her wrist and pulled back, swimming out of the

lake, running my hand through my hair. I glared at her as she slowly followed me, shock and guilt written all over her face.

"Khalid… I am so—"

I picked up her clothes and thrusted them in her hands. "Get dressed. We are leaving," I ordered, turning around and calling the palace to bring a car to the lake. I was too shaken to ride Kamil back to the palace with her sitting that close to me. I didn't look at her once she got dressed, just made sure she was close by.

Air around us hovered with uncertainty and anger as I led her to the car. One of the staff of the palace got out of the passenger seat and bowed at us before taking the rein of Kamil and jumping up into the saddle. He would bring the horse to the palace while we took the car.

I wanted to be away from her until my anger washed away, but I couldn't force her to be in a car with people she didn't know.

"Get inside the car, Valeria," I said, clenching my jaw as she sat down in the leather seat. She was shivering, her hair and clothes wet.

She looked at me, "Khalid, I want to ap—"

I cut her sentence by closing the door.

Fuck. I pinched the bridge of my nose and slowly breathed out. I sat in the passenger seat and told the driver to start driving.

Her shoulders sulked as she frowned, staring at her lap. I pulled some clean napkin from the dashboard and handing it to her. "I will ask the maid to have your warm bath ready or else you'll get sick in this wind," I muttered and turned on the radio.

Even though I was in the passenger seat, my eyes were fixed on the rearview mirror. I glared at the driver when he gave me a knowing smirk.

Valeria barely nodded, her body freezing up. I frowned

when her eyes widened, her lips moving, but no words came out.

I turned towards the backseat. "What happened?"

"S-Stop," she whispered, her face leeching of color.

"Do you want to stop the car?" I asked, worried about her. "Hey, what happened, Valeria?"

Fuck, did I get too angry at her? Was she mad at me?

"Stop it!" she pleaded, the driver giving me a concerned look.

I told him to stop the car and watched in horror when her fingers fumbled with the latch of the car door. She opened the car door and rushed out.

I followed her, quickly rushing to her aid when she fell down on her knees and hands, sobbing, her eyes red. I knelt beside her, holding her hair back when she retched, tears streaming down her face. I soothed her, stroking her back as she wiped her mouth with my handkerchief, her breath heaving as she sat back on her heels.

"Are you okay?" I asked in a soft tone, not wanting to scare her any further.

Valeria nodded, her eyes swollen. She weakly mumbled, "I want to go back."

I helped her up and noticed her tensing when I opened the car door.

Did something happen in the car? But I was with her the entire time. Maybe she panicked because I got angry at her?

"Please don't turn on the radio," she said, sitting on the backseat of the car.

Radio?

I sat with her and called her maid to ready her bath. As soon as we arrived to the manor of the oasis, I guided Valeria to Tamara, who was concerned about her, and took her to her room. I sighed as I leaned on one of the pillars in the hallway. I dismissed the staff, watching the sulking figure of Valeria fade upstairs.

What the hell happened in the car?

Valeria

The ringing in my ears had quieted down after the warm bath. Tamara had informed that Khalid wanted to dine alone. My heart shrank with guilt. It was supposed to be a prank. Hiding underneath the water, surprising him and having a small water fight to play with him. I didn't mean to make him worry or scare him.

Finishing my dinner in my bed, I wished Tamara good night and promised to call for her if I needed her help.

The song in the car played in my head and I tried to shake it out. It was *his* voice. *His* song. The same one that played that early morning when he drove me back home, assuring me I was safe.

What a bunch of lies.

Soft silk of the small nightgown felt cool over my skin as I breathed in the fresh air from the balcony. It embarrassed me that Khalid, of all people, had to witness all of that. Even though he was mad at me, he made sure I was cared for. My heart melted for his concern for me.

I wouldn't be able to sleep without talking to him.

Swallowing a glass of cold water, I braced myself to talk to him and apologize for what had happened.

I knocked on his door, my hands fumbling with the silk of my nightgown. *Oh, no.* I can't believe I forgot to wear something else before meeting him.

Stupid Valeria.

Should I quickly grab a robe and cover up my nightgown?

I would have, but Khalid was already opening his door.

"*Valeria.*" I heard his deep voice say, huskier than before.

"Khalid," I replied, and cleared my throat. "I… I wanted to talk to you about before."

He didn't reply for a few moments. I shivered, feeling his gaze rake over my face, my chest, my stomach, my bare legs. I heard the door open wider.

"Come inside," Khalid said, inviting me to his room.

15

KHALID

I poured myself a glass of whiskey as she stood awkwardly near my bed. I watched her with half-lidded eyes, still angry yet concerned for her.

"How are you feeling?" I said, stepping closer to her, the scent of fresh roses and something feminine surrounding her.

Valeria looked in my direction, her fingers closed together in front of her. She was nervous.

Hm, she should be.

"Good!" she said, nodding. "I am good! How are you?"

"I am quite furious but worried," I replied truthfully, taking a sip of the alcohol. I sat down in the armchair near the night-stand, cool wind blowing from the balcony caressing my skin.

"Why are you furious and worried?"

"Come here and I will tell you."

She looked in my direction, her gaze narrowing.

"That sounds like a trap."

I chuckled and swallowed the contents of the glass, leaving a burning sensation in my throat. I kept it on the table and looked at her, spreading my legs.

"Come here, my sweet one," I purred in a low voice, seeing

the effect it had on her half-naked body. Her hardened nipples poked through the thin nightgown as she took a small step towards me. I eyed her long legs and licked my lips.

Before she could sit down in another armchair, I held her wrist and pulled her over onto my lap. Valeria gasped, squirming on my legs, red strands framing her flushed face. Holding her waist, I settled her over me.

"I am concerned for you, because what happened in the car made me worry about you," I said sincerely, my fingers caressing the soft skin of her legs. "I thought you panicked because I had raised my voice at you. Maybe scared you."

She shook her head. "No, Khalid, it was something else. It doesn't matter anymore."

"It matters to me."

Valeria looked at her lap. "I don't want to talk about it right now." She raised her head. "But I promise, you had nothing to do with it. I am okay now, it just took me by surprise."

I stared at her honest face, her sincere words, and continued caressing her legs, slowly inching higher and higher until I noticed the change in her breathing.

"Why are you mad?" Valeria whispered, biting her lip, her voice shaky.

"I am mad at you because the prank you pulled on me wasn't funny," I said, my breathing harsh. I leaned back on the armchair, her eyes widening when she felt the loss of my touch. I continued, controlling the tone of my voice, "You acted recklessly, thinking it would be funny to scare me if you disappeared."

"Khalid, I am sor—"

"I wasn't finished, Valeria." I tilted my head. "Not only it was stupid, but it put your life in danger. If someone else had seen that, they would arrest you because you unintentionally put my life in danger when I couldn't find you and had to enter the lake when I didn't want to."

She took a shaky breath, biting her lip as I stared at her. Clenching my jaw, I looked away, slowly counting to ten.

"I wanted to tease you, play with you, but I never meant to make you so worried or angry, Khalid, I promise," she said, her voice pleading as she pressed closer to me.

I believed her every word, the innocent sincerity on her face, the sound of her shaky voice.

"Please forgive me. I won't ever scare you like that again, please. I am sorry, Khalid."

"What makes you say that there will be next time?" I threatened.

I should be in hell for teasing her like that. But I was a selfish person, enjoying the way Valeria begged me, the ample cleavage a few inches from my face as her breasts pressed against the front of my tee shirt.

"Khalid, please forgive me. I would do anything. Please tell me how can I fix this." Tears threatened to spill down as she whispered, "Let me make it up to you. Please, don't be mad at me."

Fuck it.

"You'll do anything, sweet one?"

Valeria nodded, "*Anything*, Khalid."

I smirked at her, cupping her face and caressing her cheek.

Looks like she would be apologizing to me all night.

Valeria

I leaned into his large hand, closing my eyes at his gentle, warm touch. I was glad that I could make up to Khalid somehow, no matter the cost. I would do anything he asked—

"Open your mouth."

I frowned, but parted my lips.

"*Wider*, Valeria," he said, my legs clenching at the harsh edge of his voice. It was odd to find his angry voice a turn on as I did what he asked, parting my mouth wider.

I took a shuddering breath when he pressed two fingers inside my mouth, his hot breath fanning on my neck as he leaned closer.

"You will do anything?" He asked, his voice threateningly low and smoky.

I nodded, licking his fingers, tasting them.

"Good girl. Tell me to stop if you feel uncomfortable."

I held my breath when he pulled out his fingers from my mouth, holding my hand and taking me to his bed. My heartbeat thundered in my chest.

Were we going to have sex?

"What are we doing?" I asked him, my voice soft.

"Not we, sweetheart. *You.*"

"Me?"

His fingers scrunched the hem of the nightgown and lifted it over my arms, baring my skin to him. I blushed hearing his low curse, his scorching gaze heavy on my skin.

"Yes, *you,*" he whispered, laying me on the bed on my stomach, positioning my ass towards him.

I bit my lip, my hair tickling my arms as I pressed my elbows on the soft mattress. I licked my lips, waiting in anticipation as Khalid placed a pillow underneath my hips.

"Khalid," I said his name, squirming on the bed as my arousal increased.

I gasped when he pulled my cheeks apart and pressed two fingers over my slicked slit, rubbing them over my heated sex. "You are soaking already, sweet one. I haven't even touched you properly."

I hummed, pressing back on his hand, and gasped when delicious pain singed my butt to my core. Khalid spanked me again when I pushed myself on his hand.

"You said you want to make up for me, right?"

Despite the low threat in his voice, I found it incredibly hot. His warm breath fanned over my ear. "Then don't cum until I tell you to."

I wasn't prepared for his firm hold on my thighs, the bed dipping as he blew cold air on my bare, heated sex. I whimpered, moaning his name as Khalid teased me with his fingers, kissing my wet heat with his warm mouth.

I felt him spread my lips open, his hot tongue pressing over my clit and giving a slow, long lick to my entrance. I was squirming, trying to push back towards him as my toes curled with his expert ministrations.

"You wanted to tease me, right?" He whispered hotly. "*This is your punishment for what you did.*"

So Khalid teased me. Kept me on the edge with his fingers, his mouth and tongue while I tried desperately to seek more friction so I could orgasm. But if I moved too much, he would spank my ass, ordering me to stay still.

"Move again and I will tie you up, Valeria," Khalid said, curling his fingers inside my sensitive core, his thumb rubbing over my swollen clit.

I felt overwhelmed and on the edge.

"I am sorry, Khalid," I pleaded, my hair sticking to my face as sweat sheeted my body. "Please, I won't do it again. *Ah.* Forgive me."

He hummed, "Do you want to cum on my fingers, Valeria?"

I nodded, my walls clenching around them.

"You want to release on my mouth, *hm?*" He purred, his voice velvety smooth as he smacked my cheek again. "Then do it, cum on my mouth, let me make you feel good."

I moaned, squeezing my eyes shut when the squelching sound of wetness echoed in the room when his fingers fucked me. Pleasure built inside my body, slowly rising as his mouth sucked on my pleasure nub, my mind going blank as white-hot lust melted through my body, gushing out of me.

Panting, I rested my head on the mattress, gasping when Khalid didn't stop. "I... *oh*, I am sensitive," I whimpered, his fingers twisting my nipple while he continued to fuck me, rubbing the sensitive spot inside me.

"One more, my sweet," he whispered sweetly. "I know you can give me one more orgasm. Come on."

I didn't have it in me to deny the filthy, hot request of Prince Khalid. I bit my lip, holding on to the sheets as Khalid's fingers moved inside me, precisely applying pressure on the G-spot. My body quivered and toes curled as I groaned out his name, my breathing increasing with my moans.

My body tensed just before he stopped sucking my clitoris and I climaxed, falling as I squeezed my eyes shut, orgasm rocking through my body. I had trouble keeping oxygen inside me and stayed limp when Khalid licked me clean, my sensitive muscles clenching around nothing.

He gently turned me around, my back relaxing as he spread my legs, slowly gliding his hands over my thighs.

"How do you feel, Valeria?" He whispered, kissing my knee as if he hadn't just made me orgasm twice in a row after keeping me on edge for God knows how long.

"You are a terrible tease." I shook my head, blinking in his direction. "I hate you."

Khalid chuckled softly, and I felt him move around on the bed before pressing against my side. I closed my eyes as he tucked the strands framing my face behind my ears.

"Does your ass hurt?"

"What?"

"I spanked you," Khalid said, blood rushing to my cheeks and ears. "I want to make sure you aren't hurt."

I bit my lip and shook my head. I had never thought that I would ever find *that* a turn on, but it seemed that everything that Khalid did was a turn on for me.

"I can manage."

"Promise me not to do that ever again, Valeria," he said, kissing my forehead.

"I promise, Khalid." After a moment, I asked, "But why didn't you join me in the lake?"

His muscles tensed beside me, and I knew I had asked something personal to him. Before I could take my question back, he said, "Do you really want to know, Valeria?"

16

KHALID

"Do you really want to know, Valeria?"

She nodded, her soft face peering up at me as I moved back to remove my tee shirt. I had never told anyone about it. Not a single soul, but I wanted to let her know. Even though it meant becoming awfully vulnerable.

I wanted to let Valeria know about the scars on my back.

Taking a deep breath, I turned, showing her my back. "The reason I didn't want to join you in the lake is because of my back. I... I never remove my shirt because of it."

"Okay," she said, sitting up and waiting for me to continue.

"Touch my back, Valeria," I whispered, my voice hoarse.

I clenched my jaw when I felt the soft pads of her fingers on my back. I tried not to recoil as her gentle hands moved around, freezing when they met the bumpy and scratchy skin.

I tensed, feeling both of her hands on my back.

Valeria gasped, *"Khalid..."*

I swallowed the lump in my throat.

"Who... why, what... *who did this to you?"*

"My father," I said, my shoulders feeling heavy. "Everyone knew Zain would be the Sultan, so when we were kids, he would give me *lessons* if I didn't ride a horse properly, missed my classes, mocked his name or spent too much time caring for my sister."

Valeria took a sharp breath, her soft fingers caressing my skin. The large and small whip scars splattered all over my back. "Lessons?"

I nodded, thinking back to the time he would make me stay in his study after telling Zain to leave. I always dreaded those times. His rough voice telling me to kneel and remove my shirt, ordering me to stay still while he *taught* me how to be a man. My father was many things, a pathetic man and a worse father. Whipping his own children and relishing in their cries.

Yet I never cried in front of him because I knew that if I did, he would mock me more. Threaten to hit Zain, or worse, Zara. I couldn't bear the thought of him ever hurting my sister. Hurting the people that I loved.

That was the reason why I never regretted killing him with my own hands, with his own sword. I would do it again if I could.

"He wanted me to be a perfect soldier, a noble Prince, an obedient son. My father hated that I loved painting, so he whipped me whenever he could because I won't follow in his footsteps like he wanted me to."

"Oh, Khalid." Her arms wrapped around me, her forehead touching my back.

I waited for my body to tense up or push her away, but I relaxed in her arms, relishing in her soft touch caressing my skin. I felt her warm tears on my back, on my scars, her warm breath caressing my torn skin.

"Are you crying?" I asked.

"No," she sniffled loudly.

I smiled sadly, letting her cry on my back. My mother had taught me that the best thing you can do when someone was crying is to let them cry, be there for them, and allow them to say something whatever they wanted to share.

"I am glad he's dead or else..." she threatened in her small voice.

I faced her, smiling at her adorably stubborn face. "Or else? What would you do?"

"I would scold him!"

A broken laughter erupted from my throat. The thought of my sweet Valeria going against my father just to scold him made tears glisten in my eyes as I clutched my stomach and laughed like never before. Of course, if he was alive, I would never let her meet him, but her gesture, her words, her expression made me chuckle.

"Stop laughing, Khalid," she whined, her nose scrunching up. "I am serious. I would scold him *pretty hard.*"

I shook my head, grinning at her. "Of course, you would."

Cupping her face, I pressed my lips against hers, gently prying them open and kissing her slowly, lovingly. As if I was painting on a delicate paper. My heart felt full and warm when she pressed against me.

"You are so fucking adorable, my sweet," I whispered, kissing her once more when she smiled at me.

I closed my eyes when her fingers ran through my hair, massaging my scalp. Valeria knew about my scars. I felt content letting her touch my back.

I didn't have to worry about hiding my scars from her.

I didn't know whether to be happy about it or feel concerned.

Valeria

Humming, I shuffled in the bed, taking a deep breath from the soft tee shirt that Khalid had lent me before we cuddled each other. It smelt so much like him. Woodsy, pine and fresh male scent. I would drown myself in his scent if I could.

"Khalid?" I mumbled, rubbing my eyes as I sat up on the bed, sheets lowering to my bare legs.

I heard him take a sharp breath on the other end of the bed. What was he doing so far away from me?

"What happened?" I asked.

If he was thinking about his father and his scars, I wanted to make sure he was okay. What he had shared with me the other night felt vulnerable and intimate. I knew he had never shared it with anyone else, and I felt honored that he trusted me to talk about his past, his scars.

I adored him for it.

I felt him move, the air heavy and hot in his room. It felt different from before. Like the time I had entered his room, and he had spanked me, edged me, and made me come in his mouth. My body warmed just thinking about those things, the feel of his rough, large hands holding me close, his hot tongue, mouth, and lips on my body.

"I am sorry I woke you up," Khalid said, his voice smoky and hoarse.

Biting my lip at the sound of his sexy voice, I asked, "Are you okay?"

He didn't reply for a moment.

"I am touching myself, Valeria."

It took me a moment to process what he had said.

I cupped my mouth and turned away, even though it wasn't necessary. "I am so, so sorry, Khalid! I swear I didn't know. I just wanted to make sure you were—I am sorry."

Khalid

I bit my lip and tried to focus on how to handle the situation properly. I hadn't meant to wake up from my extremely filthy wet dream about Valeria with a boner. She was sleeping peacefully beside me and I didn't want to wake her up so I had resorted to use my hand, trying to be as quite as possible.

But Valeria was a very light sleeper.

My cock was throbbing in my palm and my head was filled with lewd thoughts of Valeria and nothing else.

She was hiding her face and looking away.

I sighed. "Valeria, you don't have to apologize. I was thinking about you."

"You were thinking about me? While touching yourself?"

"Yes." I squeezed my eyes shut.

"I wish I could see that." Her voice was almost inaudible, but I heard her loud and clear.

I opened my eyes and looked in her direction. She wanted to see me touch myself.

Valeria wanted to see me.

"Come here."

She shook her head. "If I do, I will get curious."

If it was even possible, I got even harder. My dick twitching in my palm.

"What's wrong with being curious?" I crooned.

"I… I might touch you to know—to know how it feels," Valeria whispered.

Even though I couldn't see her face, I knew it was red.

I swallowed the lump in my throat. Does it mean she has never touched someone before?

"Do you want to touch me, Valeria?" I asked, wanting to know what she wanted to do.

Her back straightened, and I was surprised when she replied in a firm voice, "Yes."

"Good girl." I was extremely pleased knowing that she wanted it as much as I did. "Then crawl towards me and touch me."

I leaned back on the soft headboard of the bed and gazed at

her through half-lidded eyes when she came closer, her seductive, sweet scent making it more intimate.

I held her palm and kissed it, wanting to reassure her. She may have never pleasured a man before and even though I was excited and honored to be her first, and hopefully her last, I didn't want her to do anything she didn't want to.

I would be the luckiest man alive even if Valeria cuddled to my chest and called it a night.

Pulling her on my lap, I kissed her, moving her hair over her shoulder and running my hand through her silky red locks. She kissed me deeper, angling her face as our tongues met in a soft caress, a moan slipping out of her lips when she felt just how hard I was for her between her legs.

Valeria must have realized by now that I was completely naked.

Her fingers tightened on my shoulders when I kissed her throat.

"What is it?"

"I have never done this before," she admitted truthfully.

I cupped her cheek and kissed her softly. "Then I will teach you."

She gave me a shy smile, lowering her hands towards my abdomen. My muscles clenched at the soft caress. I wanted her to lower her hand and close her palm around me. Make her feel how hard she made me.

"Can I touch you, Prince Khalid?" Valeria asked sweetly, her lips wet and swollen with the kisses.

"Yes, but first remove this tee shirt. I want to see you naked."

Having a woman take off her top in front of you was one of the hottest things ever. My mouth watered at the sight of her round, perky breasts, but I controlled myself, keeping my hands on the dip of her waist.

"You are wet," I said, my eyes pinned on the glistening slit between her thighs.

She tried to hide her face with her hair.

I held her chin. "Don't hide from me, Valeria. Seeing you wet and needy for me is a turn on. Feel how hard I am for you."

Valeria gasped at my dirty words. I wrapped my hand around her wrist and pulled her closer, her fingers brushing over the soft, velvety skin of my stiffened member, making me hiss with pleasure.

I watched her as she wrapped her fingers around my hardened cock, her lips parting as she felt me. I wanted to close my eyes and relish in the pleasure, but it was more pleasurable watching Valeria touch me and explore me with curiosity.

"Show me how to please you," Valeria whispered, her sultry voice needy. "Please, Khalid."

I exhaled sharply, hearing her words. I could never say no to her, especially when she was naked and on all fours, begging me to show her how to please me.

"You are already pleasing me, my sweet one," I said truthfully.

Her cheeks turned red. "You know what I mean."

I closed my hand over hers and slowly stroked myself, squeezing at the shaft, teaching her. Her other hand held onto my thigh, my muscles tensing when she stroked me by herself, slowly squeezing my length at the base. The red tip leaked with pre-cum when I saw how aroused she looked.

I let out a low groan when she surprised me by leaning closer and tasting me.

17

VALERIA

I *loved* how Khalid tasted; musky, salty, and masculine. The groan of his pleasure resonated through my body, making me wet. His cock was hard, but the skin was velvety soft as I moved my hand back and forth. I wanted to taste him again and hear him moan.

Leaning down, I licked his length again, this time taking the tip in my mouth and gently sucking on it.

"Valeria," Khalid moaned, his hand weaving in my hair and holding it as I repeated my actions.

I must be doing something right, making him moan like that. It was the sexiest sound I had ever heard. I wanted to hear it again and again.

I parted my lips and bobbed my head back and forth over him, taking his aching cock inside my hot mouth as much as I could. Hollowing my cheeks, I sucked on him, loving the way he tightened his hold on my hair and guided me to do it slowly. His sharp inhales and groans made it pleasurable for both of us.

I would do anything to hear him groan like that.

Khalid

The tips of her copper hair brushed on my inner thighs when she sucked me in her mouth, my muscles clenching. I groaned at the sight of her pillowy lips stretching around my cock, her hand stroking the base gently.

"Relax your throat, sweetheart," I said, my breathing harsh and heavy. I tugged on her hair, allowing her to take a deep breath before she went back to suck me, experimentally relaxing her throat as I slowly slid deeper inside her hot mouth.

She let out a soft moan, squeezing her eyes shut. The reverberations of her moan made me tether to the edge as I clenched my hand tightly on her hair. We both lost ourselves in the pleasure as my arousal kept growing and growing.

"Let me know if you want to stop, Valeria," I breathed out, holding her hair and gently thrusting my hips towards her, guiding myself deeper inside her hot mouth. Her other hand clenched the sheets as she opened her mouth wide and relaxed her throat like I had instructed her.

I was so close to climaxing that I had to stop myself from releasing inside her.

"Why did you stop?" Valeria asked as soon as I let her go, licking her wet lips and gazing up at me.

"If I hadn't, I would've cum inside your mouth," I explained.

I didn't miss the slight clench of her thighs as she leaned back and said, "Then do it."

I couldn't say no to her when she dipped back and slowly bobbed her head over my cock, urging me to release my seed inside her mouth. I held her hair and the sheets as I felt myself uncoil. I let out a groan of her name, my legs trembling. The muscles of my body tensed kand went lax as the spurt of my seed hit the back of her throat.

I watched in awe with half-lidded eyes as she swallowed my cum, my body still going through the aftershocks of orgasm. I released the tight grip I had on her hair and held her hand when she sucked me clean.

Valeria

I leaned back, swallowing the last of his cum and licking my lips at the musky taste of Khalid. Even though he had just released inside my mouth, I couldn't wait to please him again. I loved it and understood why he spent so much time giving me oral. Giving pleasure was as arousing as receiving it, if not more.

"You are a vixen, Valeria," Khalid whispered throatily, his voice sounding huskier and deeper than before.

I flushed when he pulled me closer, pressing his lips against mine. "Are you okay?" I asked, caressing his cheek.

Khalid chuckled. "Of course, I am okay, sweet. You gave me the best blowjob of my life, and you're asking me if I am okay. I should be the one to ask you that."

I smiled. "I am great. I want to do it again."

"Not so soon," he ordered, holding my hand before it could reach him. "I am quite sensitive right now. How about we take a bath?"

"Together?"

"Yes, together. I don't plan to let you go so soon."

I let out a small giggle when Khalid took me in his arms, even though I could walk perfectly. "I plan to return the favor."

And Khalid returned the favor. After I washed his back and kissed his scars, he fingered me in the bath. After our bath, he laid me spread out on his bed and urged me to come again and again on his mouth and fingers until my body was spent and exhausted, too tired to even move.

He pulled me closer to him and covered both of us with a blanket, kissing my forehead before dozing off, his hand caressing my spine.

Khalid
(Khalid first person. Valeria third person)

"What about the color green?" I asked, dipping the flat brush in blue paint and mixing it with white and a bit of red on the color plate with linseed oil to thicken it.

Valeria hummed, her naked body lounging in the pose, her body much more relaxed. Her eyes were still blindfolded, but she wasn't tensed as before. I was glad that she trusted me.

"It is nature. Leaves, grasses, the rustles of palm tree leaves remind me of green. I sense a lot of refreshment and peace in the color."

I stopped painting, staring at her. The slight scrunch between her eyebrows vanishing as she finished speaking. Her answer was short and filled with such depth that I was intrigued. Every time I spent time with her, I discovered something new about her and was in awe of Valeria. I wanted to spend more time with her.

"What do you think about brown?" She asked, her head tilting in his direction for a flicker of moment.

I continued painting, the light blue paint melting into the plain canvas. "For me, brown is dirt. Earth." I thought over it and continued, "How the suppleness of the leaves feels like green, it is like life. But when the leaves are crispy or turn brown, they are dead, it is like death."

Valeria hummed.

"What about you? What do you think of brown, Valeria?"

"To be honest…" her cheeks and ears turned red as I waited for her to continue. "Brown reminds me of fart."

I grinned, shaking my head as she chuckled, cupping her mouth. I wished I could talk to her all day, laugh with her, kiss her smile and be with her.

A lock of her red hair fell over her neck, brushing the

roundness of her bare breast. I averted my eyes and washed away the blue paint from the brush.

We had started the painting early that morning and the first coat of paint was finished. I had finished painting the color of her skin and hair, adding shadows and depth to the curves and then working on the background and chaise. The canvas would dry the whole night as the studio was open to air and I could work on second coat the next day.

After telling her to relax, I washed the brushes, glancing at her. Her naked body stretching over the chaise. She emitted a soft sigh, lifting her arms over her head. The muscles of her stomach and legs tightened; my gleaming eyes pinned over the pink tips of her breasts.

I licked my lips.

The thump of brush falling on the ground snapped me back to reality and out of the fantasy I was having. Valeria looked in my direction when I hurriedly kept the paint and brushes away.

"Were you staring at me, Your Highness?" Her voice was sultry when she offered me a small smirk.

I raised my eyebrows at her. Standing up to my full height, I prowled towards her, her eyes still blindfolded with the silk.

"And what if I was? I have seen, touched and licked every inch of your skin, my sweet one," my voice lowered with each step I took towards her.

Valeria licked her lips, knowing Khalid was in closer proximity than before. She had heard him keep his painting tools away. She sat up in a sitting position and clenched her hands in a fist when his warm hands glided over her thighs, sending a shiver of tingles down her core. The delicious sensation of his hands on her skin made her clench her sex.

The clench of her thighs didn't go unnoticed by me as I knelt in front of her, fully clothed and in awe with her responsive body. I loved how sensitive she was to my touch.

"Are you wet for me, Valeria?" I asked, my voice low, knowing that she was dripping for me. When she failed to reply, I leaned closer, digging my fingers on her creamy thighs and purred in her ear, "I can *smell* how wet you are."

"*Khalid.*" she let out a soft teasing moan, her muscles quivering beneath his touch. She arched up at him, wanting to embrace him. "Please touch me."

I hummed, kissing the corner of her lips and spreading her knees. The heavy, musky scent of her feminine arousal wafted in the air. I let out a warm sigh on the hollow of her neck and kissed the soft skin. No one made me lose my mind like she did.

Valeria bit her bottom lip when the stubble on his jaw grazed her skin, his hands trailing all over her body but not touching where she wanted him the most. Her hips raised towards him when he licked the valley of her chest, kissing the pale, sensitive skin of her breast.

"Where do you want me to touch you, Valeria?" I asked, my voice gruff with lust.

She breathed out. "*Everywhere.*"

I gazed at the woman in front of me and shook my head. Tugging at the silk covering her eyes, I raked my hand through her hair, holding her head and kissing her lips. She melted in my arms when I held her, ravishing and tasting her lips like a starved man. My teeth nipped at her bottom lip when she groaned in my mouth at the tweak of my fingers on her hardened nipple.

Before my hot mouth could soften the burn of a pinch on her nub, there was a knock on the door of the studio making me pull away from her. I regretted moving away from her, but I didn't want anyone to find us like this, especially Valeria. She was still naked on the chaise.

"Here." I handed her the clothes when she tried to close her legs and cover her flushed breasts. "Let me help you."

I knew she could do it on her own, but helping her dress was much more intimate than removing clothes off of her body. It didn't make sense, but it felt right to me. It felt good and brought me joy.

Valeria mumbled a soft thank you when I buttoned her jeans and straightened her top. She always dressed in pastels and neutrals, which I adored.

Kissing the top of her head, I whispered, "We are going to dine in your room tonight. Just the two of us."

"I am looking forward to it." Valeria gave me a shy smile, her fingers scrunching on my shirt as she leaned up to kiss my cheek.

My cheeks were flushing as I opened the door. My guard told me about the call from an unknown number in Australia. I apologized to Valeria that I couldn't walk her back to her room because I had to make a call. It would be none other than Zara.

I needed to talk to my sister.

18

KHALID

(KHALID FIRST PERSON. VALERIA THIRD
PERSON)

"**D**id you enjoy the food?" I asked, helping her wash her hands in the sink.

The dress I had sent to her room felt like a second skin over her, dipping over her curves and making her look stunning in the ruby color. I had managed not to stare too long at her cleavage throughout the dinner and haul her over my lap, but slowly my patience was diminishing.

"I loved it. Especially the spicy curry and the sweet dessert," she beamed, her cheeks, nose and ears turning red because she had spicy food.

I patted her palms dry with a hand towel. "I am glad you did. Would you like to come to the palace next week?"

"The palace?"

"My home. Nasrin, my sister-in-law is having a baby shower and we are holding a modest party—well, not modest actually. We are holding a celebration and my brother invited you to come along with me. If you want."

Why am I nervous?

Maybe because she will get to meet my family?

Zara had called earlier, interrupting us, to ask me about the baby shower ceremony and when she had to arrive. We had talked for a while until someone, a surfer, interrupted our call, flirting with my sister in front of me. I had glared at him but he didn't care. Neither did Zara. I knew she was twenty years old and could look after herself, but she was still my little sister.

Valeria grinned, her pearly smile making my heart beat faster. She had no right to smile at me like that without a warning. No right to go around smiling like that and show her pretty face.

There I go, thinking like a caveman again.

"You mean the Sultan and Sultana? I am really touched. I would love to come and meet your fam—*oh*."

The smile fell off as she turned away.

I stepped closer, holding her hands. "What happened?"

I wanted to know what was causing her to worry.

"I don't have anything to gift your family," she said with a small pout, her voice cracking.

My God, if I didn't do anything, she might cry and truly break me.

I let out a small huff of laugh. "Oh, my sweet one. You don't have to worry about the gift. Your presence will be enough for them."

"That's not fair, Khalid. I don't want to go empty-handed. I will get all of them something in a few days. You have to tell me their likes and dislikes. What can I gift to the Sultan and Sultana? Princess Zara?"

I let her walk out of my arms and leaned back on the railing of the balcony. I gazed at her when she paced around my room with her phone in her hand to take notes on what possible gifts she could get for my family. The whole moment was so normal that I wished it could last forever.

Eating dinner in peace, holding hands, hugging and arguing about which gifts to buy for family. It was eerily normal. It was hard for me to get used to it.

"Does your sister have a painting set?" She piqued, looking in my direction.

"Of course, she does. Her favorite brother gifted it to her on the day she was born."

"Of course."

I held her arms before she could start pacing again. I pulled her closer, taking the phone from her. "Stop worrying about the gift. Nasrin would pinch my ear if she knew I was making a beauty like you worry about such a silly little thing."

"But it's not a silly little thing. I want to show my gratitude to them. To *you*, Khalid. I am meeting the royals, your family. You have treated me so well for all this time. I can't meet your family empty-handed."

Fuck. This was not supposed to happen.

I glared at her soft cheeks and the adorable stern pout on her lips that she wasn't backing away. *How dare she make me feel this way?*

I cupped her cheeks, my eyes darting over her freckles. "My family doesn't care about the presents and neither do I, my sweet. I don't want you to worry about it, okay?"

"Okay," she mumbled. "But I am gifting them something."

"Yes, ma'am." My thumb stroked her cheekbone, my eyes falling on her inviting pink lips, "Can I kiss you?"

Again, her lips curled in the stunning smile I adored. Her arms locked around my neck as she tipped on her toes and kissed me. I closed my eyes and sighed when I felt the soft pressure of her body flushing against me, my arms holding her waist. I lifted her, her legs wrapping around my torso as I led us to my bed, laying her down with a soft groan when she bit my lip.

Valeria gazed at me with a shy smile as I kissed her once again, savoring the soft taste of her lips and grinding my hips against her. She arched her back, her hair fanning out on the black satin sheets. She clutched the fabric of my shirt when our kisses got heavier and needier. Lust and passion taking over our bodies.

I pulled away to unbutton my shirt, throwing it away carelessly on the floor and ravished her lips once more with sweet intensity. Her body trembled beneath me, her hands wandering over my chest, abs, pulling me closer through the belt loops of my pants. My lips trailed down the slender column of her neck to the top of her cleavage. My hand slid underneath the silk dress and kneaded her breasts through the soft lace covering them.

"*More*," Valeria gasped out, urging me closer until the bulge in my pants pressed on the heat between her thighs.

We both groaned at the heady sensation. My cock was throbbing through the zipper, wanting to feel her as I traced my hand down her smooth skin towards her abdomen. *Lower*.

Before I could touch her where we both wanted the most, a shrill ringing stopped me. I cursed audibly on her skin, making her gasp at the filthy words as if she wasn't sure that Prince of Azmia could swear like that.

I sat back, frowning at her. "I am not going to apologize for that, Valeria. I don't like getting interrupted."

She kissed my hand, "I am sorry." She sat up and answered the call.

I scoffed at the caller's name. Of course, it had to be Brandon. He couldn't leave us be, especially when we were in such a heated moment that was leading up to sex, making love to her and fucking her in every way I had imagined.

"Yes, wait, I would need to check it." Valeria held the phone guiltily to her chest, where I had laid soft kisses moments ago. "There's a product that I need to—"

I interrupted her by pecking at her lips. "It's okay, it's an emergency. Sort it out and let me know if you need my help. I am here."

Valeria returned a sweet smile and kissed my cheek. Before

she could leave my room with her dress drooping over her breast and her bra undone, I pulled her back with a soft chuckle and fixed her clothes for her.

"I don't want anyone to see you like that," I said, hooking her bra and straightening the front of her dress, making sure it covered everything.

She raised her eyebrow. "Anyone?"

"Yes, my sweet. Only I can see you mussed up like that," I said, wanting to demonstrate how her mussed up self was not made for anyone's eyes but mine alone.

I might as well brand my name on her.

It sounds erotic—

I am going insane.

"Now get out before I lock you up in my room till tomorrow morning."

Valeria's cheeks flushed red. I wanted to pinch them and then kiss them better.

"I like the sound of that, Prince Khalid."

I gaped at her when she turned around and walked back to her room, her soft giggles echoing in my head. She did not just say that—*She really did.*

SHIRTLESS, I LEANED AGAINST THE STONE RAILING OF THE balcony, gazing at the night sky. It had only been a few minutes without Valeria, but I already missed her.

Zain was right. I liked her.

I liked Valeria.

Warmth surrounded me when Valeria came to stand beside me, my shoulder brushing over her bare arm.

"Call went well?"

"*Mhmm,*" she hummed, entwining her fingers with mine and laying her head on my shoulder.

The subtle scent of the perfume I had gifted her wafted in my nose, making me smile. She wore it to the dinner so she must have liked it and it meant a great deal to me.

That moment with Valeria standing beside me, staring at the sky, was one of the times when I was the most peaceful and content I had ever been in my life. Besides from painting, but even then, my head was filled with chaos to let out everything I had felt.

It made me feel like the time I had held baby Zara for the first time, holding her tightly, too afraid to make her fall from my arms.

I was content and relaxed every time Valeria was around me. Except the moments when I wanted to claim her like an animal.

I looked down at her, her beautiful freckled face free of any makeup as she looked over the wide span of evening sky. Her red hair was coiled over in a bun. She was still wearing the ruby dress.

When she let out a sigh, I whispered, "What are you thinking about?"

She faced me, her face concerned. "Would it be selfish of me to have my sight back? I wish I could see the sky right now. It feels beautiful to me, but I want to see it with my own eyes." Her palm cupped my face, her eyes blinking with unshed tears as she squeezed them shut. "I want to see you. See your face, your lips, your eyes. I… I really wish I could see you, Khalid."

Valeria looked away, as if she wanted to continue. Holding her palm on my cheek, I kissed it. She took a shaky breath and said, "But sometimes I think that if I get my sight back, I would lose my sense of smell. I… I love the way I can sense different notes and even built my brand of perfume because of it. I don't think I would have been able to do that if I wasn't blind. So what if I get my sight back at the cost of losing my sense of smell? It makes me…—"

"*Scared?*" I finished her sentence. She nodded sadly, still not facing me. "I don't know how you feel, but you can have both, sweet. Have your sight *and* sense of smell. And it's not selfish, Valeria. Don't ever think that for wanting your sight back. I researched about your blindness and I can help you with a donor, if that's what you wish for, my sweet one. I want you to have your sight. Help you with anything you want."

My heart felt heavy when a tear slid out of her eye. I wiped it away, kissing her cheek. I didn't want to see her cry. I wanted to help her with whatever she wanted and make her smile. Make her happy.

"Why would you do that for me? You are a famous artist. A Prince. Sultan's brother."

"Because somewhere along the way from hearing your voice and painting you, I fell for you, my sweet. I would give you my own eyes if it gave you your sight back."

Valeria gasped, "Why on earth would you ever do that?"

"Silly woman." I smiled down at her, trailing her hand to my shirt, where my heart pounded wildly. "I like you. I wish to paint you forever if I could. You are my art. My muse. My sweet. And forever will be."

She kissed me. Her soft lips pressing over me as I tasted the salt of her tears. Her body pressed against mine, her fingers feathering through my hair when I embraced her, touching her back and stroking her spine. Wild electricity trickled through both of us.

"You do terrible, terrible things to my heart, Khalid," Valeria whispered, caressing my cheek. "I wish nothing more but to be by your side."

I had no words for what I felt for her. I needed to express how much she meant to me. Breaking and mending my heart little by little with shy smiles, soft words, and whispering kisses.

Our kisses turned urgent, our hands clenching and unclenching over each other's clothes.

They had to go.

I took her inside the room, tugging the dress off of her, unclasping her bra and revealing herself to me. I didn't waste any time to remove her lace underwear as blood thrummed through my veins.

I looked at her tenderly, almost disbelieving that Valeria was spread naked on the bed. I wanted to give her everything. Everything and anything.

"*Khalid,*" Valeria spoke, her voice sultry and low, wanting him to touch her and claim her.

Her soft voice had a hint of urgency behind it as she sensed Khalid crawling up her naked body. Valeria felt the heat of his face and the warmth of his breath against her cheek. She angled her head towards him, pressing her lips on his hot skin, feeling the graze of his stubble on her palm.

I captured her lips, closing my arms around her as she melted into my embrace with a tiny moan. Our passionate kiss felt hot. Her fingers bunched in the dark locks of my hair before lowering to my broad shoulders. I sighed softly when her palm glided over my chest, feeling my abs as her body arched up to me.

Valeria's fingers trailed lower to my pants, eliciting a small moan when her palm traced the outline of my prominent bulge. Her fingers hurriedly helped undo my pants. She was eager to touch my hardness, wanting to make me feel good.

My eyes traced her parted lips when I hovered above her. Both of us naked and bare. My lips pressed against hers gently, nipping and tasting. Our kisses filled with relief and an anxious hesitancy that formed between us. I exhaled sharply against her neck when her ankle brushed against my thigh, her hands feeling the beating pulse of my neck and the tendons of my shoulder.

My fingers lowered to the center between her thighs and rubbed her slickness over her heated sex, slowly rubbing the hard clit. My cock twitched against her thighs when Valeria pressed against my front. Our need to consume each other growing and growing.

Valeria spread her legs and gasped sweetly when he dipped his finger inside her hot cavern, rubbing against the sensitive spot inside her with the tenderness she hadn't known before. She squeezed her eyes shut, shaking nervously when his lips moved from her cheek to neck and lightly pulled on her earlobe, his warm breath tickling the shell of her ear.

I cupped her smooth buttock with my free hand, her hips slowly rocking against my finger when I teased her entrance. I was aware of her body trembling beneath me, but she wasn't stopping me. The strands of her copper red hair splayed across the dark sheets, which made her alabaster skin glow. Her eyes were squeezed shut, her pink swollen lips parted as she breathed out my name when I inserted another finger.

I cursed sharply against her breasts, feeling the tightness of her walls clenching my fingers. If I hadn't known already, I would've thought that she was a virgin. Heat flowed from between her legs, coating my fingers as her fingers held onto my arms. The scent of her body and the musky perfume of wild roses enveloped my senses.

I couldn't wait anymore. I *had* to have her.

"Valeria, are you ready?" I asked, pulling away to look at her. I licked the sweet glistening nectar from my fingers, groaning at the taste.

She gasped at the sound of him sucking his fingers clean, her sex clenching deliciously. She was definitely ready. Far more ready.

"Yes," she begged. "Please, Khalid."

19

VALERIA

"Yes." I begged, "Please, Khalid."

I had never heard my voice full of lust. All Khalid had to do was be in my presence, and it turned me into such a wanton woman. Even though I was a little nervous and afraid, I trusted Khalid to be gentle. I knew he would never hurt me like *he* had. Khalid wouldn't even dare to think about that.

Swallowing the lump in my throat, I spread my thighs, feeling the hardened length of him brushing over my calf. I felt the walls of my sex clench as instinct drew me closer towards him.

When I felt him pull away, I frowned at the loss of his heat and his musky scent. "What happened?"

He let out a sigh, kissing my knee softly. "I need to get a condom from my room. I will be—"

I closed my hand around his, stopping him from retreating. "There's no need. I am on pills," I replied truthfully.

Khalid
(Khalid first person. Valeria third person)

I had never had sex without a condom in thirty-two years of my life. I was too afraid of the repercussions of a night of lust and always wore protection. But gazing at Valeria's shy, flushed face, I knew she was telling me the truth and trusted me to be clean.

"Valeria, you would have to sign an NDA, you know that, right?" I said, caressing her leg.

Her cheeks flushed a deeper shade of red as she nodded. "I know. You are a Prince, Khalid. I can sign it right now, if you want."

When she tried to get up, I pushed her down, kissing her. "Not now. You aren't going anywhere right now, my sweet one."

I released the softness of her lips when her fingers weaved through my hair. I held her waist and rubbed the head of my glistening cock on her welcoming, slicked lips. We both moaned and gasped at the intense rush of pleasure.

I clenched my jaw, holding myself back as I spread her lips, groaning at the sight of her pretty pussy. I started slowly sliding the tip inside and wondering why she felt so tight. Flickering my eyes at her, I found her face contorted in pain. Valeria was gasping, as if she couldn't control her breath.

I froze, my heart thundering in my ears when I found her fingers clenching the sheets tightly. Not in a good way.

"Valeria, what happened?" I asked, concern lacing my husky voice.

"It hurts," she gasped, her eyes opening as tears trickled down her face. "*Stop*. Please."

Her voice was barely audible in the room, but I heard her loud and clear. It echoed in my head as I quickly pulled away, wanting to comfort and soothe her. Wanting to know what was troubling her.

Valeria cowered away from me, wanting to hide as she curled up, her eyes squeezed shut, with tears streaming down her flushed face. I knew that something was very wrong. My muscles were clenched with tension, and I didn't know how to comfort her without knowing what had happened to her.

I wore my boxers and placed the warm blanket around her shoulder, her fingers clutching it tightly. I knelt down on the floor and stroked her hair.

Did I hurt her?

"Can you tell me what happened? Did I... Did I hurt you?" I asked. I couldn't comprehend that I might have become what I swore I could never be.

My father. How my father hurt my mother, sweet Isabella, grooming her, using her blindness against her and hurting her until she died.

I didn't want to be like him. I didn't want to hurt my Valeria. I didn't want to hurt anyone.

But I had caused pain to someone, someone so special and precious to me. I had done it. I had hurt Valeria. I didn't know how I was even able to live in my own skin—

Valeria's soft hand held mine, holding it close. "It's not you, Khalid. You could never hurt me."

Even though relief washed over my body, I was concerned for her. "Something did. Tell me what happened?" I clenched my jaw.

"Are you a virgin?"

She shook her head, "I never lied to you."

I frowned at the dainty face contorted in so much grief and pain. Before I could press further. Wanting to know the reason, she sat up on the bed. She was still covering herself from me as if she was afraid—not afraid of me, but of something else.

"I... I was assaulted when I was sixteen," she whispered, still holding Khalid's large palm on her lap. His warmth and tenderness reminded her of everything good in this world.

She couldn't hide the secret any longer. She had to tell him.

Taking a deep breath, she spoke, "I was forced. Held against my will when it happened."

Even though she wanted to say it in a firm tone, her bottom lip quivered and warm tears slid down her cheeks, remembering that horrid night. The cold, rough touch and the pain. So much pain and hurt. She would never wish it upon anyone, not even to the person who had done that to her.

I was frozen with shock. My pupils were dilated, my body clenched with anger, sympathy, and grief. How could someone dare think of hurting another being was beyond me. But I had seen it with my own eyes while growing up. I had done it myself and didn't regret it. I was hearing it again. Someone had touched my sweet one without her consent. Forcing her.

My body was shaking with anger. I shook my head, focusing on how soft the skin of her palm was. I stood up from the floor and gently sat beside her on the bed, rubbing her hands with mine, trying to hold her shaking hands.

"I am sorry, Khalid. I... I got nervous and thought of him when—"

I shushed her. "You don't have to apologize, sweet. If I had known, I would have been more careful. Is he rotting in jail?"

I wished he was. So that I could face him one more time before getting him executed publicly in Azmia. I would find a way to do that. I wouldn't let that man live. He didn't deserve it after what he had done to my Valeria.

Just like my father didn't deserve to live after wanting to hurt my sister.

I snapped out of my cruel thoughts when Valeria leaned on me, sighing in relief and tracing the veins on my arms with her fingers.

"He died a year later," she whispered.

"Who was he? How did he die?"

"A close friend, or so I thought. He pursued me to go to a party with him, I got drunk and he..." I stroked her back with my other hand, kissing her head for being strong enough to tell me about it.

"I was blind, but I trusted him. He was my only friend. The golden boy of our high school. Yet he… When I woke up, he pretended that it never happened. Even fooled me to trust him to take me home. It wasn't until Mabel saw the… saw the blood on my dress and asked me about it."

"Did you report him?"

"I couldn't." She shook her head. "I thought it never happened for a few months until the nightmares started and I had to get therapy because Mabel and Mr Benjamin were worried that someone had taken advantage of me. When I finally faced the truth and confronted him… his car crashed and he died."

I rubbed her back when her hand tightened.

"His name was Mark Bennett."

I had heard his name. Then it clicked. "The lead singer in the boy band? The news of his death was all over the world."

Valeria nodded. "I thought I might get the chance to prove to the world that he wasn't a good person. But the cops didn't want to believe it, he was already dead."

She shook her head and looked at me. "That day in the desert, I panicked because his song was playing on the radio. That same song was playing in his car when he took me home after that night… I should have told you then, but I was afraid, I am sorry, Khalid."

That is why she asked to stop the car and reacted in such a way. Fuck. If I had known back then, I would have made sure she was alright. But I acted like a fool.

"Don't apologize for what that asshole did, Valeria." I kissed her forehead.

"I know it isn't right, but that is why I wanted or I still want my sight back. I kept thinking that only if I wasn't blind, if I had my sight, it wouldn't have happened. It is pathetic, but I hated that I couldn't see his intentions or even fight him. I am weak for even admitting that, aren't I?"

"Don't say that." I cupped her face. "You are not weak, Valeria. You are one of the strongest and kindest women I know. I am honored to know you, be here with you."

I swallowed the lump in my throat, trying to control my anger towards him. "I wish he was alive just so I could kill him."

Valeria took a sharp breath. "Don't say that, Khalid. I know you could never hurt someone."

I smiled sadly at her. She was too innocent and pure for me.

"I have, my sweet one. I am a monster," I whispered, knowing I had to tell the truth. "I'm afraid."

"Of what?"

"The way you'd feel about me or look at me if you knew."

"I am blind. I will tell you how I feel about you. Tell me."

I took a deep breath and said, "I killed my own father."

"*What?*"

Valeria couldn't believe what she was hearing. She felt Khalid pull away. She could feel the dread and pain hovering in the room.

"Zain wouldn't forgive me for telling you, but you need to know this, Valeria. I killed him with his own sword in his room." Tears formed in my eyes as I thought back to that night. "And the worst part is that I don't regret murdering my own father."

Valeria could hear the tremble in his voice and she knew he was crying. She gently stroked his hair, wanting to comfort him. The Khalid she knew would never even think of hurting an ant, let alone kill someone. Especially his father. There must be a reason to why he did that.

"Then why did you do it?" She asked gently, as if she was asking me about my favorite color. As if she wasn't afraid that she was embracing a murderer.

"Because he was a pathetic person and a terrible father. He

hurt our mothers. Hurt Zain, me. He would've hurt Zara but I… I stopped him before he could ever touch her." His voice had gone low and despite that, she could hear and feel the pain in his voice.

He had killed his father to protect his sister. He had taken someone's life to protect another's. Valeria didn't know why, but in her eyes, he was not a monster he thought himself to be. He was still the good, kindhearted Khalid, she knew.

"It's okay, Khalid. You did it to protect your sister," she said, her voice soft as she wiped the tears from his wet cheeks.

My eyes widened at her action. "You don't think I am a monster?"

"No, silly. You are not a monster. Not in my eyes at least, you aren't." She said, caressing his cheek with extreme tenderness. Under his hard skin, he held a heart of gold that was pure despite what he thought of himself. "Even though it wasn't the right thing to do, you must have done it on impulse, right? I don't think Zara or Zain or any other person see you as a monster, Khalid."

I took a deep breath, my emotions all over the place after listening to her sincere words. Her gentle touch was a soothing salve to my heart, her scent affecting me on an intimate level. I had never been that raw or vulnerable with anyone.

I had to be a protector to Zara, a brother to Zain, a friend to Zayed and a famous Prince or artist in everyone's eyes. But with Valeria, I could be just Khalid. I could be vulnerable, be open and have her not judge me to the title I was born into.

I smiled, despite the blurriness of my vision. Cupping her hand, I placed a soft kiss on the inside of her palm. "Thank you for telling me about your past, my sweet one. Thank you for trusting me, I figure it must have been hard for you," I said, thinking about the times I had asked her to be alone with me for multiple occasions. The dinner. The art gallery. Even being alone in my apartment, trusting me completely. Accepting my invitation to come to Azmia all alone with me.

Her cheeks warmed. "It wasn't. I trust you completely, Khalid. Thank you for allowing yourself to be vulnerable with me."

I leaned closer and wiped away any stray tears from her cheeks which were dusted with rosy hue. My eyes dropped to her lips on their own accord. The urge to please her thrummed in my veins. I wanted to show and make her feel everything about the pleasures of sex.

But Valeria beat me to it.

"I want to kiss you, Khalid. I... I want to please you and have sex with you." She licked her lips, her skin prickling with growing heat.

"Are you sure, my sweet? I do not want to cause you any pain or discomfort." I tucked her hair behind her ear, her pale face looking up at me with urgency and need and... adoration.

"Yes, I am sure, Khalid. I... I want *this*. I want to have sex with you." She leaned closer to me, my soft, warm breath fanning over her cheek. *"Please."*

20

KHALID

(KHALID FIRST PERSON, VALERIA THIRD PERSON)

I wanted to do everything for her. *To her*. Anything and everything she asked, I would offer it to her. I took her lithe body in my lap, softly kissing her pale, slender neck. Valeria's hands feathered through my hair, sighing at my hot mouth licking her neck and nipping at the skin softly.

Knowing she was being so open to a man, especially me, for the first time, made me twitch in my boxers. My kisses turned rough and the primal part of me knew I had to claim her, mark her. I gave her a hickey on her collarbone, rubbing the red mark with my thumb, soothing it.

My gleaming obsidian eyes peered up at her. My heart and mind were racing at the erotic sight of her, so beautiful and wanton in the soft glow of the lamps and moonlight. Her russet waves gleamed, the splattering of freckles making me smile.

"*Khalid,*" she repeated, her voice smoky, urging me to do every filthy things I wanted to do to her.

Hearing the pure lust in her voice, I knew what she wanted. What we *both* wanted.

"You want me to fuck you, sweet one, *hm?*" I tugged down

the blanket covering her, whispering in her ear, "You want me to make you feel good?"

Her nipples were taut, exposed to the night air. My dirty, hot words made her sex pool with wetness. "Khalid… *please.*"

In a flash of a moment, I rolled us over, laying her down on the sheets, exposing herself to me. The sound of her soft moan made me stand up, hard as rock. I blew air on her nipple, watching her shudder and arch as I latched my hot mouth to the pert bud. I licked it, kissing and biting until she squirmed underneath me, spreading her legs wide.

I pulled back, mesmerized by the sight of her dripping pussy, her slicked lips parting with glistening nectar sliding out of her warm heat. I stroked her, her creamy thighs opening wide for me, her musky feminine scent hovering in the room. My fingers traced her wet lips, watching her hips rock towards me.

Valeria's breathing became shallow when he leaned down, blowing cool air on her sex. Khalid licked her succulent lips with a low groan at the sweet taste of her. He slid fingers inside her slick warmth, a gasp pouring out of Valeria when he pressed the tips of his fingers on the sensitive spot. He repeated his slow, languid movement, slowly licking at her glistening arousal and sucking her clitoris in his mouth.

Valeria couldn't stop the trembling in her legs at the pleasurable sensations that Khalid derived from her. She arched and shamelessly pressed herself on to his expert hot mouth and fingers. He groaned, rubbing his nose on her clit when he increased his pace, urging her closer and closer to her release.

She said meekly, "Khalid, I am—"

He caressed her inner thigh. "I know, sweet, let it go."

The soft touch of his hand while his fingers stroked her filled her body with hot white lust and fire. Her feet curled as flames ticked through her body. His hand trailed up from her thigh to hold her hand, squeezing her palm in reassurance when he brought her closer and closer to the climax.

Valeria came with a sweet moan, my dick twitching with need watching her come apart on the bed. I leaned down and sucked gently on the hardened nub, her cries of pleasure spurring me on.

Light danced behind her lids, her head tilting back as another groan tore out of her lips. She squirmed and gasped. My hand squeezed hers, holding her when waves of pleasure rolled through her.

When Valeria came back to earth, she felt him pull away before hovering above her. She embraced him, kissing his soft lips coated with her own arousal. She sighed breathily, locking her legs around his muscular torso. His lips moved against her with a new fervor, his hard heat brushing over her inner thigh.

No words were needed to be exchanged when I kissed her once more, trailing my hand lower to her cunt, spreading her lips. I looked at her with a gentle intensity, my gleaming dark eyes dilated with passion. Valeria moved against me, pressing closer as if she couldn't wait to have me inside her.

I lingered at her core, throbbing with need, and slid inside her. My eyes were fixed on her face, noting every freckle when she opened up to me with a faint gasp. I sighed sharply on her neck, feeling her velvety walls envelop and close around me. Clenching my fingers on the sheets, I slowly rocked back and pushed deeper inside her.

Valeria held onto Khalid's strong shoulders, clenching her fingers on his back, stroking his scars, when he stretched her slowly. She wanted to cry out at the hint of a pain, but he soothed her, stroking her hair and face. Khalid eased inside her with one last thrust, warm heat surrounding him. Scorching heat poured out of them.

With anxious hesitation, he stayed still while she adjusted to his girth. She relaxed her eyes, sighing out when he lightly circled and rubbed her sensitive nub. The fullness of him inside her made her squirm and quiver with need and friction. She could feel him throbbing inside her, her tight walls clenching him. Khalid groaned out, his hot breath fanning over her cheek, making her flush.

My face was strained, my breathing as shallow as hers, when heat poured out of our unison. But I wanted to wait until her pain subsided before I continued. I kissed away a tear from the corner of her eye, wanting to apologize for causing her pain, but no words formed in my head with Valeria wrapped around me. I loved the clench of her fingers on my shoulders as she clung to me, her legs shaking lightly around my torso. Her rosy scent wrapped all around me.

Khalid trailed his lips to hers, her ragged breath growing. Valeria kissed him gently, wanting him to know how much she felt for him. Her anxiety melted away, her body relaxing until lust and pleasure took over. The pain started to dull with each stroke of his tongue on her lips. Experimentally, she moved her hips toward him, making them groan in unison. She felt him stroke every pleasurable nerve within her, her walls tightening over his hardened length.

Valeria wished to see him, to look at him when he claimed her like that. She wanted to see his eyes, look deep into them when they made love.

She willed herself not to cry when he pulled back to gently thrust inside her. She gasped, instinctively squeezing him. A low growl elicited from deep in his throat. Valeria loved his throaty, husky voice when he pressed into her once again, forming a rhythm.

I held her close when everything but our joined bodies melted into nothing, primal pleasure taking over both of our senses. I increased my pace, her fingers raking through my hair as our breathing became one. Valeria arched up to me, forcing me deeper.

"Valeria..." I whispered, watching her lips part in a low moan. My eyes trailed to the soft flesh of her breasts, rocking to my movement as I brought her closer and closer with every thrust.

Her fingers clawed my back when melting heat poured out of her, stroking me to thrust deeper into her wet cavern. The sharp stab of pleasure shook us simultaneously as we both climbed to find our own release, holding onto each other as we climaxed together.

I squeezed my eyes and groaned deeply, my shuddering body matching hers, my jaw clenched. Valeria clung to me, rolling her head back as she found her release with a loud moan. We held onto each other for a while, my large hands stroking her waist and soothing her as waves of aftershocks rocked through us.

With slow gentleness, I slid out of her with a sharp sigh, a hint of blood coating her sex. I laid down her quivering legs, watching her body go limp with exhaustion. After telling her that I'd be right back, I went into the bathroom to clean myself and find a rag to clean her. She must be too tired and over-whelmed for a bath at the moment.

Valeria jumped when something warm touched her sore and sensitive sex. I gently stroked her leg. "It's okay, my sweet one."

She flushed. "I can clean up myself."

"I know, you can. But I want to."

She smiled in my direction, her fingers rubbing over my knuckles as she waited for me to join her on the bed. She breathed lightly when I held her close, pressing a small kiss on her lips. Her breasts pressed against the hard muscles of my chest as she went to sleep, my hand stroking her back.

VALERIA WOKE UP, CLENCHING AND RUBBING HER LEGS TOGETHER and mewling softly. Her head was still groggy from the sleep but something was getting stroked over and over on her taut nipples. It turned her on. She sighed again, arching her neck and stretching her arms.

"Hm, you are awake." Khalid whispered, "How did you sleep?"

Memories of last night came crashing into her mind, making her face flush red. Instinctively, her sex clenched, the sweet soaring pain reminding her of him. How large yet sweet and tender he was.

"I slept well." She bit her lip when he moved over her, something brushing over her stomach, tickling her. "What are you doing?"

"I am painting on you as I promised, Valeria." I gave a hard flick to her nipple with the paintbrush, her body squirming. "I am painting your beautiful tits."

She looked adorable with her red face and trying to hide from me.

I had woken up early to find her cocooned to my chest, sleeping soundly with parted lips. I had been wanting to use the edible paint on her for a long time. So when her maid asked me for the breakfast when I went to the studio, I brought a fruit basket with me to her room.

Valeria tried to sit up, her breasts and stomach covered in something cold and liquid-y. "What is this?" She asked, trailing her finger on her stomach and lifted it up to her nose to know the scent. It smelt like… *mangoes.*

"Taste it," I said in a low voice, urging her to suck on her finger.

She did, the sweet taste bursting in her mouth making her hum. "It tastes like mango."

"Yes. Mango juice. I love mangoes." I eyed her and the pot of mango juice. We were going to get sticky early this morning. "Lay down for me, my sweet one."

She frowned, "Why?"

"I have yet to paint you with my own hands. I plan to lick every inch of you."

Khalid's dirty words made her nipples harden and toes curl with anticipation. She couldn't believe herself. How erotic it felt when he licked a straight line from her lower stomach to her belly, to the valley between her breasts, kissing her neck. She cupped his face, wanting to kiss him, and tasted the sweetness of mango juice with a hint of strawberry and even watermelon.

Valeria moaned, spreading her legs. I pulled back, breathing heavily. Taking the cold glass of mango juice, I drizzled it down her neck. She shivered instantly.

"It's cold." Valeria bit her lip, her skin tingling when it traveled to her round breasts.

I hummed, my cock twitching for attention, watching it slide over her nipples. I smeared it over her perky tits, licking it off of her hot skin. Valeria let out a low moan when my hot tongue tasted her, licking and sucking on her taut nipples and breasts. Liquid heat seeped out of her when I held her waist and devoured her soft skin.

I knew Valeria was aroused when her voice turned sultrier and huskier, her body moving beneath me. I licked her belly, pressing soft kisses and softly kneading her pink breasts to soothe the assault of my mouth on them.

Her thigh brushed my hard length. I cursed, my dick straining to find her heat and take her again. I wanted to, but I knew better. She must be sore from last night, and I didn't want to cause her any more pain or discomfort.

When Valeria thought Khalid might have her yet again, she pouted at him when he pulled away, telling her that they needed to get clean. She would rather get dirty and hot with the filthy hot prince, but she kept it to herself, too shy to voice out her thoughts.

In a night, he had turned her into a minx.

"But I thought we would, you know…" Valeria trailed off, sitting up on the bed.

I shamelessly stared at her creamy skin, flushed under my gaze and covered in a bit of cold mango juice and the red strawberry juice I had painted on her stomach. Her red hair was tousled, her alabaster skin glowing in sunlight that streamed through the open balcony.

I raised my eyes at her flushed face. Someone seemed turned on. I couldn't blame her, I had been teasing her with bristles of brush on her naked body.

"We would what, Valeria?" I pressed, wanting to tease her more. But she wasn't alone. I denied us both the pleasure of sex. I was equally, if not more, aroused and sexually frustrated than her.

She looked down at her lap. "Have sex?"

I smiled at her small shy voice and leaned down on the bed, keeping my arms on either side of her body, caging her.

"Aren't you sore from last night, sweet?" I purred in my low voice, licking the shell of her ear.

Valeria breathed out, "I don't care."

Before she could reach out to me, I pulled back, frowning at her. "But I care. Taking a warm bath will help you. Come on, I am helping you clean up."

I was being selfish, wanting to be with her and caress her skin in the name of cleaning up. But it wasn't like she wasn't enjoying bathing me, softly trailing her hands all over my chest and back, apologizing for her nail marks, kissing my back. I would wear her marks proudly.

My Valeria had marked me, after all. There was nothing to hide about them.

I helped wash her hair, massaging her scalp and washing it off and talking to her about the call she had last night.

"We are launching a new product, a new scent, so Brandon wanted to ask me when I would be back in London for testing," she said as I showered her with the shower head.

"What did you say?"

"That I am busy seducing the Prince of Azmia," she said cheekily, grinning over her shoulder. I sprayed water on her face as she giggled, my lips landing on her neck and arms wrapping around her.

"He must have been jealous that you are here with me."

When she didn't reply, I turned her around and tilted her chin. "He was, wasn't he?"

She held my wrist, kissing my palm. "He wanted to take me on another date."

My eyes narrowed at the thought of him having dinner with her. Or anyone trying to date her.

"And?" I asked, trying not to be bitter about it.

Valeria was stunning and kind. I had to remind myself that she might have been with other men in the past.

"Of course, I said no, Khalid." She wrapped her hands around my chest, warm water pelting over both of us. "I want to be with *you*."

My heart thundered hearing her.

She wanted to be with me? Khalid Al Latif? A murderer?

Holding her, I kissed her head. Even though I wanted to be with her, *did I deserve it? Did I deserve to be happy after taking someone's life?*

PART III

"Rose Colored Sorrow."

2 1

VALERIA

(VALERIA FIRST PERSON, KHALID THIRD PERSON)

"Spread your legs wider, Valeria," Khalid's husky voice floated through the studio, reminding me of my position.

"I am trying," I whimpered, the teasing cool air brushing over my exposed, heated skin. Especially my bare sex.

Khalid's voice was in-between a teasing and soothing tone when he said, "Only for a while, my sweet one. I need to draw your swollen pink clit."

I glared in his direction, knowing well he was smirking at my delicious torture. It had been four days since we had sex for the first time, opening up to each other, both emotionally and physically. Since then, we had been having sex and making love in every way possible when we were not painting or eating.

That morning when Khalid was bathing me like he always did, he had told me that the painting only needed final touches which he could do by himself. Before I could get sad, he had asked me if he could paint some more of my body. Something more private and erotic. Only for his eyes.

I, of course, had agreed. *After* showing him how much I loved that idea. The water had turned cold by the time we stepped out of the bath, naked and flush with our release. Khalid helped me dress up and had breakfast with me before leading me to the painting studio.

"*Khalid*," I almost begged, my core heating with growing wetness as I sat on the chaise, naked, and legs spread. "How much longer?"

I let out a soft gasp when he leaned closer to flick a brush on my taut nipple. I wanted him to do it again.

"Be patient, Valeria. I have yet to paint your beautiful breasts. And…" Khalid shamelessly raked his eyes over her bare body, ripe and flush. "I enjoy seeing you naked. Your cunt dripping with need. You must be really turned on, *hm*?"

I clenched my legs, nodding slightly as liquid heat seeped out of me at his dirty words.

"We must do something about it," Khalid said, dipping the small brush in pink color and outlining her slicked lips with the color on the canvas. He was painting her pussy, her lips blooming like a flower, sweet nectar pouring out of her.

"Touch yourself, Valeria," he said. "Use your finger and rub your clit."

My cheeks turned red upon hearing the command in his voice. I supported myself on my palm, leaning back and trailing my middle finger down my smooth stomach. My muscles clenched with anticipation, my skin prickling with Khalid's heavy gaze. I let out a soft sigh when my finger found the hardened button.

"Good girl. Now keep rubbing it," he said in a husky voice, watching me pleasure myself.

"I… I need—"

"Shh, my sweet. Do as I say and keep rubbing your clit. Don't cum just yet, I am not finished with you."

I bit down on my lip, my body quivering with the need to release while my fingers kept rubbing the clit which was getting over stimulating. I moaned, feeling my wetness slide out from me to my inner thigh. I gasped when his calloused, warm finger swiped over my thigh. My legs clenched with need, hearing him suck on the finger.

Khalid

I groaned at the sweet taste of Valeria.

I eyed her wet cunt, her arousal dripping out of her, her slicked lips clenching and pulsing when her fingers kept rubbing over her little nub, taunting me to hold her thighs down and have her for lunch. My cock was aching in my confines, hardening, and bulging in my pants.

When I found her finger teasing her entrance and pushing inside her, I almost lost it.

"Valeria, didn't I tell you to rub your clit?"

I finished painting her outer lips, loving the sounds of her little moans and heavy pants. "Khalid, please…" she begged, her moan ringing in my ears like a sweet melody.

"Please what, sweet? I didn't ask you to touch your pussy, did I?"

Valeria shook her head, her fingers stopping their decent when the air became heavier. I stood up from the stool and stepped towards her. Calm dark eyes staring down at her naked figure. Sitting beside her, I raked my hand through her silky red hair and pressed a passionate kiss over her lips. She scrunched her fingers on my shirt, groaning in my mouth when I kneaded her breasts, tweaking the nipple roughly between my fingers. I took her pink nipple in my mouth and soothed the burn with my tongue before biting it again.

I turned her around on the chaise, bending her over as her delicious pale ass faced me. I was careful to rest her head on the soft chaise, spreading her knees on the Egyptian rug. My hands slid to her shoulders, dancing over her hot skin and brushing over her spine, making her arch her back to my touch. I let out a low grunt when Valeria pressed her ass towards the erection straining in my pants.

"Dirty girl," I ground out, moving her hair to the side and licking her neck, biting the soft skin. I purred, "What do you want, my sweet? Do you want me to fuck you like this, *hm?*"

"Yes," she gasped. "Please Khalid."

I removed my shirt, cupping her breasts and pinching the nipple gently. "Then say it."

"F-fuck me, Khalid."

"Good girl." I smiled at her, pressing a soft kiss on her neck and lowering my hand to her sex, slowly rubbing the sensitive clit. "Now say please."

"*Please.*"

"You know what I meant, Valeria." I let out a low chuckle, giving a soft spank to her ass, making her gasp in surprise. I watched the pale skin turn pink before rubbing it tenderly. "Say it, sweet one. I know you want to."

She took a shuddering breath. "Please Khalid, fuck me."

"That's my sweet. It wasn't hard, was it?" I teased her, my dark eyes gleaming down at her.

I lowered the zipper of my pants, her breath hitching at the sound. I pressed against her. My hands kneading the soft skin of her ass, parting her lips and rubbing the tip of my cock from her tiny bud to her dripping sex.

Back and forth.

Back and forth.

"Khalid! Please take me." Valeria let out a frustrated moan, rocking her hips back when I teased both of us.

My jaw clenched tightly, her ass rubbing over me. Holding her hips, I aligned myself and thrust inside her in one slow move, pushing all the way to the hilt. We both groaned, feeling the scorching heat burn and burn around us, clenching and throbbing. Her snug walls clenching me tightly, her muscles tensing. My cock twitching inside her, wanting to move and fuck and slam inside her.

I wound my fist in her red hair, slightly tugging at it when I rammed inside her again, her legs quivering. Valeria's neck arched, her hands clutching the soft material of chaise as her entire body rocked with the force of me *claiming* her, *taking* her, as she had asked me to. Her breasts pushed against the chaise again and again when I went faster and harder.

I pulled at her hair, holding her stomach and planting her back against my chest as I thrust upwards in her clenching heat. Her rosy scent wafted in my nose when I breathed her hair, gently pinching her nipples.

She arched up to me, spreading her legs and laying her head on my shoulders, meeting my lips with a shy, anxious kiss. My teeth teased her lips, biting them while my other hand rubbed her bud, her release teetering on the edge. She kissed me back, moaning in my mouth when our bodies rocked higher together. Our need to release climbed higher as it kept growing and growing.

"I am going to come inside you, Valeria," I whispered, licking her neck and kissing the soft skin below her ear when my legs shook, my abdomen coiling with need.

Her reply was a loud groan as her walls clenched me, wanting me to release inside her. Valeria wanted to hold back her own orgasm and let go of her own release together. With a little tremor spiraling across her body, she cried out my name when I pushed inside her, the fullness stretching her walls as she climbed her orgasm.

My soft grunt echoed in her ears when I dug my fingers in her hips, my warm breath caressing her neck as I released inside her. Warm spurts of my seed coated her inner walls, making her shudder. I trembled, my hold on her waist softening as I glided my palms over the red marks that were imprinted on her pale skin by my fingers.

I sighed, letting Valeria support herself on the chaise and slid out of her, our release seeping out of her making me clench my jaw. *Not so soon*, I scolded myself. She must be too sore for another round. I cleaned us both with a warm cloth, curling her body on my lap. I stroked her back, kissing her head, and murmured soft words to her, her fingers gliding over my stomach.

"Was I too rough?" I asked. The question had been bothering me for a while. "Did I… did I hurt you?"

"You didn't, Khalid." Valeria caressed my cheek, planting a soft kiss on my jaw. "I… I enjoyed it."

I smiled down at her flushed face, making her straddle me. My eyes trailed over the hickeys on her breast and down between her thighs. I moved my thumb over her inner thigh, her sex pink and flushed.

"I am glad you did, my sweet," I said, letting out a low groan when she bucked her hips over me, her red locks of hair brushing down her breasts when she clutched my shoulders.

I held her hips, frustrated with myself, trying to stop her. "We can't right now, Valeria. We have to leave for palace after lunch—"

Valeria gasped out, feeling Khalid twitch underneath her sore, heated sex. She wanted him again. His musky male scent and the scent of their sex surrounding her made her feel heady.

"Please," she whispered, kissing down his sharp jaw, trailing her soft lips over his neck and muscular chest.

"You're making me crazy," I groaned out, thrusting my hard member over her soft lips, teasing her opening.

We embraced each other once again in the heat of pleasure, lost in our own cocoon of lust and passion. We had to scramble for our clothes when one of the maids knocked on the door, letting us know that our lunch was getting cold.

Valeria giggled when the hook of her bra got stuck in her

hair, making me chuckle. I hooked her bra, hating to see her beautiful round tits getting covered and zipped my pants.

If I could, I would keep her naked every day.

I patted down her hair and kissed her passionately, leaving her breathless for more, and opened the doors. I knew that the staff were aware of my relationship with Valeria and I didn't mind it. I had the reputation of sleeping around as soon as I turned eighteen. Bringing different women to my room overnight, sometimes even more, but I never brought them to the oasis. None of them saw my studio or observed me in a vulnerable state like Valeria had.

It was not just lust with Valeria. It was different.

I wanted the entire world to know that Valeria was with me. We hadn't discussed about where we stood in terms of relationship. We both were enjoying the time spent with each other, kissing, making love, painting, and talking about life and death.

But deep down, I knew we would have to talk about it. Sooner or later.

I PEERED AT VALERIA, HER HAND ENTWINED WITH MINE AS SHE constantly looked around, trying to figure out her surroundings. The hushed chatter of people watching her in awe as they moved our luggage to my room and her guest room in the palace. I squeezed her hand, wanting to know what was going on in her head as we stood at the front hallway of the palace, my home.

I tried to look at the palace as if I was visiting for the first time. The white and golden shimmering walls and pillars that held the palace for over a hundred years, covered in intricate designs. The floors covered in soft red carpet that pressed with each step. Fire lanterns were placed by each pillar, and the chandelier shimmered with golden diamonds. It exuded opulence.

"Do you want me to describe?" I asked in a hushed voice.

She looked up at me, a soft smile tugging at her lips. "Yes, I want to know how your home looks."

I spoke, pulling her by my side, describing the details of pillars, paintings adorning the walls and how I used to play hide and seek with Zain and Zayed when we were young. Sometimes even our mothers joined us, pretending that they didn't know where we were hidden by the soft giggles and acting surprised when they lost. But they were only allowed to play when my father was in some other country, far away from Azmia.

Valeria chuckled when I mentioned that Zayed would still be excited to play, but Zain had banned him to run inside the palace. He had caused a fire last time.

Valeria listened to Khalid's soothing, deep voice with patience and curiosity. How it would have felt to grow up with a house full of love and playful mothers. Having arguments with his brother and cooking with his mothers. She had a smile on her face the entire time, listening to his tales of childhood and how much he adored his family.

"Am I getting too old that you have forgotten to meet your favorite *jadati*, Khalid?" A soft raspy voice spoke, making the couple turn toward the voice.

I grinned at my grandma. Her face—even though withered with old age—still radiated her charm and wit. I took Valeria towards her and bent down to hug her. The scent of old books and rosemary made me remember my childhood, how I would annoy her by making her sit in one place and practice painting her portrait.

"You are our *only* grandma." I grinned down at her, her wise eyes smiling at me as she patted my shoulder.

Valeria was standing behind me, not knowing where to go

or what to do. I squeezed her hand when my grandmother spoke. "And where have you been hiding this beauty, Khalid?"

I agreed with her and introduced Valeria. "She is Valeria, *jadati*. My... my friend from London. Valeria, this is my grandma."

Before Valeria could greet her with a bow, she was wrapped in a tight hug that made her cheeks flush. Khalid watched the exchange with amusement.

"You are lovely, my dear. It's a shame that my grandson has kept you hidden for two weeks, but now that you are here, I can't wait to make you *roz bel laban*. It's his favorite dish." His grandma patted her hair and talked to her, telling her about all the different food and clothes she had to try as she was their guest.

I had warned my family that Valeria was blind before we arrived, and I was glad that grandma treated her as our equal.

"Khalid!"

I knew that voice. Before I could turn around to greet her, her lithe frame stumbled into my chest with a small laugh as her arms wrapped around me. I let out a small chuckle and hugged her close, kissing the top of her hair—*hair* that was much shorter than before and colored in white platinum dye.

I didn't care, she was here and safe in my arms. In our home.

"How have you been, Zara? You said you wouldn't arrive until the baby shower." I looked at my little sister—little was exaggerating it as she was a twenty-year-old woman, living on her own, but for me, my sister would always be the innocent girl who used to braid my hair when we were young.

Her hazel eyes were filled with warmth, her short hair framing her elfish face. The beauty spot above her upper lip twinkled as she grinned up at me, her pale face flushed with excitement. Zara's mother was Isabella, so she had her pale skin tone, but her hazel eyes were similar to our father. The same eyes Zain and I had. She was dressed in a short white shirt that grazed the top of black straight jeans. She looked barely over eighteen with her elfish face and young grin.

When did she get so big? When did she turn eighteen? Where did all the time go?

"I wanted to surprise you. I even bought gifts from Sri Lanka and Australia—*oh*, hello!" Her hazel eyes flitted from me to Valeria, who was trying her best not to eavesdrop on the siblings.

"Valeria, this is my little sister, Zara. Valeria is my friend, and she's staying with us for the baby shower."

Valeria's face morphed into understanding as she smiled in her direction, not looking straight at her, which made Zara frown.

Zara's eyes gleamed with mischief and scoffed, "Friend, my *ass—*"

"*Zara,*" I warned her.

She poked her tongue out in return, which was pierced with a metal barbell. I did not want to know what my sister had been up to or the reason for her piercing. I trusted her to take care of herself.

"It's so great to finally meet you, Valeria! Khalid has told me so much about you, but he must have forgotten to mention how pretty you are," Zara gushed, smiling at her and carefully hugging her so that she wouldn't shock her with a sudden touch.

My cheekbones slashed with color. I scratched my neck when my sister and my lover started bonding instantly. Seeing her with my family made my heart swell. I wondered what would it be like if they accepted Valeria as their own family. She could be a part of my family… if she wanted.

Only if I was brave enough to admit my feelings towards her.

I swallowed the lump in my throat, wanting the images of a

potentially brighter future with Valeria to vanish from my head.

"You have changed, my son." My grandma's warm hand patted my arm. "You look happier. Relaxed. I haven't seen you smile like that in ages."

"What do you mean?"

She nodded at the two women, who were grinning and chatting animatedly. They were acting as if they were long-lost friends.

"I approve of her."

"Zara?" I stalled.

"*Ow!*" My grandma pinched my cheek as if I was eight again.

"You know what I mean, and you are man enough to know what's good for you. Don't break her heart, and if you do, remember that I will only have one grandson and one grand-daughter. I will replace you with Zayed," she warned me, walking away with a raised chin, her maid cautiously walking beside her.

I rubbed my cheek and gazed at Valeria, hating the idea of ever causing any pain or hurt to her. I wouldn't be able to live with myself if I did.

2 2

KHALID

(KHALID FIRST PERSON, VALERIA THIRD
PERSON)

"**V**aleria, would you like to come see the stables with me tomorrow?" Zayed asked, showing off his pearly whites with a charming smile.

I clenched my jaw, shooting daggers at my close friend, who was invited to have dinner with us. Zara hid her smile while *jadati* raised her eyebrow. Zain, my brother and the Sultan of Azmia and Nasrin, his wife and my sister-in-law, had taken up residence in one of Zayed's private oasis for a week. Zain was calling it a baby honeymoon and had told me that they would arrive the next morning.

Valeria swallowed her food. Even though her hair was in a bun, a few wisps of it framed her face as she looked in Zayed's direction. I had seen their exchange from afar before the dinner, and I didn't enjoy how Zayed had dared to hug her and grin at me over her shoulder.

"I would love to join you if it's no trouble," she replied shyly.

I mentally groaned, clenching the spoon in my hand.

Would it be rude to throw a spoon at Zayed's face?

I wrapped my hand around hers under the table. "We have

painting session, Valeria," I said, glaring at Zayed who still had the stupid grin on his face. With a dimple.

"A painting session? Are you painting her? You didn't tell me, Khalid," he said.

"Yes, I am."

Valeria frowned at Khalid. *Why was he getting mad?* She thought.

"But we do that in the morning. I can see the stables in the evening," she said with a small smile. She had loved petting Khalid's horse back at the oasis.

"Great, it's settled then," Zayed announced. "I will take you to the stables—"

I interrupted. "I will come along."

Zayed grinned at me, knowing well he did that to get under my skin.

After the dinner, Zara announced to walk Valeria to her room and talk to her. It seemed like I would have to resort to sneaking into the guest room in my home.

👑

I KISSED VALERIA'S TEMPLE AS SHE SLEPT SOUNDLY, SNUGGLING the dark blanket as her red golden hair splayed across the pillows. Her face was the picture of innocence, her pink lips parted as she sighed, mumbling something incoherent.

I smiled at her, tucking her hair behind her ear and stood up from the bed, reaching for my clothes which I had removed hastily as soon as I had sneaked inside her room well after midnight.

She had just gotten out of the bath and I had ravished her with a kiss, seducing her and taking her against the wall. We had slept in each other's arms after both of us were satisfied. But I knew that even sharing these few moments with her wouldn't satisfy me.

I was selfish. I wanted more. More of her and her time. I didn't want her to leave for London, I didn't want whatever we had to end. *Ever.*

Because I wanted forever with her alone.

Clenching my jaw, I zipped my pants and buttoned my shirt. I gazed at her sleeping profile for one last time before getting out of the French doors of her guest room. I hated leaving her bed, but I had to get ready for the meeting. Zain would arrive that morning, and that meant other guests would arrive soon.

I was in the main study before the sun rose, going over the files of royals, their servants, maids, and guards that would be attending the ceremony. Nasrin's family, the Sultan and Prince of Maahnoor would also visit for their sister's baby shower, so I needed to make sure neither of our people broke into a fight. The relationship could still be a little bit tense at times, despite the shared respect as leaders.

Zain had worked hard to settle a peace between Azmia and Maahnoor. If some people didn't understand that, I would make sure they did. Punishments in Azmia were treated with keeping injustice toward victim in mind. For example, if a man had harassed a woman, forced her, then he would be beaten by the officers and shot in front of the public, daring anyone to ever think about hurting another being again.

My hands clenched into fists, dropping the file on the desk as I leaned back on the chair. I wished I could have done something to protect Valeria, even though it was a fool's wish.

"I have been looking everywhere for you, little brother."

I looked up at the lean frame of my brother, the Sultan of Azmia, Zain Al Latif, and smiled. I stood up to greet him, hugging him as we both grinned at each other. We looked almost identical, standing side by side wearing suits early in the morning. We had father's hazel eyes and strong aquiline nose with our mother's sharp features. I had an inch over him with broad shoulders while Zain's form was lean and muscular. He looked like a true leader, while I looked like a soldier. Zain always told me that I could have been a better Sultan, but I knew it was his own doubts speaking. I preferred to be in the low light.

"How have you been?" I asked, pouring us a glass of scotch. "How is Nasrin? The baby?"

As soon as Zain had told me about their baby, all of Azmia was waiting to welcome a new child to the Al Latif family. Our family knew the baby was a princess. I couldn't wait to meet my niece, play with her, and spoil her with affection and anything she wanted. She had everyone wrapped around her tiny little chubby finger, and she wasn't even born yet.

Zain clinked the glass and gulped down the strong drink. "Nasrin and the baby are well. She is getting ready for breakfast. I heard you brought that special guest with you. I want to meet her."

I looked away, unable to meet my brother's teasing eyes. There was something piercing and intense about them. "She would be at breakfast. I checked all the details of royals that would be attending—"

"Why are you changing the topic?" My elder brother narrowed his eyes at me, crossing his arms. He leaned against his desk and spoke. "Is she truly that special as Zara mentioned?"

So he must have talked to Zara before meeting me.

"*Precious*," I met his levelling gaze. "Like Nasrin is to you."

Zain's face morphed into a big grin at the realization. "You are in love, Khalid. *Ha!* I can't believe my player brother is whipped. I have been waiting ages for you to profess your love for someone and—"

"I can't," I stopped him. "She is… she is *too* good. She is everything that I am not. Sweet, innocent and *pure*. She reminds me of everything that is good in this world while here I am… filled with every wicked thing—"

"You don't mean that."

I glared at him. "I do. You don't know what it was like to see life leave out of your own father's eyes while piercing a sword through his heart."

I took a deep breath to stop myself from shaking, to stop my hands from shaking. Even years of therapy hadn't erased those memories from me. I could still see the betrayal in my father's angry face, the warm trickling of his blood coating my palms when I stood in front of Zara to protect her. The look of horror on Zain's face.

Zain laid a hand on my shoulder. "You did it to protect our sister, Khalid. It was impulsive and reckless, but you did it to protect our Zara from a monster. You are still the kind brother who cried when he stepped over a caterpillar. Don't let that one thing ruin you from accepting love of others."

I forced down the overwhelming emotions. I shook my head, "I don't deserve her."

Zain scoffed, rolling his eyes, "Don't make me punch you."

When I remained silent, Zain continued. "It's not about deserving each other, Khalid. It's about accepting each other. And if she is here, in our palace and sleeping in your bed at night, then I am sure she *has* accepted you. *All* of you. All you have to do is talk to her."

We were interrupted by a maid letting us know that the breakfast was ready and everyone was waiting for us.

Zain gave me a hard look. "Talk. To her."

I nodded, hoping I had the courage to talk to Valeria as soon as I could.

Valeria
(Valeria first person. Khalid third person)

"And when little Khalid didn't like the food, he would start crying and stay hungry until we ran after him all over the palace to make him eat," Khalid's grandma said with a smile in her voice which made me chuckle with others.

I was sitting beside Khalid, holding his hand under the table and having a delicious breakfast. I had met his in-law, Nasrin, who had a melodious husky voice when she hugged me. It seemed that everyone in his family were huggers.

My excitement flew over the moon when I felt the bump on her stomach and she allowed me to feel the baby kick. I almost cried and burst out into a small laugh.

Khalid and his brother had watched the exchange from the hallway with smiles on their faces. Zain was proudly smiling at his wife while Khalid had a gleam in his eyes. How Valeria would look with a pregnant belly and how beautiful their babies would be, with red hair and hazel eyes, running around the palace with paintbrush in their fists, their clothes splattered with paint.

It seemed that they needed to talk as soon as they could. About their relationship and feelings. Not about marriage or babies, *pfft*, of course not.

I had greeted the Sultan, Zain, with a bow, but he let out a chuckle and told me that there was no need for me to do that. That I was already a part of their family. I had flushed with joy but didn't know why he had said that with a deep meaning in his tone. Again, I wished I could have my sight to see what he meant and look at Khalid to see the emotions on his face.

I pushed away all those thoughts and focused on the warmth of Khalid's hand as his fingers entwined with mine. The same fingers which had been cupping my breasts, pinching my nipples and then slipping inside me when he had visited me last night. My core clenched, remembering his hot whispers against my ear when he claimed me against the wall. Although

I was sad that I had woken up alone, I knew that he must have his reasons. He was a Prince after all.

"Elena was going to join us for lunch today but couldn't arrive," Khalid's brother, Zain, announced. They had almost similar voice but Khalid's voice had deeper baritone and turned low when he whispered.

"Oh, I would have loved to meet her. We haven't met in years," Khalid replied with ease.

So she must be a friend. A close friend, like Zayed. I knew I shouldn't be jealous of hearing about his female friend, but I couldn't help it. I felt guilty because I hadn't even met the woman and yet, I couldn't stand the thought of Khalid meeting a woman while I didn't know what her relationship was with him. My appetite fell as I swallowed the lump in my throat.

"I am sorry, I am not feeling well," I mumbled, standing up from the low seating. "I will be in my room. Thank you for the breakfast, it was really lovely."

I bowed and hastily left the dinner hall, mentally thanking Zara for walking with me yesterday. I had mapped out the route from my room to the hall, remembering the right number of steps. I closed the door behind me and sighed, swiping my hand across my face.

Fool, I was acting like a complete fool.

Oh, God, what have I done?

Someone knocked on the door and thinking it must be Khalid, I opened it and blurted, "I am so sorry, I shouldn't have rushed to my room like that, Khalid. I didn't know—"

A soft feminine laugh echoed in my ears. I flushed when the woman walked inside the room, closing the door behind her. By the exotic floral scent, I knew that it was Zara. Her voice was husky and sultry.

"My brother is too naïve to come after you when Zain mentioned Elena," Zara calmly explained. "Forgive him, he truly thinks that you have a headache and will visit you soon to give you proper medicine."

"Oh, I don't have a headache."

"I know, Valeria. Come sit down with me."

Both women sat side by side on the low sitting area in the balcony, warm sunlight caressing their skin. They looked total opposites, sitting like that. One had bright long red hair while the other had pixie platinum white hair. One was wearing neutral-colored clothes while one was in dark clothes, just like her brothers.

"I know you must be thinking about Elena, his friend, but I want to ease your worry and tell you that there's nothing between them." Zara took a deep breath. "When Zain became the Sultan at the age of twenty, many rulers wanted their daughters to get married to him and Khalid for power. Elena's father was one of them."

I listened to her words carefully, wondering what it must have been like to be in their place. To rule over a golden country instead of going to college and focusing on growing into a better person.

"He is a nice man, but at that time, Azmia needed the support of a neighboring country. Khalid and Elena met, and they were too young, so when she turned eighteen, they were announced to get married for the benefit of both the countries."

My heart crushed hearing that. He was betrothed to her, he still might be.

Oh, God.

Zara held my arm. "Valeria, they were betrothed. But the arrangement ended when Khalid didn't want to marry his friend. Neither did Elena. By then, Azmia had good connections with the neighbors, so the marriage wasn't needed. They are still good friends and that's all I know. I don't think my brother ever found someone to love… until *now*."

Even though I was relieved hearing that Khalid wasn't betrothed to anyone, my heart clenched hearing Zara's last words.

"What do you mean?"

I felt Zara stand up. "I think you know what I mean, Valeria. Khalid has feelings for you. I have never seen him so content and relaxed. The way he talked about you… it felt special. And by the look of your flushed face, I know that you do too."

I was shocked that my attraction and affection towards Khalid was easily noticed.

"My sweet, can I come in?"

Both the women shared a knowing smile, hearing the muffled, husky voice of Khalid. Zara squeezed her shoulder and opened the door, winking at her brother's shocked face when she passed by him. Khalid was more surprised when his sister whispered, "If you don't confess your feelings towards her, then I will."

2 3

VALERIA

(VALERIA FIRST PERSON, KHALID THIRD PERSON)

My body kept tensing and relaxing as I tried to control my breathing, sitting naked in front of Khalid while he painted me. I didn't know what to do. I felt nervous with anticipation. My skin was prickling with anxiousness. My fingers clenched the soft suede of the armchair he had asked me to sit on.

Even the air seemed thicker and boiling with tension in Khalid's room. It had been like that since Zara left us alone. I had told him that I was feeling much better than before, and he had asked me to have a painting session.

I couldn't wait any longer. I needed to talk to him.

But all my courage left when I had to expose myself for the umpteenth time in front of his piercing eyes in his childhood room. Which smelt of something musky with his signature masculine scent.

Khalid dropped the paintbrush with a sigh as he stared at her face. "Valeria, what is troubling you?" He asked, wanting to know what was causing her so much discomfort that she couldn't even stay still for a few seconds. He wanted to comfort her.

She looked down on her lap, her hands entwining with each other. Khalid suffered and tried to fix the bulge in his pants and scolded himself. She was anxious, and he was getting hard, for fuck's sake. He couldn't help himself. She was naked and sweet and looked so alluring with her red hair glowing, caressing the soft alabaster skin.

"I am sorry. I have a lot on my mind. I can't seem to relax." Valeria offered him a sweet smile, which made his heart beat faster.

"You don't have to apologize, my sweet one. Is there something—*anything* that I can do to help you relax?"

Khalid didn't mean to make his voice deeper and almost teasing, causing her to blush. Oh, what he wouldn't do to lick her sweet neck and thrust inside her, feeling her tightness as she softly gasped his name over and over.

He was hard as steel now. *Fucking great.*

"I… I wanted to talk to you about something," I said, my voice wavering, looking in his direction.

"What do you want to talk about?"

By the way she was tensed, he knew it was important and a serious matter for her.

I took a deep breath. *Just ask him, Valeria.* "About our relationship."

"Relationship?"

"Yes." I continued with a firm but soft voice. "I don't want to be confused regarding where we stand in all of this. Where I stand in your life. What is it that we are doing, Khalid? I… I want to know."

Khalid wasn't expecting that. He clenched his jaw and closed his eyes to take a calm breath. "You know I like you, Valeria. You are special to me. I want you in my life if you feel the same."

"I do," she said. "If not more."

He gazed at her, his lust long forgotten. That woman, with a kind heart and kinder spirit, had feelings for *him*? He rubbed the sore spot on his heart and looked away, not understand the why.

Why would she do that to herself?

Khalid clenched his fist. "I am afraid I don't know where we stand, my sweet."

"What do you mean by that?"

He didn't like the way her voice had lost its softness, as if she was pulling away from him.

"I want to wait and see whether whatever we have right now blooms into something else. Something more important."

I didn't reply for a while, letting my thoughts process his words. Khalid wanted to wait and see how everything turns out for us.

"What if I don't want to wait?" I whispered to myself, heart-broken and wanting to sort out what I wanted.

Khalid didn't hear what I whispered, the sudden change in air making him worry. "Valeria… what is it? Say it, sweet," he coaxed her, wanting to know what was bothering her. *Was it his reply? Did he say something wrong?* He wanted to stroke her back, inhale the sweet scent of roses from her hair, and talk to her.

I abruptly stood up. My hand wrapped around the flimsy robe as I tried to push my hands through the armholes, my actions frantic. "I am sorry. I need some space right now," I mumbled. I needed some space and time to think, which I couldn't do if he was in my presence.

Khalid understood her, even though it hurt him that he couldn't be of more help. He stood up and walked towards her, her dainty face so vulnerable with emotions that he wished to hug her, caress her, and whisper that everything would be okay. Instead, he maintained his space and helped her delicate hands through the armholes and tied the robe for her.

Running a finger down her cheek, he lifted her jaw, boring his dark eyes into her face. Her lips. Leaning down, he brushed a gentle kiss over them. "Promise me that you will talk to me tonight, my sweet one. Promise me that you… that you will *stay*," he whispered, hating how weak his voice was.

I cupped his cheek, caressing his cheekbone with my thumb as he leaned into my soft palm. "Oh, Khalid, of course, I will stay. I just need to have some time alone where I won't make a decision overpowered by you because you distract me." I smiled at him, my cheeks warm. "I promise I will talk to you. Tonight, I will sneak into your room."

"I look forward to that, sweet one." His lips lifted into a smile, kissing her palm. "Now leave my room unless you want me to bend you over the armchair, spread your pretty legs and have your sweet pussy for lunch."

Khalid smirked, loving the way red blush creeped over her slender neck to her face. Her freckles brighter than before.

I shook my head stepping away from him. "You are a filthy hot prince, Khalid."

Valeria let out a small squeal of giggle when Khalid smacked her ass as she walked pass him. She was grinning when she turned around to give him one last look in his direction before leaving his room. Leaving him alone with a silly grin on his face that he couldn't seem to wipe off even after finishing the final touches of the painting.

Even with all the silly talks with Valeria about his feelings, deep down, he knew that he was *done for*. Valeria Dunne *owned* every inch of him, his mind, his heart, and his soul. For he was in love with her. Deeply and ferociously.

I WAS AT EASE DURING THE LUNCH WITH KHALID SITTING BESIDE me. I had called Mr Benjamin and talked to him about my stay in the Golden Palace of Azmia and how welcoming Khalid's family was. Mr Benjamin and Mabel were happy for me, but they missed my presence back at home.

I had to sort out my thoughts and decided that I wanted to continue whatever I had with Khalid and see it develop into something deeper and meaningful. I wanted to be with him as much as he did me. Some part of me felt empty without his scent surrounding me. He was my anchor, and I didn't want to know how it would feel if we ever parted ways from each other.

Khalid's hand squeezed my thigh, making me snap out of my thoughts when Zayed asked me a question related to my business, asking me to release a scent after his name. Khalid scolded him while Zara and Nasrin laughed at their banter.

For the first time in a long time, I felt accepted. I had made so many friends who didn't see my loss of vision as a disability, who treated me as an equal. Treated me as their friend.

All thanks to Khalid, the man who sat beside me chatting away with his brother and best friend.

I squeezed the hand on his thigh and kept it there finishing the delicious *kunafah* for dessert. I would later show him how much all of it meant to when I would sneak into his room at night and touch him.

After the plates were cleared up from the table, I frowned. "Where is grandma? I didn't hear her teasing the Prince or the Sultan."

Khalid smiled down at his sweet while his brother chuckled. Nasrin replied with a small smile of her own, "She had her lunch in her room. She has a minor cold. Don't worry, she will join us for dinner and make up for the teasing."

"AND THIS SWEET GIRL IS YASMINE, SHE IS VERY GENTLE WITH everyone unlike Khalid's horse, Kamil," Zayed commented, walking beside her, allowing me to pet his horses. He was the Sheikh of Azmia. As an orphan, he had grown up with the Al Latif siblings, earning the title of the Sheikh through hard work, even though he tried to hide it behind his charm and addictive laughter.

I chuckled, remembering the horse ride. "Not really. Kamil was kind when I sat on him for a brief ride. He doesn't like you because you always tease him."

"True enough," Zayed said with a smile. "Here, touch Yasmine, she has a white mane."

I lifted my arm, and he carefully led it to the flaring nose of the horse and down her jaw. Yasmine grunted happily, allowing me to scratch and rake my fingers over her jaw, petting her silky mane. I chuckled softly when Yasmine huffed loudly.

"Valeria, there you are!" Khalid exclaimed, trying to hide his jealousy when he found Zayed standing too close to me.

I lifted my hand from the horse and looked over in Khalid's direction. I could hear some sort of restraint in his voice.

"Hi."

"*Hi?* I have been looking all over for you in the palace. Zayed, why didn't you tell me?"

Zayed raised his slashing brow at his friend, who was obviously jealous. "I asked her yesterday, Khalid. You were there, promising to join us, but we couldn't find you so I brought her here."

Khalid
(Khalid first person. Valeria third person)

I glared at him. Zayed grinned, with his charming dimples and easy-going smile.

"Well, I will leave you guys here. I have an important call to make. I am sure you can escort Valeria to her room." He winked at me when he left.

"He doesn't have any important call to make, does he?" Valeria asked, frowning at me.

"He doesn't."

"Then why did he—*oh.*"

I grasped her hand and took her to an empty smaller shed where we used to store horse tack. I pressed her against the wooden wall, grasping her jaw in my hand and kissing her. I growled, biting her lip and pushing my hip towards her, trapping her.

"You have no idea how angry I am at you, my sweet, do you?" I whispered throatily, grazing my teeth on the shell of her ear making her gasp.

She squirmed when I wrapped my hand around her wrists, holding them above her head. Her breasts, covered in cotton tee shirt, pushed towards me, her nipples hard.

"You're a-angry at me? But why?" she asked, her voice husky with arousal. Valeria could feel the outline of his bulge against her stomach, his huge frame looming over her, surrounding her. Khalid let out a wicked laugh that made her sex clench deliciously.

"Because you made me worry for an hour and then I find you in a stable, alone with Zayed, laughing with him."

Valeria grinned teasingly. "Are you jealous, Prince Khalid?"

"You have no idea." I dropped my head, kissing her neck and biting the skin. "Tell me to stop if I get too rough, okay?"

"*Too rough?*"

"We are having angry sex, Valeria."

"But I am not angry at you. And neither are you," Valeria replied with a chuckle, willingly rubbing herself on my thigh as I got harder and harder in my pants.

I grinned down at her, her sweet innocent face looking at me, full of adoration. I kissed her nose. "You are so fucking adorable, my sweet one. You are right, I could never be angry at you, but you have caused something to go up that needs your utmost attention."

She smiled, her freckles bright. "Then we need to fix it now, Prince Khalid."

I was about to remove her clothes when she stopped me, "Wait, I need to ask you something."

I bit back a groan and pulled away. "What do you want to ask?"

"Is it true?" Her wide eyes blinked up at me.

"*True?*" I tilted my head.

She swallowed the lump in her throat. "About *Limerence*. Zayed told me what inspired it."

Oh, I didn't see that coming.

"You really want to know about that right now?" I asked, my eyes flickering between her hard nipples and my boner.

"Yes."

I scratched my neck. "I met this cute ginger haired girl when I was fifteen. Even though my father was terrible, he liked to pretend he was a good person by donating to foster charities. I went with my mother to London because the Queen had invited us."

Valeria gasped, "You have met *the* Queen?"

"Of course, I have. She is just like my grandma but kept feeding me a lot of biscuits."

"Remind me to ask about Buckingham palace," she grinned, making me poke her cheek.

I continued, "After meeting the Queen, we went to a lot of foster homes and I was tired of pretending to be a perfect Prince in front of so many people. I was also a teenager, so I was always moody and angry. Until I met that girl in the back-yard of the foster house."

I could remember that day, that time, as if it was happening right in front of me.

"She was sketching something on a paper, so I helped her. She asked me if I was a Prince Charming and I pinched her cheek."

"What did you say to her?"

"I told her that I was and she scoffed at me, told me that I don't look like one." Corner of my lips quirked thinking about her, how no one had ever dared to talk against me, yet a seven-year-old child had told me that I didn't look like a Prince.

Valeria smiled, caressing my arm, waiting for me to continue.

"I couldn't get her name, but she told me her age was seven. We drew a little house together with a baby giraffe in the garden because that was—"

"Her favorite animal and she wanted it as her pet," she finished my sentence.

I stared at her. "What… how did you?"

My brain scrambled with memories as Valeria pulled back her arm.

"Khalid… the girl that you met? It might have been me," she said in a soft voice, tucking a piece of her hair behind her ear.

That same red hair.

I swallowed the lump in my throat. "You were wearing a yellow tee shirt and had this big—"

"Carrot hair clip on my head to keep my hair from falling on my face," Valeria chuckled, covering her mouth. I held her wrist and pulled it down, wanting to stare at her grin.

It was *her*.

I leaned closer, pressing my forehead against her. "You don't know how much I looked for you, you silly girl. I begged my mom for months to remember the name of the foster we visited together but she had forgotten."

"Why?"

I stroked her cheek. "Because I liked you when I first saw you. It was pure amusement and adoration to see a small girl like you tell me that I am not a Prince. Telling me that you could color better than me when I colored out of the lines to banter with you."

She nodded, biting her lip. "I didn't like boys who could color out of the lines."

I let out a soft laugh, kissing her neck, and looked at her. Really looked at her. She had the same nose, same freckles and even the same I-want-to-pinch-your-cheeks-every-time-you-smile cheeks. She had her sight back then. I remembered everything.

I was a fool not to notice it before.

"You were my muse for *Limerence*. I couldn't get the color of your red hair out of my head. It looked so vibrant in the sunlight that I had to pour it out." I raked my hand through her hair. I couldn't believe I was holding it. She was real. In my arms.

"You are my muse for *Limerence*, my sweet one," I whispered.

Valeria leaned up and pressed a soft kiss on my lips. "I want to share a secret with you, Khalid."

I hummed.

"After you colored with me, I had decided that I wanted to marry you," she giggled, looking away. "Then your mother found us and she hugged me. She smelt so wonderful that I asked her what perfume she was wearing. Your mother was the one who inspired me to be a perfumer, Khalid."

"You wanted to marry me? After coloring with me?" I grinned, shaking my head.

"I knew you were a prince, and you took time to talk with me…"

"In my defense, I was bored with social gatherings and was looking for a place to sit in silence. But I found you." I kissed her, just to make sure she was real. I pulled away, "If my mother was alive, she would have loved to meet you."

"You really think so?"

"*Mhmm*. She would get shy that her signature fragrance inspired you."

Her fingers threaded over my hair, massaging my scalp. "You must miss her so much."

I nodded, pulling her close, tightening my arms around her. "Now that I know you are the same girl I have been looking for all these years… I want to fuck you even more. I want to bend you over and fill you with my cum, Valeria."

"*Filthy Prince*," she gasped, grinding her hips down my thigh.

Valeria loved how he emitted a low groan, kissing her mouth before removing their clothes and bending her over the nearest table, like he had promised. She gasped when he pushed everything off of it to make her comfortable and pressed his hard erection against her dripping wet folds.

"You drive me so fucking wild, Valeria," I said, tangling my fingers in her hair and tugging them back when I smacked her ass.

She moaned sweetly, her fingers stretching over the table to hold the other hand. I stroked the pink hue on her ass and nudged her legs wider. I pressed a kiss on her neck and rubbed her clitoris, slowly pushing myself inside her warm heat.

Valeria gasped, and I sighed, both of us burning together at our unison. Her tightness clamped around me, clenching me deliciously, and sending shivers of tremors all over my body. I groaned, trailing my palm over her smooth back before holding her neck and slamming inside her with more force. Her supple body rocked forward, the table hitting against the wooden wall of the shed, when I repeated my action with powerful thrusts.

The muscles on my back clenched with tremors, my deltoids tight when I leaned over her smooth back, rolling her hard clit and feeling her stretch around me.

"H-how do we look?" She whispered, looking over her shoulder.

"Fucking beautiful, my sweet," I grunted as I rocked inside her dripping heat. "You are so wet for me. Your, *fuck*, cunt coating my cock with all your juices. Here, feel it."

Holding her wrist, I made a V with her fingers and slid it over our unison. Her soft gasp as she felt us fucking was the sound of angels in my ears. I squeezed my eyes shut and leaned my head back as I lost myself inside her warmth.

Valeria moaned loudly, the fullness of my girth and the pleasure of my thrusts making her tether to the edge as she clutched on to the wooden table underneath her.

"I… I am going to—"

"*Yes*," I hissed, my thrusts deep and gentle. "Cum on me, my sweet one. Let me feel your cunt clench me."

Valeria whimpered, his dirty words brushing over her ear, his warm breath caressing her neck. After a couple of thrusts, she was clenching him tightly, her walls spasming with the orgasm, when she came with a loud groan. Loud enough to alert anyone outside the shed that someone was definitely fucking inside there.

I gripped her hips and shuddered, coating the insides of her walls with my release. I squeezed my eyes shut to remove the images of Valeria pregnant with my child, making love to her and holding our baby together with her in my lap.

It was too much, it felt too much.

I was not ready for that.

I pulled out, cleaning us with my shirt and apologizing for my handprints on her hips. I embraced her in a hug, wanting to feel the warmth and softness of her skin against my hard skin. Kissing the top of her head, I was ready to confess my feelings for her. In a shed where we had just fucked like animals.

Nonetheless, I was more than ready.

"Do you feel it?" Valeria whispered, caressing my back and cupping my neck.

I knew what she was talking about. The air remained musky with sex, but with a sizzle of electricity, something raw and vulnerable.

"I do," I replied, and pulled back to cup her cheeks.

"I love you, Valeria."

24

VALERIA

y lips parted and heart pounded wildly against my ribcage, ready to burst out hearing Khalid's confession.

He loved… *me*? It couldn't be, I must be dreaming.

Yes, we had great sex, and I passed out and I am dreaming about—

"*Yes.*" I could hear the smile in his voice, pure joy lacing it. "I love you, I love you, I love you, my sweet one. I want to yell to the entire world—*omph.*"

I tipped on my toes, kissing his lips and relishing in the softness of them when he kissed back, weaving his hand in my hair. I savored the relief and comfort and… *love* that came from him, showing him how much his confession meant to me, kissing him harder.

He asked between the kisses, "Is this… your way… of—"

"*Yes,*" I gasped, grinning up at him. My heart was bursting with pure joy from hearing his confession. "Yes. I love you, Khalid. More than I can ever convey in words. If I could, I would like to spend my forever with you and more."

Tears gleamed in his hazel eyes. His pupils dilated as he

gazed down at her serene face, her emotions raw and sincere. "Then let's work on it. Let's spend eternity, forever, side by side," he murmured, his hands caressing her smooth skin.

We sealed the deal with a passionate kiss before melting into one, rocking the table against the wooden wall yet again until the sun dropped low over the horizon.

👑

"I can't wait to fuck you in this dress, my sweet," Khalid whispered, his eyes gleaming with lust when they raked over her gorgeous face, her red lips, her diamond earrings twinkling in the chandelier light. The deep red dress that was made just for her, leaving shoulders bare as the velvet material hugged her supple figure.

My cheeks turned the color of the dress. "It's Nasrin's baby shower, Prince Khalid. Control yourself," I replied in a teasing voice as the crowd around us chatted around, laughing and enjoying the delights of royal ceremony.

I could hear small kids bubbling with laughter and Zayed's laugh when he charmed other people by doing what he did best —*being Zayed.*

"How can I, my love? You look stunning and I absolutely can't wait to take you away from these people awing at you and ravish you," his voice dropped an octave when he said, "With my mouth, hands and my co—"

"*Khalid,*" I gasped, clamping his mouth, feeling him smirk underneath it. "You are unbelievable."

He chuckled in his low voice, that made my underwear wet with arousal. Ever since we had confessed our feelings to each other, we both had been feeling hornier than ever. Embracing each other and having sex for hours until either of us (most of the time it was me) got exhausted and passed out.

My sex was still throbbing with dull soreness after sharing

his bed in the afternoon.

"Am I doing it right?" I had asked, holding the pencil tightly and touching the paper with the other hand.

Khalid hummed over my shoulder, doing a miserable job at hiding his laughter. After the painting session in his room, I had decided to try my hand at drawing. He was kind enough to teach me but the lack of my sight created a minor problem.

"What?" I prodded, looking over my shoulder. Smiling when he kissed my nose. "Why are you laughing?"

He took the paper I had been using to draw and hummed as if he was thinking really hard.

"What were you trying to draw here, Valeria?" He asked, his voice almost teasing.

I squirmed over his lap, rubbing my ass over his boxers. "A penis."

Khalid chuckled, tickling my waist and pulling me back on the bed. "I knew it, you dirty girl. You were doing your menacing giggles the entire time!"

I gasped, trying to pull away from his tickle attack. "I do *not* have menacing giggles."

Yes, I do.

"*Liar!*" He spanked my ass, holding my hands above my head. "Do it again, I want to hear it."

Taking a deep breath, I giggled menacingly. Khalid laughed, hovering above me, kissing all over my face and settling between my legs.

It made me so happy that I could make him laugh like that. I wanted to record his laughter and show it to the world and say, 'See?! That's Khalid snorty laughter and I was the one who made him laugh. See, isn't he adorable?'

"I love you so fucking much." I could hear the grin in his voice. "My little giggle monster."

I wrapped my arms around him and hummed against his chest. "Rate my penis," I said.

Khalid laughed again, pinching my nipple just because he could. "I rate it two out of five."

"*Shut up!*" I gasped, pushing him away. "My penis is world star."

He laughed more, then the bed dipped beside me and I could imagine him clutching his stomach with tears in his eyes. "Stop saying your penis. You *don't* have a penis. You just drew a small dick that has been through a lot."

I crossed my arms, glaring in his direction. "You are just jealous that my penis is bigger than yours."

Khalid pulled me over his lap, a small gasp escaping my lips when he held my palm and guided it over his stiffened member. I bit my lip when I touched him through his boxers, feeling the hard, throbbing skin underneath. That *is* definitely big enough to be a world star penis. Too bad I wasn't willing to share it with anyone.

"Now whose dick is bigger, my sweet?"

"*Mine.*"

"Do you want to feel my enormous cock thrusting inside you, *hm?*"

"You did *not* just say that." I grinned and crawled off his lap, looking for the paper where I had drawn my art. "I will ask Zara if the penis I drew is big or not. I don't trust you to tell me —*omph*, Khalid!"

He pinned me on the bed, spreading my legs and tearing my underwear. "You will not tease me and leave my room just because of a penis you drew."

"But it's my pe—"

"Don't you *dare* say it, Valeria," he growled, leaning over my face as his warm breath fanned over my cheeks. "Or else I will—"

"*My penis.*"

Two hours later, I realized my mistake. I shouldn't have said that. Khalid had tickled me mercilessly, that had turned into kissing, that had turned into rough sex. He only stopped because Tamara had knocked on his door, because I had to get ready for the ceremony.

That Prince had the stamina of a horse.

And yet, I wanted him. Craved to be touched by him and be held in his arms.

I never thought I would be lucky enough to have someone love me as much as Khalid did.

"Grandma and Zara are five paces away from us," he said, kissing the top of my head. "Stay with her, okay? Zain needs my help."

I nodded, holding Zara's arm when we both talked about the dress. Zara had a teasing tone when she mentioned that Khalid had never looked that happy before.

"So what do you think about it?" I asked her.

She leaned in and said, "The one you drew is pretty big."

"I know right!"

Zara chuckled. "You guys are going to make me puke. So stinky cute."

Grandma piqued in, "I agree with my granddaughter. You both are glowing. Only love makes you look that young and joyous. It has changed my Khalid for the better." Her warm hand patted my arm. "I can't thank you enough, my dear Valeria. I know I shouldn't say it but... in a way, I wished that I could help you see how much love you both share whenever you are close."

Words of *jadati* pierced my heart, my eyes brimming with tears. "I... I wish I could see him too, *jadati*. See him smile and see you all tease each other."

Zara rubbed my back and said softly, "I am sorry for being curious, but I asked Khalid about your blindness. He...He mentioned that you need new cornea to have your vision back. If you want, we can have you treated here in Azmia, we have—"

"Oh, Zara, it means a lot to me," I replied with a sincere

smile. "But there are others who need them more than me."

"That is true, my dear. But sometimes you have to accept what you deserve too," grandmother replied in a firm yet soft tone, leaving me speechless. Zara agreed with her grandmother.

When other royals and guests came to meet grandma, I let myself dream about how it would feel to finally have my sight back after so many years. How it would feel to gaze at Khalid, look at his paintings and see him laugh. How it would feel to look at sunset and stars at night. To look at Zara's smile and her beauty spot Khalid had mentioned. To see people's emotions on their face instead of always guessing it by their tone.

Zara interrupted my stream of thoughts. "I am sorry, Valeria, I have to leave you in grandma's hand. I have to go avoid the suitors who are actively trying to pursue me, so I will be in a hiding. I will see you again during the dinner!"

I accompanied grandma and her maid, hearing people gushing about the Sultan and his wife, blessing the unborn child with priceless gifts. Other people seemed to be more focused on asking if Zara had been betrothed to another prince or not, and whether Khalid had any relationship. Grandmother patted my hand when one female commented that he could be having a secret mistress as he was a prince and she would be the luckiest girl alive to have his attention, even physically.

"People will talk, no matter what you do. Don't let those rumors get to you, dear Valeria," she said.

I nodded, agreeing with her. It didn't affect me, but I didn't enjoy how anyone so openly judged the man I loved and cherished. Yes, he drank and used to sleep around and even got in a fight, but beneath all of that, he was just a man with a terrible past.

He felt ashamed and guilty for living when he killed his father, even though he did it to protect himself and his family.

All I wanted to do was be with him and help him when he needed me. Embrace him, feel his muscles and body relax against me as he slept with his head on my chest, holding me close.

When grandma was busy greeting a royal guest, Tamara came up to me to ask me about Zara.

"Why?" I asked her, "What's it about?"

"Someone wants to meet her in the palace library."

I couldn't exactly tell her that she was hiding away from suitors.

"I don't know where she is, Tamara. Can you tell them to find and talk to her during the dinner?"

Tamara said, "Why don't you come with me, Princess Valeria? I don't want to defy the orders of a royal. I would be glad you are with me."

"Oh, sure. We can take the guards with us."

I informed grandma's maid that I was going in a library even though unease filled my nerves. Why would someone want to meet Zara when cake cutting was about to happen? Maybe I was getting worried for no reason. Khalid had told me that the palace was littered with the guards and I had my personal guard with me.

The end of my cane tapped against the marble floors of the hallway. It smelt musty when Tamara walked me to the library. The air felt damp despite the scent of old books.

I couldn't hear just one person. There were a lot of them. The hair on the back of my neck prickled when I heard someone groan with annoyance.

"Where's the fucking princess? Who is this redhead?"

I backed away when I felt the stranger walk in my space, trying to touch my hair. "Don't touch me," I said, trying to keep my voice from panicking.

Stop.

No.

Please, it hurts.

But you are enjoying it, Val, aren't you?

"She is Khalid's mistress," I heard Tamara reply, shock rippling through me.

What was she doing?

I heard him scoff. "We don't want something that has been used. What happened to that Princess? He wouldn't want *this*."

I felt his disgusted stare on my body. I ignored the urge to cover myself and cower away, trying to find the door to the library. I needed to get out of there. They were talking about Zara, the Princess of Azmia, as if they had planned something conniving.

"I told you she disappeared as soon as she entered the Court Room," Tamara complained.

Someone sneered close to me, roughly grabbing my arm. "Where the fuck do you think you are going? I always hated Khalid, so full of himself. We take her instead of the Princess, she is his lover after all."

"Stop, help me!" I shouted at the top of my lungs, hitting the man with the cane.

He cursed, letting go of my arm as I made a dash towards the doors. "Help me! Help!" I screamed, trying to open the doors, struggling to find the handles.

I yelped when someone grabbed my hair and pulled me back, slapping my face. My ears started ringing when my head hit the table, warm blood trickling out of my pained nose. It hurt so much.

"Shut up, no one's going to save you."

I cowered back, trying to find something to hold on to. I had lost my cane. I didn't know what to do.

"What is wrong with her? Is she blind?"

I slapped and kicked when the man tried to come near me. I grabbed the spine of a book from the bookshelf behind me and threw it blindly at him.

The book fell with a *thump*, people laughing at me as I held the books like a weapon.

"Yes, she's blind," Tamara replied.

"W-why are y-you doing this, Tamara?" I pleaded.

"A-and she s-stutters!" They all laughed, my anxiety growing and growing.

If there were guards around here, I needed to get out of the library and call someone for help. Or… no. I was not a weak sixteen-year-old anymore.

When a cold hand held my arm, I yanked away, kicking on his leg as he fell down on the floor. "Help! Someone help me!" I screamed, my throat aching as warm tears burned my eyes when someone grabbed my hair.

I bit the hand when he tried to shut my mouth, twisting out of his hold.

"Shut up, you slu—" I heard Tamara come towards me and I backed away, wincing.

But the hit never came. I jumped when I heard Tamara scream loudly before it stopped, her body falling on the floor with a *thump*. I held my breath when I felt someone else near me.

"Now, now, that's no way to talk or treat a woman," a woman with a husky voice said in a mocking tone.

I stayed back on the wall when people charged towards someone who had just saved me. I was armed with books as I heard the woman huff and breathe sharply, men groaning and falling on the floor. If someone came close to me, I was ready to slam a hardbound, heavy book at them.

"It's okay," the woman panted, lightly touching my arm. "You are okay. You are safe. Let's get you out of here, I think there are more—yep, there they are."

I stayed still, not in the right position to trust someone. "Who are you?"

"I am Elena."

I closed my hand around her as she dragged me out of the library, my steps failing to meet hers. Khalid and Zara had told me they were friends, but I didn't know he had an assassin as a friend.

Before we could reach far, I heard the loud chatter of the people coming towards us. The thumping of the feet running together.

"Don't worry, they are our guards. A little late but they are here," Elena explained as they rushed past us, in the direction of the library.

Even though we were safe, she held my hand as if she knew how scared I was. I wanted to thank her for that.

"*Valeria!*" I heard Khalid, his arms closing around me as I sighed in relief, melting into his embrace. Tears streamed down my face when he cupped my cheeks.

"I swear I will kill everyone who dared to hurt you, my sweet one," he whispered, his arms wrapping around me once more. I didn't care what he said or if he meant it. I wanted to be in his arms.

I wanted to feel safe.

Khalid

I had meant every word I had said. I was going to behead anyone who had laid a hand on my Valeria and impale their head on a spike in front of the palace gates, daring anyone to try to even think about hurting my sweet.

"Tamara was there," Valeria said, squeezing my hand. "S-she took me to the library. She wanted Zara but I…"

"*Sh*, sweetheart," I hushed her, keeping her close as more guards went past us. "It's okay. I will take care of everything. I will make sure you are safe. Stay with me, okay?"

Her hair was ruffled, her dress had a slit till her thigh, and her cane was missing. A bruise was already forming on the top of her head and I had wiped away the blood from her nose, lying to her that it wasn't much. I had already asked for the royal doctor, but we didn't know how many intruders were in the palace. My main priority was to protect my family and Valeria. Keep them safe.

Valeria nodded, not leaving my hand when Elena updated me on how she heard Valeria's scream and went to check the library. The Court Room where the ceremony was going on was in the opposite wing of the library. So even if guards were everywhere, no one had heard her scream. Even I was called to make sure Zain and Nasrin were protected. We were lucky that Elena had heard her or else I didn't know what would have happened.

It seemed like everything was planned for the ceremony. Making sure everyone was away from the library where there was easy access from windows, even though it was pretty high. They must have used ropes to get inside.

"Long time no see, *puppy*," Zayed said, walking towards us.

I sighed when Elena snarled at my friend, "You too, shitface. You turn uglier each day."

Not again. They could never tolerate each other.

Zayed scoffed, his tone different. "Thanks to you, I would need to wash my eyes with bleach. You look—"

"*Guys*," I warned them, my arm wrapping around her waist. "Not now. Where is Zara?"

Zayed eyed Valeria and looked at me. "She is safe. Zain, Nasrin, *jadati* and Rahim are all together. But the royal guests are getting anxious. They heard the guards running towards this wing."

"Then we need to secure the palace grounds. Don't let any guest, no matter how royal they are, leave the palace."

"Prince Khalid," a guard rushed forward. "You need to see this."

25

KHALID

My nose flared as I saw the sight of the library. Eleven people. Eleven people had tried to abduct my sister and decided to take Valeria. And they were all dead.

"They took a poison," Elena announced, checking the pulse of Tamara's limp body. I had trusted Valeria in her hands. And she betrayed us. "They knew the risks of coming here."

Elena Hill was my betrothed before we both broke it and she left Azmia to continue her training in order to become a better sharp shooter. At least that's what she told us. She had worked along with CIA and FBI before Zain called her for her help with security when he married Nasrin. She knew better than any of us what had happened in the library.

Zayed was patting everyone's clothes, checking what they had. They all were holding an empty small glass bottle, which likely had the poison they took. I pulled my suit jacket over Valeria's dainty shoulders and pulled her to my chest, wishing she didn't have to hear any of that. But I didn't trust anyone to keep her safe.

The guards checked the windows of the library and I had

guessed they had broken in from one of the windows, breaking it and waiting for Tamara. The maid I had trusted.

"Khalid," Zayed called out. "You need to see this."

He shook his head when I tried to bring Valeria along with me. I clenched my jaw and sat her on one of the couches. She clutched the sleeve of my shirt when I tried to move back. It pained me to see her so hurt and scared.

I tucked her hair behind her ear and gently kissed her hands. "I am not going anywhere, my sweet one. Just say my name and I will be with you. There are four guards watching over you. You are safe, Valeria."

She swallowed the lump in her throat and nodded, letting go of my sleeve and holding the suit closer to her. I stood up and the guards nodded at me before I went towards Zayed, who was looking over a small cloth.

"What is it?"

"It has a pattern over it. *Look*," he held it in his palm, a single wave on the cloth.

"A wave?" I questioned, thinking about all the political history lessons I had to learn during my childhood as a Prince.

Elena walked towards her, still in dress, her left heel missing. "Everyone has the same patterns."

I glanced at the eleven small waves and turned one around. "It could be a letter."

"Like Batman?" Zayed frowned.

"It's a letter S, you imbecile." Elena glared at him.

He repeated her sentence, mocking her voice.

I ignored them.

S? What for?

"We found him hiding in between the bookshelves." Two guards held the stranger in black clothing on his knees in front of us. He glared at us and I took a step back when Elena punched him in the face.

"What was that for?" Zayed asked her, lightly rubbing his stubble as if she would hit him next.

She glared at the man as he spit out blood and a tooth. "He broke my favorite Louboutin."

I turned towards the intruder, asking the guard to search his clothes. A similar cloth like the others was in his pocket. "What does this mean?" I held it up for him.

He didn't reply.

I glanced at his hands, noticing the reddish marks on his knuckles. So, there you are. Anger fueled my body as I wrapped my fist around the collar of his tunic.

"Should I gouge out your eyes or cut your arms?" I whispered, glaring at his face.

"Calm down, Khalid." I ignored Zayed and punched the man in front of me. Even the guards backed away as I held him down.

"Tell me. Your eyes or your arms," I ordered, my nose flaring at him.

"Khal—"

"He touched my Valeria. He *dared* to hurt her," I seethed. "I am not letting him go unpunished."

"You don't want to answer me? It's okay." I glared down at him, asking the guards to hold his arms and legs as I rolled my sleeve over my elbow. "You mocked her blindness, didn't you?"

I wrapped my hand around his neck, enjoying the quickening of his pulse, the fear on his face, his eyes widening as he thrashed around the floor. I ignored Elena's and Zayed's words as my fingers inched towards his eyes.

"Let me hear your screams," I said, pinning him down, wanting to hurt him for what he did to my precious, my sweet.

"*Khalid.*"

I stopped and looked over my shoulder.

"Khalid." I stood up, hearing the weak voice of Valeria as she stepped towards me. Zayed ordered the guards to take away the man to the dungeon as if he knew I would have taken out his eyes with my fingers.

Zayed was right. I would have if Valeria hadn't stopped me.

I frowned when she massaged her head. Valeria pulled off my suit and pressed it against her mouth.

No, her nose?

"Khalid, I... I can't—" tears gleamed in her eyes as she stared in my direction.

I held my breath.

"Khalid, I can't smell."

26

KHALID

My eyes widened when Valeria tried to walk towards me, but fainted. I reached towards her, holding her arms and head from crashing before she fell. My heart rate increased when she didn't wake up, Elena pushing me away to check her pulse and her head.

"Is she okay?" I asked, my voice low.

"She possibly has a concussion. If what she said is true, we need a doctor to check her olfactory nerve."

I nodded mindlessly, stroking her hair and taking her to my room, being close to her.

What if she lost her sense of smell? And it all happened because of me?

"You look like shit."

I raised my eyes from Valeria's face to my brother. He was still wearing his clothes from the ceremony even though it was the next morning, bags under his eyes. Zain, Zayed and Elena had taken care of the break in while Rahim and Zara had managed to calm down the royal guests with the help of grandma.

I was too afraid to leave Valeria alone, even in my bedroom. I had stayed with her the entire night, hoping she would wake up soon.

"You don't look any better," I said, my voice hoarse.

Zain sighed and poured me a glass of water, and sat down on the chair beside me. I took a sip of the water and looked at her pale face. I had changed her into one of her comfortable tee shirts and sweatpants, tucking her in the bed.

"What did the doctor say?"

"That she will wake up soon."

"Did he tell you the reason?"

I clenched my jaw and kept away the glass. I might have broken it from my hold. "It is most likely a concussion but Benjamin told me she used to get a headache that she had to stay in bed for a couple of days." I had called her parents as soon as I had settled her in my bed, apologizing for not following with my promise of protecting her. Benjamin and Mabel were concerned about Valeria but wanted to make sure everyone in my family was safe.

"I sense a but coming," Zain said, leaning back in the chair.

I looked down at the floor, clasping my shaky hands. "If she lost her sense of smell, then she fainted because of the shock. She was held against her will. A stranger manhandled her under our roof and hit her. Of course, it shocked her."

And I wasn't there to protect her. Keep her safe, like I had promised I would. She trusted me and I…

"And you are blaming yourself?" Zain guessed, concern lacing his voice.

I shrugged, flickering my eyes at her unconscious body. "I wasn't there to keep her from harm."

She must have felt so alone and scared when so many

strangers crowded her personal space, mocked her, and held her against her will. Especially considering her past.

Zain spoke, "It wasn't your fau—"

"I don't want to hear about it," I cut him off and straightened up. "How is Nasrin?"

"She is with Zara and Elena. Even though she is six months pregnant, she won't sit down until I force her to stay in our room or lock her up."

I smiled at him, the soft gleam in his eyes when he talked about his wife. "I don't think that would work with her."

He chuckled. "It never does. But I try."

We didn't say anything for a moment. He stood up, patting my shoulder. "Call me as soon as she wakes up. I want to apologize for not being a better host. Or Sultan."

Before I could say something, he walked towards the door and paused. "It is not your fault, Khalid. Don't blame yourself for what happened."

I didn't say anything. My eyes averting to the mirror of the vanity. I glared at my reflection.

Valeria

A throbbing headache woke me up from the slumber. My hand going to the bandage on my head and to my clothes. I was wearing my underwear. I sighed in relief, but it only lasted a few moments until I remembered what had happened to me.

I could hear the soft pattering of shower coming from the bathroom. I lightly touched my nose, nothing broken. My skin was soft like before. I lifted the ends of my hair to my face, waiting for the scent of roses to waft in my nose. But I couldn't sense it.

No.

Patting the soft sheets around me, I knew I was on a bed.

But whose bed? I couldn't sense Khalid's woodsy pine scent or my delicate scent.

No.

I stood up, thankful for the cane near the nightstand. I gently touched it, my view full of darkness, and lifted a glass to my nose. I sniffed and nothing happened. I dipped my finger inside it. Water, it's water.

With the help of the cane, I walked to another table, slowly holding and lifting things to my face, trying to make sense of what it was.

But I couldn't comprehend a single thing.

"Valeria," Khalid gasped, a door closing shut behind him as I lifted something warm to my face. It was yanked away from me before I could do so. "What are you doing?"

I swallowed the lump in throat and faced him. I could sense it was him because of his voice, his tall height, his familiar body. Other than that, *nothing*. I couldn't make out his scent, especially if he had just taken a shower.

"You could have burned yourself, my sweet," he whispered, cupping my face. "Why were you trying to hold a candle to your face?"

I took a sharp breath. "Was it scented?"

He didn't reply. The air around me felt heavy and damp, sticking to my skin, making me feel small.

"Khalid, tell me. Was the candle scented?"

"Yes."

Tears burned my eyes, my throat clogging up as I pulled away from him, hugging myself. "I can't smell anything," I said to myself, hiding my face in my hands. Warm tears slid down my face. "I can't even notice your scent or mine. I don't know... I don't know—"

Khalid gently touched my back, rubbing it as if he was afraid. "*Shh*, it's okay, Valeria. We will figure something out. I promise."

But he didn't understand me. I had lost my sense of smell, the only thing that I cherished the most about me. I didn't care about my body, my hair, how I looked. But I cared that I had a better sense of smell. It had brought me joy, creating new fragrances and scents. It had made me successful. It had made me rely on myself without other's help.

And I had lost it. It was my worst fear, losing my sense of smell, and it had happened.

I felt empty without it. Like I had lost a limb.

Khalid kept murmuring sweet things in my ear with his soothing voice, picking me up from the floor and laying me down on the bed, feeding me as he talked about the doctor's visit.

"It will come back, my sweet one. The doctor said that it might take a couple of months but it will," Khalid said, rubbing his thumb on the inside of my wrist.

"What if it doesn't?" I said, hating how weak my voice had turned.

I hated it. I hated what I had become. So weak and small and... *useless*.

"What if it never comes back?"

I broke down and he was saved from lying to me, hugging me as I buried my face in his chest, crying out my heart.

VALERIA

"And you're done!" Zara beamed, stepping back. "Khalid is going to pray as soon as he sees you."

I smiled at her. The light makeup she had applied made me feel better. It had been a couple of days since the baby shower. Khalid was making sure I ate regularly and bathed me, always being gentle when he touched me as if I would break.

He was right. I might break if someone grabbed me out of the blue.

"Do you want me to take you to his room?" Zara asked in a soft voice, keeping away the products.

I had talked to her about her studies when she had knocked on my door just as the sun set. She was studying photography and traveling the world all on her own. Even though she was a Princess of one of the richest countries in the world, she earned her own money and lived by herself. I was glad that Zain and Khalid had done a good job spoiling their little sister with love and not materialistic things.

I shook my head, "I can manage, thank you, Zara."

"You can call me anytime you need someone to talk to,

Valeria, okay?" Her dainty hand held mine as she squeezed it. "I promise to listen to you and scold my brother if he ever hurts you."

I let out a chuckle, hugging her petite frame, noticing that she was as tall as me. "I promise, Zara. I am here if you need to talk." I pulled back, wishing I could sense her scent.

Khalid

"Did you enjoy the dessert?" I asked, noticing she had eaten more of it than the main course.

Night air flew around us as the balcony of my room glowed with the lantern lights. I had set up a date night because we both needed it. I had asked Zara to spend some time with Valeria, and she was more than willing to do it.

"It's tasty," Valeria replied, leaning back on the low sitting.

Her hair was in a braid, few wisps framing her dainty face as she gazed up at the night sky, closing her eyes.

When I tried to caress her hand, she visibly froze. My hand hovered over hers. Clenching my jaw, I pulled away, but she closed her hand around my arm, entwining our fingers together and keeping it in her lap.

I didn't know how I could help her. I didn't know how I could make her happy.

"Are you okay, my sweet?" I asked, forcing myself to stay seated and not pull her onto my lap. I had avoided touching her in a way that may lead to more intimacy.

She lifted our entwined hands to her face, pressing her cheek on the back of my palm. "I am trying to be okay, Khalid," she whispered.

I cupped her face, a light flush on her cheeks. "Tell me how to make things right."

Valeria pulled away, looking from me. "I don't know. I am mad that I lost my sight. My sense of smell. I would do anything to have it back, but I can't and it makes me feel weak."

"You are anything but weak, Valeria."

She glared at me, tears gleaming in her eyes. "How would you know?" She shook her head, wiping away her tears. "I don't want to talk about it right now."

Valeria didn't give me time to reply and continued, "Tell me about the painting. Is it finished?"

I took a deep breath and answered, "Yes, almost done. I need to apply retouches." I didn't tell her that I needed to draw her eyes, and I was making excuses not to draw and paint them. I didn't know why I felt scared to do them.

She hummed, hugging her knees to her chest. "Did you think of a name?"

"I was thinking along the lines of roses. I am not sure."

Valeria faced me. I leaned back on the sitting when she willingly climbed onto my lap, her fingers feathering my hair. "How about *Rose Colored Sorrow*?"

"Maybe."

She pressed her lips against mine, cupping my jaw in her hands, slowly moving her kisses down my neck, unbuttoning my shirt.

"Valeria," I said, stopping her. "What are you doing?"

It didn't feel right. It felt forced. All her actions felt forced.

"I am trying to… to—"

I kissed her forehead, caressing her body through the dress. "You don't have to try with me, sweet one. You don't have to do anything that you don't want to."

Valeria didn't reply, her fists scrunching my shirt.

"Let's watch a movie and cuddle, okay?" I asked, her chin dipping in a nod as I took her inside my room, settling her against the pillows.

We watched a Disney movie with audio descriptions, her head against my chest as she cried with the princess in the movie. I was content that Valeria was trying so hard, but I didn't know what I could do to help her. It was tearing me apart as if I was watching something terrible happen to her from a sideline.

Valeria

I woke up with someone's arm cinched around my waist. My entire body froze as I swallowed the urge to scream and touch the arm. I sighed when I felt the strong veins of Khalid's arms, his tall body spooning me from behind.

I hated that I couldn't recognize him every time he tried to touch me.

Standing up from the bed, I went to the bathroom, stripping out of the dress that I had worn the night before for the dinner date. Untangling my hair from the braid, I opened the cabinet of bath oils.

Biting my lip, I took a small glass bottle and opened it, taking a sniff. Nothing happened. I still couldn't smell. In anger, I poured it all into the bath. Taking another bottle of oil, I took a sniff and when I couldn't smell anything, I poured it into the bath.

No matter what happens, I am getting my sense of smell today.

I repeated my actions, taking a bottle, sniffing it and pouring it all in the bath. I was angry for not protecting myself. For getting into the accident, the people who adopted me dying, leaving me alone and blind. For trusting Mark with me, who used my body and died before I could get my justice. For not fighting back and getting hit on my face only to lose my sense of smell. The only thing that I felt was important to me about my body.

I emptied all the exotic oils in the bath, turning on the tap and searching for the perfume bottles I had placed in Khalid's bathroom suite. I took the spray bottle and sprayed it in the air.

A frustrating sound left my lips as I sprayed it again, all around me, waiting to smell the wooden or oriental notes.

Nothing happened.

"*No,*" I sobbed, my hands shaking as I struggled to open the perfume bottle, wanting to pour it on my skin so I could—

"Valeria!" I pulled away when Khalid tried to touch me. "Stop it. You will hurt yourself."

"I can't smell anything, Khalid. Not even those oils or the perfume that I gifted you. The one that I designed myself."

I was crying, fat tears rolling down my face as I struggled to open the bottle.

"Valeria, it's okay. Give me that bottle. You will hurt yourself."

I hated the pity in his voice.

I threw the bottle against the floor, the sound of glass shattering ringing in my ears as I broke down. Khalid held me before I could fall on my knees, taking me in his arms as I sobbed.

"I hate that I can't see or smell anything, Khalid," I gasped, his hand raking through my hair as he hushed me. "I don't know what to do. I hate it. I feel empty and useless."

"You are not empty or useless—"

I felt the warm trickle on his face. I touched his cheek, hearing the small wince from his lips. My heart beat increased, my body freezing.

"Did the glass hurt your cheek?" I asked, my voice low and weak.

"Valeria, it's not—"

"It did, didn't it?" I shook my head. "I hurt you."

"It's okay, my sweet. It was a mistake. It's a small scratch."

I knew he was lying to me. I said nothing when he showered with me, washing my hair and drying my body with a towel before telling me to stay on his bed, wearing his clothes as he went to fetch our breakfast after cleaning the pieces of glass from the bathroom.

I couldn't even help myself and I had managed to hurt the person I love. If I had my sight, I wouldn't have thrown the bottle of perfume to the floor that hurt his cheek. If I had my sense of smell, none of it would have happened.

I called My Benjamin to book an airplane ticket for me.

28

KHALID

"Do you have to leave?" I frowned, staring at her suitcase as Valeria kept her toiletry bag inside the suitcase, asking me to help her zip it closed.

"We already talked about this, Khalid," she grunted, sighing as she zipped another suitcase. My grandma had ordered me to give her a lot of sweets and snacks from Azmia so she had more bags with her than she arrived with.

"I know that you have a new launch coming soon but... can't you stay for a week?" I asked, almost begging her not to leave.

After that incident in the bathroom, I hadn't left her side for more than an hour, wanting to make sure she was safe. No one had commented on the slash on my cheekbone if they noticed it. I knew she felt guilty for it, but she didn't hurt me intentionally. I was the one who stepped towards her, wanting to make sure the glass didn't hurt her when it slashed through my skin.

"I have to prepare for interviews and photoshoots for the launch campaign, Khalid." She walked towards me, hugging me and murmured against my shirt, "You know I have to go."

I sighed, hearing the sadness in her voice. I kissed her

golden red hair, tightening my hold on her warm body before pulling away. "I know, sweet one. I will visit you as soon as I can," I promised her.

She smiled at me and I ignored the instinct to ask her for a day more, to talk to her about how she felt. I had cancelled her plane ticket and set up my private plane for her to take. It was the least I could do for her.

Zara had already said her goodbye to her before she left the day before to Australia. She was still in the process of making her photography portfolio and we were proud of her that she was going to take clients. It felt weird to have her earn her own money when she was the only Princess of Azmia, but she wanted to live all by her own. We had helped her with a new citizen ID so that she could live as a normal person without her title as the Princess.

"I hope you can visit soon, and I will take you on a ride with Yasmine," Zayed flirted with her in front of me, daring enough to kiss her knuckles. Valeria flushed red and promised him that she would come to Azmia soon.

"Stay away from Zayed, Valeria. He is an imbecile," I warned her, wrapping my arm around her waist and blocked his path when he tried to hug her.

She had met Zain and Nasrin before the lunch and spent some time alone with *jadati* who still had some minor cold.

I kissed her cheek when the helicopter started, the pilot giving me a signal.

"I love you, my sweet one," I whispered in her ear.

Valeria pulled away, smiling at me. "You take care of yourself, my prince."

I rubbed the sore spot on my heart, hearing her call me *her* prince. It made me want to do terrible spontaneous thing. Like ask her—demand her to marry me so she can never leave my side again. But my family, especially Zara, would be disappointed in me if I ever proposed to Valeria like that.

No, I needed a more solid plan.

My hands and arms felt empty when she walked towards the helicopter, her hair flying as one of the guards held her cane, helping her sit in the helicopter.

In a month, I decided. I will surprise her by visiting her in a month. I could wait for a month. I had been waiting for over twenty years to meet her, the girl who inspired *Limerence*, my first ever muse.

I could wait for one more month.

Valeria

I settled in my room after chatting with my parents for the entire evening, having dinner together. The food of London felt a little bland compared to the exotic, spicy food I had in Azmia.

Changing into my light nightgown, I settled into my bed, covering myself with the blanket. It felt cold. I felt cold. I couldn't even snuggle with his warm body.

I hadn't said it back. *I love you, my sweet one.* Khalid had said it so casually that I was shocked and I couldn't even say it back.

I sat up. I couldn't sleep without making sure I told him that I loved him. Before I could ask *Siri* to call him, my phone started ringing. It was his call.

"I was just thinking about you," I said with a shy smile.

Khalid didn't say anything for a few moments.

I frowned, "Khalid?"

"*Valeria...*"

His voice sounded broken, hoarse, and extremely sad. I sat up straighter. "Khalid? What happened? Are you okay? Are you hurt?"

"No... my grandmother. *Jadati...* she passed away."

I took a sharp intake of breath, my hand pressing down on my heart. "What? I-I met her before I left and..." I shook my head. "Are you okay? You don't sound too well, Khalid. Where are you?"

"She shared a dinner with all of us in her bed. We knew that she would stop breathing soon, but she pretended that it was just another family dinner, teasing all of us," Khalid said, shuffling on the other side of the call. He took a deep breath. "We all said our goodbyes, and she passed away in her sleep."

"Oh, Khalid." My heart broke hearing his voice. I wished I had been with her, close to Khalid, so I could soothe him. Take care of him.

A sad chuckle left his lips as he continued, "She asked for a hookah and the oldest whiskey we could find in the palace."

A grin tugged my lips despite the burning tears in my eyes. "Of course, she did."

"We tried to convince her not to drink it but Zayed sneaked a bottle to her."

I swallowed the lump in my throat and said, "I wish I had listened to you and stayed with you for one more week. I will book a ticket for tomorrow—"

"*Valeria*," Khalid said, his deep voice floating through my ears. "No, it's okay. I am fine, sweet."

I bit my lip, hearing the sorrow and anguish in his voice.

He cleared his throat. "I have to go."

"*Khalid*," I called out to him, clenching my fists. "I love you."

When he didn't reply, I added with a small smile, "I will wait for your call."

The call disconnected, making me lose the breath I was holding. I fell back on the bed, hoping that *jadati* was resting in a better place. Maybe I can visit Khalid in Azmia as soon as the new fragrance launch campaign is over.

⚜

A month later

"WE TRIED BUT HE WOULDN'T COME OUT OF THE STUDIO," Nasrin said, her husky soft voice talking to me through the call.

I swallowed down the emotions that had been swelling inside me since I last heard of Khalid. The night when his grandmother died. He had ignored my calls, texts and voice-mails. I wanted to visit him and demand an explanation of his ignorance towards me, but I couldn't leave my team to do all the launch by themselves.

"Has he been eating?" I asked, hoping he did. Even though he was acting like a jerk, pretending that I didn't exist, I still cared about him.

"Yes, thankfully," Nasrin sighed. "Even Zayed cannot make him talk."

"Oh, no."

If Zayed couldn't talk to him, then I didn't know who could.

"Yes. He has never acted this way before. Zain told me he would often shut himself in the studio, but he still came to family dinners and lunches, but this is different."

I frowned, leaning back on the chair as one of the staff knocked on the door, asking me if I was dressed. "Give me a minute!" I called out, hearing the hustle in the shooting studio.

I had an interview for my launch that would be aired live all over the world. I was nervous, but I felt sad hearing how Khalid wasn't taking care of himself.

"Sorry about that," I said to Nasrin. "Do you think it's about grandmother's death?"

"We were all broken up about her death, but I don't think so. He was acting fine afterwards. It all started the next morning."

The night he talked to me.

Was it because of me?

"We will try to reach out to him, Valeria. I promise," Nasrin said, her voice firm. "Until then, good luck for the interview and the launch campaign! We are all excited to purchase the new fragrance."

I smiled sadly, hearing the excitement in her voice. "Thank you, Nasrin. I will call you later."

The call ended, leaving me alone to think and wonder if Khalid was acting strange and ignoring me because of the call we had that night. Was he angry that I left and punishing me by ignoring me? No, Khalid can act moody, but he wasn't immature enough to do that.

Then what was it? I wanted to know what bothered him.

"So why did you decide to be a perfumer?" The interviewer asked, soft light falling over my skin, making me feel warm.

I hummed, thinking over her question. With a small smile, I said, "When we dress up to go out, the last thing we apply is a perfume that defines us. Whether we want to appear delicate, manly, fresh or sweet. The perfume we choose to wear defines us. If it's a formal meeting, we will wear something light yet rich. If it's a date, we will wear something heady or musky.

For me, as a blind person, I can define someone by the tone of their voice, the scent they are wearing. I attach scents to people and the idea of creating new scents for others and how I wanted people to see me, just based on how I smell, seemed very exciting so… here I am."

"That's a lovely answer, Valeria. Tell us something about your new launch."

"The new fragrances of *Delicate Dew* are my representation of basic every day perfume keeping everyone in mind." I continued, picking up the bottle with one bump on the side and telling her about the distinct notes and who would wear it.

Ever since I had the meeting where I told the employees that I couldn't smell, they had been extremely supportive towards me. I had thought that they would want to appoint a new CEO, but instead, they had been working harder.

"You must have heard how beautiful you are, Valeria and I hope you don't mind me asking, but we saw a few pictures of you with Khalid Al Latif, Prince of Azmia," the interviewer said, almost gushing as if we were two close friends. "You two looked so good walking together to his art gallery."

I bit my lip when she continued. As a Prince, Khalid had the power, money and connections to erase the videos some of the people had taken when he fought with those three men when we had walked out of the art gallery. They had never surfaced the internet and didn't harm his reputation. It was hard to believe that we had met two months ago.

"I am sorry, can we please not talk about that at the moment?" I asked the interviewer, interrupting her.

She smoothly transitioned to another question, and as soon as the interview was finished, I had to take a few pictures with a few male and female models for the campaign. I was glad that the photographer guided me where to stand, where to look and smile, so it was over within a couple of hours.

After changing back to my clothes, I asked *Siri* if I had any new calls and got disappointed when she listed no texts, calls or voicemails from Khalid.

It's okay, I have to wait two more weeks, and then I can visit Azmia and confront him about it.

Just two more weeks.

PART IV

"Ruin me if you wish to. I am all yours, Valeria."

29

KHALID

"You look pathetic," the old woman with grey hair mocked me when she entered my room. She scrunched her face at the scent of oil paints and fumes, eyeing the red mess on the canvas. "Did you do that, boy?"

"You know what my name is, *jadati*," I said, staring at the painting.

I wanted to tear it apart. Burn it.

"Zain seemed concerned about you. Ever since Salman died, you haven't stepped out of this room," she said taking a good luck at the painting.

I shrugged. "So what? Why are you here anyway? You have never been around."

If you were, you could see what your son did. You could have savedwho was I kidding by overthinking about it. He was dead. I had killed him.

"I wanted to make sure how you were coping, Khalid," she whispered.

Grandmother never knew what her son did, she lived in another palace even though our grandfather had passed away.

My father rarely allowed her to visit but when she did, it felt like she brought sunshine with her to the gloomy Golden Palace. It wasn't her fault that she didn't know how pathetic her son was. The entire country looked up to him, deemed him as some God.

I could feel her eyes on me but I didn't care. I couldn't look away from the painting. When I had woken up from the nightmare after trying to sleep that night, I had seen red and poured it all out on the canvas. The red glowing hair in the sunshine and the red of my father's blood.

I had never painted such an abstract before but I couldn't stop it, feeling overwhelmed and complex painting. My hair was mussed and the shirt was red with the splatter of red paint, oddly similar to the night where it was splattered with blood instead.

"Come, eat with me."

"I am not hungry."

"You haven't eaten anything for three days"

"I. Am. *Not*. Hungry," I glared at her, finally meeting her eyes.

"You did not hear me, child," she chided. "I wasn't asking you. I was ordering you to eat with me. Until your brother accepts the crown, I am here to look after Azmia."

I scoffed, turning away. "Put me in dungeon for all I care, *jadati*. I am not going to eat."

"So you would rather starve yourself to death?"

I shrugged. I didn't care. Zain would accept the title of Sultan and Rahim would be his advisor. Zayed was already a Sheikh and Zara would be cared after by the people who adored her. there was no place for me to exist. I wasn't needed. The broken prince who had no ambitions to follow his father's footsteps, who had murdered his own blood.

I was better off dead.

"Suit yourself," she said. "I will be sending someone to make you eat." Before she left my room, she said, "You should paint more, Khalid."

I ignored her comment and braced myself for the soldiers she would send to my room to hold me down and make me eat

But no soldiers appeared. Just my little sister, balancing a huge plate with various bowls of curries, bread and sweets. Including a dish full of *roz bel laban*. My mouth watered and stomach growled in hunger as Zara glared at me, puffing her cheeks in anger.

I took the plate from her and set it on the table.

"Eat it," she demanded, putting her hands on her hips staring at me with narrowed eyes even though she barely reached my hips.

"I don't want to," I said, trying to keep my tone down. I had to give it to grandmother, she knew I could never win an argument with my sister. "Why don't you eat it?"

She raised her chin at me, "I won't eat it until you do. Grandmother told me that my first task as the Princess of Azmia is to make sure you eat everything from this plate."

"And what if I don't?"

Zara's eyes widened as if she couldn't believe I was saying no to her. I might have spoiled her too much.

But I couldn't hold in my small smile when she stood up on the table, her small fingers holding the spoon filled with sweet rice and hovering it across me.

"*Eat!*" she exasperated.

My throat clogged with tears as I stared at her. I had done it to protect her. That's what Zain, Rahim and even Zayed who had followed the advisor that night and seen everything had said to me. Zara had asked me if I was alright after killing our father.

She made an airplane motion like I used to do to make her eat. I smiled at my sister, her hazel eyes.

"*Khalid,*" she drawled my name as if she was tired of me not eating the food. "My arm is hurting, eat it or I am smacking the food on your face and grandma will scold you!"

I took the bite, savoring the sweet taste even though tear slid down my face.

That night, after having dinner with my family, I cried on the lap of my grandmother, allowing her to stroke my hair as I clutched her hand like a small child. She knew I was hurting and she saved me from it.

Even though I couldn't share what I had done, she accepted me and cared for me.

I FELT NAUSEATED, MY HEAD THROBBING PAINFULLY, AS I stumbled off the lounger to the floor. I coughed, reeking of whiskey and sweat.

I felt miserable, my whole body aching from sitting on the stool in front of the canvas for hours. My only fuel was water, whiskey unless someone dropped a platter of food for me. I couldn't eat much when I didn't deserve it.

Pressing the heels of my palm on my eyes, I stood up on weak legs, going to the washroom and washing my paint splattered face and arms. I sighed, looking at my pathetic reflection.

My hair was growing out and so was my beard. So unruly and unkept. My eyes had dark bags underneath them and my skin looked ashy from not going out in the sun. I felt dead. Drinking and trying to make sense of the paintings I made when I felt so unfamiliar in my art studio.

It didn't feel familiar without Valeria's warmth.

But she was better off without me. She had lost her sense of smell. It was her biggest fear and it all happened because I couldn't protect her. I broke her promise.

Maybe if I drink enough, I will eventually wither away, and

maybe then I can donate my eyes to her. Be useful. I could at least do that.

Shaking my head, I stepped under the cold shower.

I HAD FINISHED THE PAINTING. HER PAINTING. IT LOOKED beautiful, sensual, but sad. Her body was a work of art, and I don't think that even my painting did justice to her incredible figure. Sun rays fell on her skin, a white cloth draped over the navy lounger behind her in contrast to the red colors I had chosen for the painting. It was painted in unique tones of red, light pink for her lips, tips of her breasts and her knees. Lush red for her stunning silky hair. Maroon for the floor.

Despite the different tones of red, her hair stood out the most. Her green eyes gleaming as she stared out of the open window.

Even though everything seemed pleasant and appealing in the painting, her face had a solemn expression.

Valeria was right to name it *Rose Colored Sorrow.*

I pulled away from the canvas and picked up my phone, ignoring her worried texts with a heavy heart. I saw her interview, proud of her work when she explained the unique perfumes.

She looks so beautiful.

I frowned when she ignored the question related to me. The pictures of us walking together and smiling showing up on the video. She was holding my hand and grinning while I was smiling down at her. Had two months passed already? I felt like I had spent a lifetime with her and still wanted more.

My face hardened when I saw the pictures of her on her social media page, posing with male models on either side of her.

I shouldn't, but I was jealous of them.

"Khalid?" Zayed called out from the door, making me put away the phone. "I know you are in there, shithead. Come out and play with me, I am getting bored."

I didn't reply.

He sighed, "You know, one of these days, I am going to break into this studio and punch you *so fucking hard* for being so stupid." As if he was imagining my face on the locked doors, he punched the door, cursing like a pirate when it didn't budge. "Valeria has been calling every day, asking us if you ate or stepped out of your cave. If you don't come out by this evening, I swear to God I will marry that woman *just* to spite you."

"But I can't do that to her. She is too sweet for—*wait*… is that why you are rotting in here?" He paused for a moment. "You dense *fuck*. Stop blaming yourself or doing your broody shit that you don't deserve her."

I swallowed the lump in my throat, but he continued talking through the door.

"I know you feel responsible for what happened, but stop hiding like a baby. You are a Prince. The Khalid I know would make up to the woman he loves *before* his charming, handsome best friend in the whole world proposes to marry her, do you hear me?"

I bit back my smile. Zayed was so full of himself.

"I will come back again this evening and if you don't open up, I am flying to London and broadcasting my proposal to Valeria in front of her office and uploading it on my YouTube channel for you to see." His words were full of promise and I wouldn't put it past him to do that. He would, most definitely, fly to London and propose Valeria to marry him out of spite for me.

After hearing what Zayed had said, I had put a little effort to look better. I trimmed my beard to my usual stubble, noticing that the slash on my cheekbone had disappeared. I wore a clean shirt and pants when I walked out of the art studio—

"My best friend!" Zayed yelled, tackling me on the ground.

I winced when my head hit the floor, his heavy weight pressing me down as he yelled in my ear.

I pushed him away, glaring at him, "Touch me again and I will cut your arms."

He grinned at me, his eyes almost tearing up as dimples popped on both sides of his cheek, hugging me again. "I missed your death threats so much, my best friend!"

He even kissed my cheek.

I pulled away, wiping his saliva, disgusted. "I hate you."

Zayed followed me, making kissing sounds. "I love you too, honeybun."

I shook my head, "There's something seriously wrong with you."

"Chicks dig it," he smirked, winking at me.

"Nice of you to show up," Nasrin mocked me, walking towards me and pulling me into a light hug.

"You look bigger than before," I commented, looking down at her baby bump.

I frowned when Zain's eyes widened over her shoulder. He mouthed 'Cut it out' while Zayed made slicing head action.

Nasrin glared at me, pulling away. "You are not getting *kunafah* for dessert."

What did I say?

"Oh, forgive him, darling." Zain talked to her in a sweet voice. "He hasn't socialized with anyone for over a month. Give him some break."

We settled on the low dining table, crossing our legs as the staff served the food. I swallowed the lump in my throat, noticing the empty spot of grandma and Valeria's seat. Zara was in Australia and Elena had left for States, the mystery of letter *S* still unsolved.

"I know this is not the right time, but I need to know what the fuck happened to you," Zain said politely.

I opened my mouth, but Nasrin glared at me. "Don't even think of lying to us. We know it's related to Valeria."

I closed my mouth, staring at the food.

"I couldn't protect her when I promised I would. I killed father to protect Zara, but she still gets nightmares because of him. I tried to protect Valeria, but she still lost her sense of smell."

"Khalid," Zain spoke. "None of it was your fault. Father was a terrible person. That man who is rotting in the jail is a terrible person for what he did to Valeria."

Zayed said, "She never blamed you, did she?"

I stayed silent.

"Did she ever tell you she was mad at you? Did she tell you she hates you?" Nasrin asked.

I shook my head.

"Then don't spend time blaming yourself for what happened." Nasrin paused. "Grandma did something for... Valeria."

I looked at her. They all shared a knowing glance. "What is it?"

"She donated her eyes but they were already used for a successful transplantation and wrote Valeria's name so that she can get her sight back," Zain said, a hopeful gleam in his eyes. In everyone's eyes as they stared at me.

"Why are you guys staring at me like that?"

"I have an idiot for a friend." Zayed sighed. "We are telling you so that you can man up and talk to her."

Oh.

I shook my head, "She will slap me if I go meet her—"

"She won't."

"She *definitely* will."

"Oh, I would pay to see that."

Nasrin, Zain and Zayed said, the couple glaring at each other.

"What?" Zain said. "You punched me and I almost fell off the balcony."

"Now, I would pay to see *that*," Zayed commented.

"You deserved it because you acted like a complete fool."

Zain pointed at me. "So did he!"

"Hey," I frowned at them, eating *kunafah* to feel better.

They stopped bantering as I slowly swallowed the food down my throat. "So you guys think I can make up to her? Apologize and tell her about the eyes? Would she accept me?" I asked.

"You have to try, Khalid," Nasrin said with a small smile.

Try. I could try for Valeria. For my sweet one.

"And please check the packaging for any leaks. Yes, I want you to go the factory and check them personally—"

Someone knocked on the door, I pulled the phone from my ear and said, "Give me five minutes, please."

I continued talking to the employee until he understood what he had to check after visiting the factory and the chemical lab.

"Come in."

I read the paper in front of me, my fingers tracing over the Braille. The person who had entered wasn't light on their feet like my assistant. The feet felt heavy but soft. There was a change in air as someone deposited something on my desk, looming close to me.

Before I could ask them who were they, I heard him.

"Hello, my sweet one," Khalid greeted me, standing in my office. In London. In front of me.

I stood up, ready to hug him but held back, remembering the times he had made me scared and worried about him for the past month. Ignoring me as if I didn't exist.

I cleared my throat. "Hello, Khalid. What are you doing here?"

He seemed nervous. I could sense it in his voice. He wasn't here as the Prince of Azmia, he was here as Khalid.

"I came here to apologize for being a stupid fool, Valeria," he said, taking a deep breath. "I may or may not have gifted your painting to you. It's at your house by the way."

My lips parted. "What?"

"Uh, yeah. I didn't feel right keeping it with me, so I decided to give it to you. *Rose Colored Sorrow* is yours, Valeria."

I blinked at him, walking into my office, feeling him close to the desk as I paced. Khalid was in my office in London, apologizing for being stupid and gifting me the painting he had made.

"Why?"

"Because I love you."

He said it as a fact.

I didn't reply as he continued. "You don't have to say it. If you want to slap me, do it. But all I want is to talk with you, sweet one."

"I don't want to slap you." I frowned at him. *Was he okay?*

"Thank God," he sighed. "I have something else to say."

"Sure." I didn't care what he had to say. He was in my office, apologizing—

"My grandma wrote your name for corneal transplantation. We have them ready and you have a week to think about it. If they match with yours, you can have your sight back."

I had to lean on the desk. I had known so little about her and yet she…

"I couldn't believe it too, Valeria. But she even wrote it in her will with the help of Rahim, our advisor, so you can have your sight back."

I swallowed the lump in my throat and straightened up. I fought back my tears and said, "So, you show up in my office after ignoring me for a month to apologize to me, gift me your painting, and tell me I can have my sight back?"

"Well…*yes*. That's about it."

"I hate you."

He took a sharp breath upon hearing me. "I can understand that you would, I ignored you—"

"I hate you so much, Khalid."

"Now don't rub it in the wound, you can keep the painting, the roses on the desk and the corneas—"

I smacked his chest, pulling him into a hug. "You stupid, stupid fool. I can't believe it took you a month to pull your head out of your arse!"

"*Ouch*," he muttered, hugging me back.

"I promised that I would wait for you, Khalid," I said, pulling back to cup his cheek. Feel his warm skin on my hands. "I have been waiting."

I felt a small drop on my cheek. "Are you crying?" I asked, my voice soft.

He sniffed, hugging me again. "Maybe. I didn't think you would want me after what I did to you. I truly thought you hated me and would probably call security to drag me out."

I chuckled, stroking his hair and kissing his neck. "I don't hate you, but I am angry at you for ignoring me instead of talking to me about what troubled you, Khalid."

He hummed, the vibration of his chest against me making me melt in his arms. I felt safe. I felt home.

"Don't tell Zayed I cried."

Khalid
A week later

"Stop tapping your shoes, Khalid, you are making me nervous," Valeria said, sitting on the hospital bed wearing a mint green gown, her red hair in a braid. Even in such a bland setting, she looked like an angel.

"I am sorry, sweet one, but I am worried about you," I said, waiting for the doctor. "They said I couldn't be in the room when they perform the surgery."

She chuckled, squeezing my hand. "Of course, you can't stay in the room, silly."

"Then who will look after you?"

"You are being clingy again, Prince Khalid," she teased, her grin making me smile.

Valeria needed time, and space after I talked to her in her office. I had given her that and everything she wanted from me. Telling her why I never called back and ignored her. She had accepted me, ordering me to stop blaming myself for the circumstances. She had lived with her loss of smell and even though it was difficult, she could endure it. The doctors had told her that her sense of smell could come back in six months span or it might not and she had accepted either of the reality.

My Valeria was a brave woman.

It took her time to face that she could get her sight back and even though she would rather have her sense of smell, she didn't mind having her sight back. After various checkups, the doctors had told us that there was a seventy percent chance of getting her vision. She won't have twenty-twenty vision, but enough to live by. There was a chance of eye infection if her body rejects it but she had accepted it.

She was ready to regain her sight. So was I.

When I had dinner with Mabel and Benjamin at her house the night before, they had thanked me for making her the happiest she had ever been. I had cuddled with her in her room when she asked me,

"Why would you do so much for me, Khalid?"

"Because I want to. I care about you, I love you and because it's my responsibility. I am never repeating the same mistake again. I want to make up to you. Forever."

"You would do that all for me?" She had asked with a small smile.

I had kissed that sweet smile and said, "The question is what I wouldn't do for you, my sweet one."

⚜

"Are you sure everything is settled? Did you keep the fresh roses in the vase like I asked you to?" I said through the phone, my eyes drifting to the surgery room where the red sign glowed red.

Zayed sighed through the phone, annoyed. "Yes, Khalid, I did. Are you done pestering with little things? The maids already decorated the room last night with you, and now you are just scaring everyone. Do all of us a favor, remove that cane up your ass and sit the fuck down."

I sighed and sat down on the chair, glaring at the white wall in front of me. "You're right, I am sorry. I am scared of what—"

"Of what she will think of you once she sees how ugly you are?" Zayed asked in a playful voice.

"Watch that mouth of yours before I cut that tongue out myself," I heard Nasrin's voice through the phone, "Ignore Zayed's words, Khalid. We always do. Valeria is not a woman to judge a person by what they look like. She loves you for your art, mind, your heart and your soul. She couldn't care less if you looked ugly or handsome. You of all people should know that beauty is nothing but subjective."

I pondered over her words, thanking her in a small voice before ending the call and looking over the picture of her painting which I had stored in my phone. It didn't capture every stroke of paint on the canvas, but the photo was enough to ground me and think of the memories we had shared at the oasis and the palace.

Or the time when Valeria had touched my face and explained how I looked to her, and I didn't think that Valeria thought of me with such stern face yet so beautiful. It had certainly been enough to kiss her and be my muse.

"You can meet her, Khalid," Benjamin said when Mabel wiped tears from her face after walking out of the room where Valeria was resting after her surgery.

"Is she okay?" I stood up from the chair.

"Why don't you see for yourself?" Benjamin smiled, squeezing his wife's shoulder, allowing me to have some privacy with Valeria.

With a deep breath, I pushed the door open and entered the room, noticing her untangling her hair from a braid.

"Hello," I said, awkwardly looming near the edge of the hospital bed.

Valeria looked at Khalid, holding her breath. Even though the doctor had warned her about the little fogginess, she could see him. He looked devastatingly handsome. No one had warned her of his beauty. His sun-kissed skin, his dark hair, his cutting cheekbones, his slashing brows, his warm hazel eyes, his sharp jaw peppered with stubble or the lush lips. She had kissed those lips so many times, not knowing that the face it belonged to looked like pure sin.

I stared at her vibrant green eyes as she blinked at me. I froze when she tilted her head. "I'm sorry. Who are you? Where's Khalid?"

Valeria held back her laughter, seeing the look of horror on his face. His skin going ashy as he gaped at her, as if he truly thought that Valeria didn't recognize him.

I was going to pass out.

"*Valeria,*" I said her name like I was pleading. "It *is* me! I am Khalid. Khalid Al Latif. The Prince of Azmia. *Your* Prince."

She licked her lips, a small smile tugging at the corner. "You don't look like a Prince."

I clenched my jaw when she burst into tiny fits of laughter, cupping her mouth and stomach as if she enjoyed tormenting me, scaring me like that.

I sat on the chair beside the bed, shaking my head at her. She must have spent too much time with Zayed. "Had your fun?" I asked.

Valeria sobered up from her laughter, gazing at him. In awe at his beauty. He was dressed in a crisp shirt, a dark navy suit, and slacks. She suddenly felt shy for being in a hospital gown.

"Hi," she said, her voice shy. It was unbelievable that he was holding her palm in his big hands, the white shirt stretching over his broad shoulders, revealing a hint of tan skin. *This was her Khalid, he was hers as much as she was his.*

I smiled at her small tone, her eyes raking over my body. "Hello."

"I can't believe it," Valeria said, meeting his eyes and squeezing his hand to know he was real.

"Believe what?"

"That you are… *you.*" She raised her hand and cupped his cheek, feeling the warmth beneath her skin. She could see it and feel it.

"Is that good?"

"*Better.* You are so much more than what I had imagined." She caressed his cheek. "And very tall."

Khalid chuckled, and Valeria was left speechless yet again. He looked beautiful when he laughed, and knowing that she made him laugh sent flutters to her belly. She wanted to make him laugh more, make him happy.

"Can I kiss you?" She asked, her eyes wide as she looked at his handsome face, her cheeks flushing when his hazel eyes became molten.

"You don't have to ask, my sweet one." I leaned closer, my warm breath caressing her pink cheeks. "You own me."

Her lids fluttered close when she felt the soft press of his lips against hers. Her hands tightening over his shirt, pulling him closer and kissing him harder, parting her lips. They both ignored the sound of her heart rate increasing on the monitor and kissed each other until they were left breathless.

Before I could say anything, my phone started ringing. We both saw the name of Zara, my little sister, flashing on the screen. She would have wanted to know about Valeria's surgery. But I sent it to voicemail. I needed more time alone with her.

"Thank you, Khalid."

I caressed her cheek, gazing at her bright green eyes. "For what?"

"For *this*. For being with me."

My voice was firm when I replied, "You don't have to thank me for being with you. You are more than my lover, Valeria. I am dating you and in a broader way that means, I am courting you."

"Courting me?"

I rolled my eyes at her playful grin and kissed her forehead when the nurse came to check up on her. She would have to stay a few more days at the hospital, but I had talked to the doctor and I would be taking her to my apartment in London, where I would make sure Valeria was taken care of.

I would do more than just take care of her.

Valeria

We stumbled into his bedroom, kissing and touching each other, gasping and moaning into each other's mouth. I unbuttoned his shirt, his fingers removing my top and unclasping my bra.

"Shower," I breathed, pulling him towards the shower.

I had been given a leave that day, my vision seventy percent clear while it got foggy in the morning. But I enjoyed having my vision back, being able to see people when I talk to them, see the different colors that I had missed and awing at Khalid's talent when I had asked him to take me to his gallery.

"What are you doing?" Khalid whispered, his voice hot when I stripped him naked, pushing him into the shower stall and peppering his broad chest with kisses.

I gazed at him, his dark hazel eyes, his wet hair and sharp cheekbones. "I always wanted to touch you and take care of you like this."

He smiled, full of adoration and lust. He rubbed his thumb over my bottom lip and whispered, "Ruin me if you wish to. I am all *yours*, Valeria."

Words couldn't convey how I felt so I decided to show it with my actions.

"So am I, Khalid," I said, licking my lips. "Let me take care of you."

I slowly pumped his hardened length, not believing that I took *that* much inside me. No wonder I always felt a little sore afterwards. Khalid Al Latif was packing.

I kissed and licked down his abs, loving the way his muscles tensed underneath my tongue. My eyes flickered at him when I lowered on my knees, slowly stroking him and sucked the thick head inside my mouth, humming at the taste of pre-cum.

"*Fuck*, Valeria," Khalid groaned, craning his head back as I took more of him inside me, cupping and fondling his heavy balls. Arousal seeped out of me hearing the husky sounds of pleasure he made.

"S-stop," he heaved, both of us wet with water as he pulled me up, kissing my lips sweetly. "I want to cum inside you."

I nodded, my sex clenching. Before I could get out of the

shower stall, he pulled me back, chuckling, "Let's shower first. We have all night to ourselves, Valeria."

I flushed, watching his large hands soap my body, touching me and teasing me until I squirmed in his arms. I returned his favor, lathering up his large body in soap and kissing the scars on his back.

"Show me how ready you are, Valeria," Khalid whispered, hovering above me, both of us naked on his bed.

I spread my legs, my hands cupping my aching breasts as his eyes turned feral, looking between my thighs, my sex flushed and wet for him.

"Please fuck me, Khalid," I said, watching him through my half-lidded eyes as he crawled over me. Kissing my legs, caressing my skin with his hand, licking my belly, biting my nipples.

I wrapped my arms around his neck, pulling him in a kiss when he settled between my legs, rubbing the tip of his cock on my slicked lips and clit, teasing us both until he slowly slid inside me. My warm walls clenched around him as he swallowed my moans, allowing me to settle with his girth inside me.

I groaned when he reared back and slowly slid deeper inside me, his movements slow and hard. Khalid was taking his time with me, making me feel every inch of him as he slowly stretched me.

"My precious Valeria," he moaned, kissing my lips clumsily before rolling us over.

I gasped when I felt his length going deeper inside me, my legs straddling him. Khalid groped my breasts, pinching the nipples and looking at me through his half-lidded obsidian eyes.

"Ride me, Valeria. Ride your Prince."

So I did, holding onto his shoulders as he held my waist, slowly moving my hips and riding him, looking down at our unison. I whimpered, hiding my face in the crook of his neck as pleasure took over me, waves after waves rocking over my trembling body.

Khalid fucked me harder, thrusting inside me by tightening his arm around my waist, making my walls spasm around him. He wanted me to come again, his length hitting the sensitive spot while his thumb rubbed my clitoris, asking me, ordering me to orgasm once more.

The look in his eyes was feral, filled with passion and love for me as we moved together in unison. I groaned and thrashed in his arms when he fucked me while I rode him, his hands on my pale breasts.

He rolled us over, our lips meeting in a clumsy kiss before Khalid held my leg over his torso and thrust deeper inside me. We both groaned in unison, reaching climax together and falling apart on each other.

I hummed softly when release washed over me, my mind turning black and white, feeling the warm spurt of his climax coating the insides of my walls.

"I love you so fucking much, my sweet one," he whispered, bringing me closer to him as I laid my head on his chest.

I kissed his skin, pulling away to look at his face. So handsome and rugged.

I couldn't believe he was mine. And I was his.

"I love you, Khalid."

THE END

READ EXPLICIT BONUS SCENE HERE
Or type this link into your browser:
https://mailchi.mp/577206f09a91/filthyhotprincebonusscene

Thank you so much for reading Filthy Hot Prince! If you

enjoyed reading this book, I would be grateful if you could leave a review on the platform(s) of your choice.

Reviews help other readers like you find this book and are hugely appreciated by authors!

Love always,

Mahi

EPILOGUE

KHALID

I lounged on the blue velvet armchair as if it was my obsidian throne. That time, a male interviewer was sitting across me, taking notes and stuttering, asking me questions. I wished he could hurry so I could be with—

"Your painting, *Rose Colored Sorrow*, has been auctioned for over three-hundred million dollars. Do you feel that it is because of your fiancé and your love story or purely because of the art?"

With my smooth, deep voice, I said, "I would need a moment to ask her myself, if you'll excuse me."

Without waiting for his reply, I stood up and walked off the small stage for the interview and searched for the stunning red-haired woman who had my heart in her palm. The art show was buzzing with people whispering about Valeria's and my recent engagement.

I found her talking with my old friend and his wife, Ethan Kane and Kiara Kane. I wasn't surprised to see Kiara pregnant, as Ethan had shared that they had been trying for a while. I hadn't seen Ethan so carefree and smiling when we had first met, but it had changed, as he couldn't stop smiling with Kiara around him. She was his best-friend, and he had loved her since her family became his neighbor when they were just children.

Ethan was whipped, just like I was.

"Congratulations," I said, wrapping my arm around Valeria, kissing her cheek.

"Thank you, Khalid." Ethan's blue-green eyes shone with happiness. "We heard you are engaged to this lovely woman, Ms Valeria, and I had to make sure if you were threatening her to be with you."

Both women shared a laugh and Valeria winked at him, "I assure you it was me who did the threatening, Ethan."

I chuckled at her answer, squeezing her side. After talking to them for a while, Valeria and I walked together, talking about the paintings. I glared at any men who dared to stare too long at my sweet.

When the art show ended with all the lights dim and my paintings on the walls, I pushed Valeria into the empty space between the two paintings. I kissed her, letting her hair free of the bun to fall over her pale skin, tugging down her dress and tasting her skin, her sweet breasts.

I stripped her naked until she was only wearing the diamond ring and took her against the wall, kissing her and whispering filthy words in her ears as she came around me.

She panted when I pulled her limp body over my lap, leaning back on the wall. I hummed softly when she raked her hand through my hair, smiling at me.

"What?" I whispered, caressing the red finger marks on her waist where I had held her.

"You really don't look like a Prince, Khalid," she chuckled, her cheeks flushed with a soft glow. "But I don't care, you are my filthy hot prince."

"How many were killed?" I asked, seeing the endless sand out of the car window.

"Eleven, sir," he answered.

Eleven people died to kidnap one woman.

"And they couldn't even reach the princess, could they?" I said, giving him a pointed look.

His eyes lowered to the sleeve of my shirt which were splashed with blood from my previous… *detour*. Even the gold cufflinks were red. Pity, I liked them.

"No, sir, they couldn't reach princess Zara. She was heavily guarded along with Sultana."

I hummed, giving the signal to the driver.

"Nasrin is pregnant, isn't she?"

The man in suit didn't reply, only swallowed the lump in his throat.

"I take that as a yes then," I smiled. "I told you that I wanted her dead the last time, didn't I?"

"Y-yes, Sir, but we couldn't sneak inside the Golden Palace, it was heavily—"

I cracked my knuckles, rubbing the sore muscle on my

neck. "I received a report from a source that both Zain and Nasrin were at that sheikh's oasis. Khalid was with his blind lover at another oasis. The Golden Palace was empty for a day and you wasted that opportunity."

He didn't reply so I continued, "That princess was either in hiding or her brothers were hiding her outside of Azmia. Zara has never stepped out of the palace until last year. Do you know where she was?"

"Sri Lanka. But when we reached to her location, she had left—"

"To Australia," I finished him, fixing my cufflinks. "You were too late. You missed one opportunity to bring me that princess and countless ones to bring me head of either Nasrin or Khalid's now-fiancée."

"We didn't know she was blind."

I deadpanned. "Do I look like I fucking care? You had a blind woman in your hands and you couldn't even kidnap her. It is your fault that your people took the poison and killed themselves. Not to mention, one is still missing, isn't he?"

"He probably snuck—"

I chuckled darkly when the driver stopped the car by the empty highway, dessert on each side of the road.

"No one can sneak out of the Golden Palace. They are probably torturing him for information in their dungeon. He is as good as dead to us."

"Why did we stop here?" He finally asked.

"I have a question for you," I said, looking at the scar on his forehead. "Did you tell them my name?"

"Who?"

"The twelve people who went to abduct little Zara during the ceremony," I said, tilting my head. "Did they know my name?"

He shook his head, "I would never sell you out like that. You are our one and only high-paying client."

I smiled at him, patted his shoulder and pulled him into a hug. "I am honoured to hear that…" I pushed the blade in his stomach, slicing through his abdomen as warm blood trickled on my hand. I ignored the sound of his choking and said, "But your words are meaningless without your actions."

I pushed him away, wiping the blood from the red blade and my hand with a handkerchief. His eyes were wide as he tried to cover his wound. The driver opened the door to his seat and pulled him out of the car.

"Sir?" He asked, waiting.

"Kill him," I waved him off, sighing when I heard the sound of a gunshot.

The car started moving after a moment, the smell of metal, gun powder and blood hovering in the air.

It was a shame that I had to kill such a good puppy but he was too reckless trusting his cronies. I didn't want anyone to find out that I was the one who had ordered to get Nasrin's food poisoned when she was in Maahnoor and plan the kidnapping of Zara during the baby shower.

I clenched my fists, thinking about the little princess. So beautiful and so carefree. What I wouldn't do to hold her as hostage, have fun with her, make her watch as I kill every one of her family until Zain is nothing but crawling on his knees, begging me not to harm his sister. If I felt like giving mercy, I wouldn't fuck her in front of him, make him see just how much power I had over him and just slit her slender neck. Blame him for his sister's death, for everyone's death.

Smiling, I made a call and said, "You know where the princess is."

"Australia?"

"Yes."

My hands were itching to hold her beneath me, strip her out of her rich clothes and take every ounce of freedom from her until she has nothing left to give.

"Do you want her alive?"

"Yes, very much alive, thank you."

"Can I hurt her?"

"Not this again, sweetheart," I sighed. "You know I don't like my toys to be played with."

"I will hurt her. Just a little bit." I could feel her smiling just thinking about hurting someone else, especially one of the most protected royal princesses. *Such a sadist.* "How long do I have?"

I thought about the birth of Zain's heir, how protective they would be in coming months and years.

"Take your time but I need little Zara alive to burn down Azmia to ashes."

PREVIEW OF TEMPTING REBEL PRINCESS

ZARA

"I want you to hurt me," I breathed, staring at his eyes. They were a dark, sexy shade of blue. They compelled me to do terrible, dirty things to him and for him. Things I had never imagined I would ever want but… there was something about him that made me want to be just Zara.

Not the Princess who had her own castle, who ate with golden spoon every day, who was spoiled rotten since the day she was born.

No. With him, I just wanted to be Zara, a woman who wanted to be pleased and do the pleasing.

"Where do you want me to hurt you, Princess?" Hayden asked, a hint of smirk on his lips as his eyes gleamed with unknown emotion.

"Here," I placed his, calloused hands on my breasts, still covered in the satin fabric of the beige dress. His eyes darkened, his face becoming sharper when he clenched his jaw. I licked my lips, trailing his hands to my waist. *Lower.*

"Everywhere."

His nose flared, pulling his hands away from my touch as he glared at me. I took a sharp breath when he pressed closer to me, my back pressing against the closed doors of his hotel suite.

"Don't mock me, Princess. I will bruise your lips, kissing them, fucking them until you cry," he rumbled, swiping his thumb over my bottom lip. His hand lowered to my neck, wrapping it around my throat. My eyes widened when he pressed lightly, my pulse getting slower as anticipation and pleasure burned through my core. "I will choke your slender neck, just like this, making you hold your breath until you cum for me."

I gasped, tears blurring my vision when he lowered his hand to hold my breasts. I blinked at him, at the sight of his large palms holding me roughly.

No one has ever touched me like this before. As if they were claiming me with their touch, their words.

I never wanted him to stop.

"You like this, Princess?" He asked, his voice gruff with desire. He squeezed my breasts until a whimper tore out of my lips. As if satisfied with my answer, his hands lowered to my thighs, yanking the hem of my dress over my hips and between my legs.

I held my breath, staring at him through my half-lidded eyes, waiting for him to be rough with me.

But he didn't.

Hayden ran a finger against my drenched underwear, from my slit to the pleasure nub, rolling his finger around it. He leaned closer, his musky scent wafting in my nose as he whispered, "I will spank you *right here*, Princess. Get your clit red and swollen before I stretch your pretty little cunt with my thick cock. I will fuck you hard and rough and won't stop until you scream. You know why?"

"*Why?*"

He pulled back, trailing his finger over the side of my cheek, the same finger he had between my legs. I could scent my feminine musk on it. My legs clenched.

"Because you *begged* me to hurt you, Princess."

I gasped when his fingers clenched around my hair, tugging them back and pulling me closer. I felt the hardness of his length against my legs and I knew he wasn't kidding about stretching me.

"You can leave right now, Zara, or stay here and allow me to hurt you."

I didn't even give it another thought.

"I want to stay."

He tugged my hair harder until it hurt. His ocean eyes narrowing on my face, "Then for this night you belong to me."

The dominating tone made something click inside of me. As if this was what I wanted for the longest time after being caged and coddled as a Princess. I could have whatever I wanted but not… *this*. This pleasure, this need of getting hurt through pleasure because who would ever hurt the Princess of Azmia? No one but *him*. Hayden.

He didn't know I was a Princess.

He *wanted* to please me. Hurt me.

I wanted him to please me. *Hurt me.*

My stomach dipped as if I knew the answer even before he had asked me. I felt my pussy moisten when I sealed my fate and said, "My answer is yes, Hayden."

His hold on my hair loosened but he didn't let me go. No, I didn't think he would let me go until next morning. I didn't think I would complain even if he tied me up on his bed and held me captive.

Bringing his face closer, he crooned, "Such a pretty Princess." He smiled and there was nothing sweet about it when he whispered, "I'm going to enjoy breaking you."

EXCLUSIVE CONTENT

Want more exclusive content? You can sign up for Mahi's Patreon to read steamy one shots every Saturday!

As a supporter, you get access to early drafts, exclusive VIP content, deleted scenes, deleted chapters, cat pictures and YOUR NAME in the Acknowledgements of my books.

www.patreon.com/mahimistry

PREVIEW OF TWISTED THERAPIST

IVY KNIGHT

"I am so sorry, Aiden, the traffic was so bad," I heaved, taking support of my knees to control my breathing. So much for dressing up in cute dress, applying light makeup and curling my hair in waves just for the session. I wiped down the sweat from forehead and straightened up, daring to peek at him.

Aiden looked like he always did. His face stern and no emotions showing on his face. His eyes travelled down my body and I held in my shiver when they raked over my bare legs.

He made a dramatic point of checking his wristwatch that cost more than the car that I drove and hummed. "We will talk about your tardiness after the session. *Sit.*"

I quickly sat down and drank some water, the breeze of the air conditioner cooling my skin. The session started, and we made usual talk about my day, what happened that week or if anything exciting happened that I wanted to share with him.

"How did your journaling go?"

We talked more about the days where I would write two-three pages a day or days when I could barely write a paragraph. He listened to me and asked questions when I would stop talking, urging me to drink water and keep going.

"Do you mind if I see what you've written?" He asked, his dark eyes soft.

My muscles tensed as I met his obsidian eyes. They ran over my body and noticed how stiff I had become. My eyes lingered on his crisp white shirt, stretching over his shoulders, the sleeves rolled up to his elbows with a dark-coloured tie. Maybe it was my imagination when I thought his eyes had stayed far too long on my chest and my legs. I shuffled in my seat and tucked the strand of my hair behind my ear.

Aiden's eyes flickered to my face, and he closed them for a moment, as if he was taking his time. He finally said, "You don't have to if you don't want me to read. I will understand and respect your privacy."

I licked my lips, trusting my instinct. "I-it's okay, I don't mind. You can read it."

I handed him the diary, frowning at the ruffled separate pages that I had shoved between them. He silently read the entry of my first day while I squirmed in my seat. I may or may not have drunk too much water, so I excused myself to the washroom.

When I came back, I could feel the change in the air. Aiden was sitting on the couch, but his posture was stiff. He barely addressed my presence when I sat down in my seat. I saw the diary was placed beside him and his jaw was clenched.

"Is everything okay?" I asked, my voice small.

He finally looked at me and the corner of his lips twitch. Leaning back on the couch, he said, "Yes, I suppose you could say that. I want to ask you something, Petal, and I want you to be honest about it."

Frowning, I nodded.

His eyes darkened, and he said in a stern voice, "Use your mouth."

"I—*um*, yes, Dr. Aiden."

I didn't know why I *felt* the need to address him seriously.

"What were you doing this morning?"

My eyes widened, my heart pounding in my ears. I glanced at the diary and it struck me. Those ruffled pages. *Shit, shit, shit.* After journaling every day for a week, I wrote my fantasies regarding Aiden, my brother's best friend, on different torn pages. I always tucked them back in the diary, reminding myself to pull them out before I brought it to the session. But I was in such a hurry that I had completely forgotten about them.

Did he read it? I hope he didn't. I would rather eat raw broccoli than have him read all those pages.

Looking away from him, I lied and carelessly shrugged my shoulder, "I was meditating."

I mentally winced at my lie. He had tried coaching me to meditate, but I could never do it.

He is right. I am a terrible liar.

Aiden raised his eyebrows. "Is that so?"

I didn't like the tone of his voice. He seemed serious, and I prayed that the ground would swallow me up. He waited for my answer, crossing his arms over his chest. I got distracted by the way his biceps bulged, the veins on his forearms getting prominent.

He noticed me staring. I glanced down at my lap, twiddling my thumbs. "Y-yes, Dr Aiden, I was meditating and I-I focused on my breath like you taught me—"

"Why are you lying to me, Ivy?"

My head snapped at him. I shook my head, "I-I am not lying."

Aiden tilted his head and my throat went dry when he said, "Then why did I hear your voice moaning my name when you orgasmed with your fingers inside your pussy?"

PREVIEW OF DON'T DATE YOUR BEST FRIEND

KIARA

"If you don't want to kiss me then . . . let's swim."

"Yeah, sure."

"Naked."

"*What?*"

"I always wanted to try skinny dipping." I pursed my lips and said, "And I really want to get out of these clothes."

When I thought about it, I wasn't feeling self-conscious about my body when it came to him. Yes, he had seen in me in bikinis and accidentally walking in when I was busy writing something on my Post-it in my underwear and bra. But I was never self-conscious about what he would think of me or my body. I did have stretch marks, but I wasn't uncomfortable about them. What I was most worried about was *myself*. If he got naked and my hormones spiked up, I didn't know if I would control myself and not jump on him.

Gosh, I sounded so bad in my head. Not to mention, my best friend would be the first guy I would ever see naked. *Way to go, Kiara.*

His voice was strained when he said, "What if someone catches *you* . . . me, both?"

I moved my damp hair over my shoulder. "We will be in the pool, Ethan. And no one can see us from the living room." I smirked when I said, "Unless you want to watch me while I swim, you can stay here."

The thought of Ethan watching me with his intense green-blue eyes while I was swimming naked in the pool sent a delicious shiver down my core.

His eyes darkened and he looked away, probably thinking the same when I noticed red blush creeping up his neck and making his ears and cheeks flush. *Cute.*

I prodded, "Come on, Ethan. Don't be a chicken . . ."

"*Fine.*"

He stood up, his tall frame towering me. I forgot how to breathe when his dark eyes seared me, slowly trailing down my body as if he had all the time in the world. His voice was rough when he said, "Remove that sweater first."

I raised my eyebrow at the sudden change in his demeanour.

Ethan said, "You have an extra piece of clothing than me."

I grinned. "Who said I was wearing any underwear?"

I loved the way his pupils widened in shock, surprise and then they were clouded by scorching desire. Biting my lips, I whispered, "I was messing with you."

Holding the hem of the sweater, I tugged it up and removed it. I straightened my damp hair and shivered. But it wasn't because of the cold air.

His eyes averted down my breasts, which were barely covered by the ivory lace bralette. As it was wet, he could easily notice my hardened nubs, which were begging for his attention.

We were crossing a dangerous line right now. And I knew neither one of us wanted to step back.

"Your turn," I managed to whisper.

ALSO BY MAHI MISTRY

Have you read them all?

Alluring Rulers of Azmia Series

Dirty Wild Sultan

Filthy Hot Prince

Tempting Rebel Princess

Charming Handsome Sheikh

Alluring Rulers of Azmia Complete Series Books 1-4

The Unfolding Duet

Don't Date Your Best Friend: Best Friends to Lovers

Don't Date Your Ex Best Friend: Second Chance Best Friends to Lovers

The Unfolding Duet Books 1-2

Dominating Desires Series

Twisted Therapist: Brother's Best Friend Age Gap Romance

Tempting Teacher: Student Teacher/Dad's Best Friend Age Gap Romance

Scan to easily access all of my books:

ACKNOWLEDGMENTS

I won't ever be able to do justice to these two wonderful characters that I got the chance to write if I didn't mention the one person who inspired me to write this story.

To Anjali, the blind physiotherapist, who visited our house regularly to help my grandmother. I was so in awe and inspired by you, how you moved so freely and bravely that I knew I had to write a blind character, especially a woman.

My knowledge regarding blindness is limited and I take full responsibility for any places where my research fall short. I am thankful to the Blind subreddit and the wonderful people who helped me with the research of corneal blindness. You guys are brilliant!

To my readers, I am tremendously grateful for your kindness, generosity, and support. I don't have words to express how much YOU inspire me each day to keep writing and have faith in the process. Thank you for taking time to read their story and share it to the world, it means a lot to me. You guys are my rock!

To my family and two Devils' spawns, my cats, thank you for always believing in me, supporting me and for your unconditional love.

To the best editor I could have ever asked for, Jeanie, thank you for your incredible hard work and pushing me to be a better writer with each book. I can't begin to tell you how grateful I am to have you as my editor. You are a gem!

To all my beta readers, proofreader, arc readers, bloggers

and book lovers, bookstragramers, I couldn't have done this without you.

Thank you to everyone who accepted the ARC edition of this book and helped me share this book with the world.

If you enjoyed reading this book, please don't forget to leave a review. I would really appreciate it. It helps find more readers like you and they are very important for authors!

Mahi Mistry has been writing since she was in middle school. Soon, she fell in love with writing passionate, steamy romances. Her stories have elements of humor, suspense and character development. Mahi's main purpose in her life is to make one person happy every day, even if that is a stranger reading her book and rooting for the main couple or her cats by giving them extra treats.

She enjoys simple things in life, like spending time with her family and friends, cuddling with her cats, reading and writing drool-worthy characters while sipping on hot chocolate from the wineglass to validate herself that she is actually an adult. She is an avid reader of fantasy, romance and thriller books and thinks writing about yourself in third person is atrocious. She firmly believes that cats rule the world.

www.mahimistry.com

9 789354 732058